THE FRIENDS OF PANCHO VILLA

Also by James Carlos Blake

Novels

The House of Wolfe

The Rules of Wolfe

Country of the Bad Wolfes

The Killings of Stanley Ketchel

Handsome Harry

Under the Skin

A World of Thieves

Wildwood Boys

Red Grass River

In the Rogue Blood

Borderlands

The Pistoleer

THE
FRIENDS OF
PANCHO
VILLA

A Novel

JAMES CARLOS BLAKE

Grove Press
New York

Published simultaneously in Canada
Printed in the United States of America

First paperback edition: Berkley Books, 1996
First Grove Atlantic paperback edition: July 2017

ISBN 978-0-8021-2688-7
eISBN 978-0-8021-8910-3

Grove Press
an imprint of Grove Atlantic
154 West 14th Street
New York, NY 10011

Distributed by Publishers Group West

groveatlantic.com

17 18 19 20   10 9 8 7 6 5 4 3 2 1

For
Carlos S. Blake and Estrella L. Blake . . .
and
my sister, Chris Lucas

"I too love the great pagan world,
its bloodshed, its slaves, its injustices,
its loathing of all that is feeble."
                        —George Moore

"What thou lovest well is thy true heritage."
                        —Ezra Pound

"What joins men together is not the sharing of
bread but the sharing of enemies."
                        —Cormac McCarthy

"Salud, amor, y pesetas—
y tiempo para gastarlas."
                        —a longtime Mexican toast

THE
FRIENDS OF
PANCHO
VILLA

PROLOGUE

The greatest tragedy that can befall a man is never to know who he really is. So I have heard. I have also heard that the greatest tragedy a man can meet is never to find something to love. It seems to me these notions mean the same thing, but even if they don't, I cannot agree with either. Who has not known men who discovered the truth about themselves only to be tortured by it for the rest of their lives? Is a man worse off when he doesn't know who he is or when he learns he is truly a coward? When he is ignorant of his true nature or when he knows he is a traitor at heart? My point, I think, is clear. Not that I pity either cowards or traitors. To the contrary: in a just world they would all be made to face the hard truth about themselves before they died. In my fashion I made many of them do exactly that.

As for the misfortune of never finding something to love, I'll tell you what's worse: to find it—whether it's a woman or gold or God, whether it's power or fame or the exercise of one's own will—to find it and yet lack facility with it. *That's* the greatest tragedy that can happen to a man: to discover his true love and then be no good with it. I saw it happen to many.

I suffered no such misfortune. I loved the Revolution. I loved its rolling thunder and brute power, its exhilarating rage. It set free the man I truly am. It let me do what I do best as well as it can be done.

I was lucky.

Pancho was lucky too. The Revolution made him a hero. It made him the legendary Centaur of the North, the most famous of us all. He was the Revolution's incarnation and its eagle of a soul. And he was the only true friend I ever had.

He himself had many friends, and many of them loved the Revolution too, and also found their best selves in its fierce, wild beauty.

But some, of course, did not love well, and they were not so lucky.

PART ONE

THE DISCOVERY OF MY LIFE

"It is the Revolution, the magical word, the word that is going to change everything, that is going to bring us immense delight and a quick death."

—Octavio Paz

ONE

In 1910 I killed a policeman and went to prison for two years. The details don't matter except to say the bastard had it coming. After I'd been in the joint two weeks, nobody—guards or inmates—gave me any more trouble. Some of the political prisoners could pay me to protect them from the brutes, so I always ate well and I never lacked a woman on days of conjugal visits. Most of the politicos were overeducated fools, but a few had served in the government and some of those were sometimes interesting to listen to. All in all, I did my time without too much discomfort. When I got out, I drifted back to my old job as a mechanic for the railroad. By then the country had been at war with itself for almost as long as I'd been behind bars, but I wasn't about to join anybody's army just to take orders from assholes and get blown up into buzzard food. Late one night a federal press-gang jumped me when I came out of a cantina. I broke one's neck and scattered the rest like yelping dogs. Nobody tried to grab me again after that.

In those days my sense of injustice transcended fury. I was in a constant rage at the imbalance of the rightful order of things. There I was—a man of my intelligence, *my* caliber—laboring like some donkey under the authority of ignorant loudmouth fools who answered meekly to men in silk suits, men whose arrogance was made of money, men with soft hands and gross bellies who rode in plush railcars and ate off glass plates. My wrath defied intelligible expression. It dug and twisted in my soul like a knife. There were days when I wanted to howl, nights when I did.

One day a new foreman began cursing me for a slacker as I stood watching a passenger train pull out of the railyard. Its windows framed one infuriating vision after another: cuff-linked men in high collars, sipping from brandy glasses and puffing big cigars, laughing and shaking hands, patting one another's backs; and powdered women in lace dresses, unreachably beautiful, smiling at one another over teacups and utterly indifferent to the passing world, to *me*. My blood pounded. I knocked the foreman down and beat his head on a rail until it felt like a bag of broken tile under my hand.

None of the witnesses was a lawman, but one was a scar-faced railroad boss who wanted to know my name and if I knew how to use a gun. I told him to hand me his revolver and I'd show him how I could shoot. He had balls, I'll say that: I was still heaving with the thrill of smashing that skull, and it must have crossed his mind that I might as easily shoot him as the two empty bottles he pointed out in the cinders about twenty yards down the track. I blew them apart, then shattered the headlamp on a locomotive steaming on a siding another ten yards farther on, then yelled for the frightened engineer to hold his cap out. I shot it from his hand—then made it jump twice more along the ground. The boss man was all smiles. He wrote my name in a little notebook, and before the foreman's blood was dry on my hands I'd been promoted to freight guard.

A few months later Tomás Urbina and his boys stopped a train I was guarding. They swarmed into the cars shouting "*Viva la revolución!*" and shooting every man in uniform or in the clothes of the rich. Passengers jumped from the car windows and tried to run for it. Women were shrieking.

I made my decision on the spot: I put the shotgun aside and left my pistol in its holster, shoved the freight car door wide open and yelled, "Help yourselves, boys! *Viva la revolución!*"

I went forward to the locomotive, where the engineer was sprawled dead beside the tracks and Urbina was arguing with some of his boys about the proper operation of the huffing engine. It was an ancient French model that had undergone dozens of makeshift modifications to keep it running all those years. None of its gauges was accurate. It took an expert to get it under way and keep it rolling along.

Urbina noticed me listening to them with amusement and said, "Who the fuck are *you?*"

"The guy who can run this thing," I said.

By nightfall I was engineering that pile of iron onto a siding a hundred miles away, in Urbina's main camp. He stood beside me in the cab for the whole trip and told me one story after another about his love life, including a recent affair which had ended sadly.

"My God, what an ass that one had!" he said, and kissed his fingertips. Then one afternoon her husband—who happened to be the local police chief—caught them in bed and grabbed for his gun. But Urbina was prepared for this possibility and had his own ready gun under the pillow.

"Imagine this fool!" he said. "What the hell was he so jealous about? Fucking a general of the Revolution isn't cheating, for Christ's sake—it's a woman's patriotic duty!"

Whatever the case, the wife thought her husband was a lousy brute and didn't mind at all that Urbina killed him.

"But I couldn't enjoy her after that," Tomás said. "I mean, she was such a *happy* widow. Smiling, laughing, making jokes. She gave me the creeps. I suddenly felt like I was fucking Mother Death. I had to stop seeing her. But I tell you, hombre, I miss that sweet ass."

Urbina was short, dark, and red-eyed, and usually wore several days' whiskers. He couldn't read, and so he always "signed" his name with a little drawing of a heart. He was drunk as often as he wasn't. But he was cunning as a coyote and an absolutely fearless leader, and his men would follow him straight to hell. They called him the Lion of Durango.

He and his boys had just won a big fight with a federal detachment near Durango City, and they were still in high spirits about it. For good measure Urbina had robbed the Durango branch of the Bank of London of more than a quarter million pesos. "For the cause, of course," he said with a grin. Now he was getting his troops ready to join with Pancho Villa's army in Jimenez for an advance against the federals at Torreón.

He had been close friends with Villa since their boyhood, and he loved to tell stories of their bandit days and their run-ins with the Guardia Rural—the *rurales,* the suede-and-silver uniformed national mounted police force that patrolled the countryside and was infamous for its brutal efficiency. I learned that Pancho's real name was Doroteo Arrango, but at age seventeen, after killing the landowner who raped his sister and escaping to the high country, he joined Ignacio Parra's notorious outlaw gang and took the name of a famous old-time bandit named Francisco Villa. Eventually he and Urbina formed their own gang, and for years they did well for themselves, rustling cattle from the great herds of the Terrazas family and robbing payroll wagons and outland mining companies.

Yet always the Guardia Rural was on the hunt for them. Most *rurales* had been bandits themselves—before being captured and given the choice of jail or joining the police—and they knew the sierra wildlands as well as most of the outlaws they pursued. There were shoot-outs and plenty of close calls. Over the years, many of Pancho's gang were caught or killed. And all those years of hiding in the mountains gave Urbina a chronic case of rheumatism which he claimed was the main reason he drank so much— to ease the pain in his joints.

<hr />

Just before we joined Villa at Jimenez, I made the discovery of my life.

One of Urbina's bunch was a captain named Fausto Borunda. He was called El Matador because he always shot his prisoners. "Be careful of that one," I was warned by several of the boys. "He kills just to make himself smile." But the first time I got up close to him I sensed the secret truth. His hard lying eyes could fool others but they didn't fool me. I knew he was not the true killer his *compañeros* believed him to be—but he was greatly afraid not to be thought so. I understood completely: few things can hide a man's fear of death as well as a killer's reputation. My understanding, however, in no way softened my outrage. A coward who kills is the worst sort of fake. I watched him for a week and I knew I was right.

One evening I roughly shoved up against him at the bar of a cantina and made him spill his drink. He whirled on me, his face clenched like a fist. "Hey, prick!" he said. "You tired of living?" I looked him dead in the eyes and laughed. In that instant he knew he had been found out. His grab for his gun was an act of panic— but I caught his wrist and drove my knee into his balls. As he sagged to the floor, I twisted his arm to turn him away from my boots just before he puked. When he looked up again, the bore of my pistol was inches from his wide red eye. "Say hello to the truth, you phony fuck," I said, and squeezed the trigger.

After that, nobody called him Matador anymore. All they called him was dead. *I* was the true Matador. *El Carnicero*, they would come to call me—the Butcher. *El Señor Muerte:* Mr. Death. *I, Fierro.*

Goddamned right.

TWO

The Revolution had been coming for a long time, and it wasn't hard to understand why. Anybody with brains, with a sharp eye and good ears and a nose that knew the difference between fact and bullshit, could fill you in fairly well.

Allow me.

For more than thirty years Porfirio Díaz ran the country like it was his personal estate. The enemies he didn't kill he bought off with hacienda grants, political office, or generalships in the army. The only choice Díaz ever gave anybody was his bread in their mouth or his club on their head. He personally appointed the governor of every state, and any problems the governors and their henchmen couldn't handle, Don Porfirio's *rurales* or his army sure could. Army generals lived like lords, and the rich landowners—the *hacendados*—had the power of God over the peons who slaved on their land. The *hacendados* loved Porfirio Díaz. So did the foreign businessmen—the Brits and the Yankees, especially—who got such friendly and profitable deals from him on grazing land, mining rights, oil leases, shipping ports, railroad rights-of-way—anything they wanted.

What the hell, I would have loved Don Porfirio too if I'd been in their shoes. But of course I wasn't.

Thirty years Díaz ran things. Most Mexicans didn't live that long. The only thing to beat the old bastard was age. He was eighty before things finally started to slip away from him—and then they slipped away fast.

Francisco Madero led the movement against him. He was barely five-foot-three, with a melon head, a goatee, and a squeaky voice. At first the Porfiristas treated him like a joke. But he came from a wealthy family, so he had the means to make himself heard. (I always thought it interesting that so many fervent liberals happen to be rich. Are rich liberals too stupid to know where their own interests lie—or just too damn guilty to care? In either case, I never could respect a man who sided against his own kind.)

Madero had been to school in Europe and the U.S., and he came back to Mexico with his big head full of democratic notions. They say he meant well, but his own loyal brother Gustavo once called him the only foolish dreamer in the family, and their family was very large. When he ran for the presidency against Díaz on an anti-reelection platform, old Don Porfirio ridiculed him, calling him "the runt" and "the little madman." But when Díaz saw how popular the mad runt was becoming and how much he was stirring folks up, he figured enough was enough. He sent Madero running for his life across the Rio Bravo into Texas and then announced himself reelected by a landslide once again.

But up in San Antonio, Madero declared himself the provisional president and called for all freedom-loving Mexicans to take arms against the Porfiriato. He began to assemble an army, and the Revolution was on.

Abraham Gonzalez recruited Villa in Chihuahua. I never knew Gonzalez, but Urbina described him as a serious, courtly man who spoke with great eloquence and conviction about the ideals of the Revolution. "Pancho was always a fool for talkers like Don Abraham," Tomás said. "But hell, I didn't waste any time joining up, either—not when I heard we'd get full pardons for all our crimes if we did. Don Abraham said Madero understood that men like us had been driven to rob and steal by the cruelties of the dictatorship." Urbina grinned at me and winked. "Such great understanding is a rare thing, no? One has to admire it."

Six months later the Maderista rebels defeated the federal forces in a three-day battle at Ciudad Juárez and Díaz was finished. He resigned the presidency and shipped out for Europe from Veracruz. The old bull would spend the next four years living in Parisian luxury and then die in bed under silk sheets.

—➤●◄—

It was during the victory celebration at Juárez that Villa became one of Madero's most devoted disciples. Urbina was there, and the way he told the story to me, the whole thing happened because Pascual Orozco demanded the execution of the captured federal commander, an old warhorse named Navarro who was given to bayoneting rebel prisoners. Orozco had been a Chihuahua mule driver before joining the Revolution and forming his own army called the Colorados. They'd fought well for the Maderistas, and Orozco naturally thought Madero owed him a few rewards for his service—including the small right to shoot a captured enemy officer. But Madero insisted that Navarro's rights as a prisoner of war had to be respected, and rather than risk having him killed against his orders, he arranged for the general to be spirited to the river and allowed to escape to the U.S.

When Orozco heard about it, he was enraged. Villa had also been in favor of shooting Navarro, and he was swayed by Orozco's fury. "That little shrimp don't know shit about running an army," Orozco told him. "I say we take over."

They went to Madero's headquarters with a hundred armed men behind them. Orozco rushed through the door, grabbed Madero by the collar, and demanded his resignation at gunpoint. But Gustavo Madero, who had plenty of guts for a man with a glass eye, jumped on him and pulled him off his brother. Madero managed to push his way through the melee and get outside, then clambered up on the hood of a motorcar and started making a speech to Orozco's men at the top of his little voice.

The shouting Orozquistas gradually began to listen as he praised them for their victory over the federal army and the great blow they had struck for Mexican liberty. Orozco, he told them, was a fine man and a superior general who was simply feeling an excess of revolutionary spirit. "But *you* make the choice," he said to the soldiers—and he stretched out his arms like Christ on the cross. "*Kill* me if you wish! *You* decide whether I or General Orozco shall be your president!"

For a moment there was stunned silence. Then someone shouted, "Viva Madero!" In an instant the cry was taken up and chanted again and again, louder and louder. Madero smiled widely, then reached out his hand to Orozco.

"Well hell," Urbina said, "with his own men shouting 'Viva Madero!' all around him, what could Orozco do but put up his pistol and accept his hand? He sure as hell couldn't match words with him. But he was plenty pissed off, you could see it in his face."

Villa, on the other hand, was moved to tears by Madero's speech. He shoved through the crowd around the car and clutched at Madero's sleeve with one hand and tried to give him his pistol with the other. "Shoot me—*shoot* me, señor!" he cried.

"Punish me for my treachery!" Madero's readiness to die right then and there for his revolutionary ideals had impressed Pancho more than anything he'd ever seen in his life.

Madero smiled and patted him on the shoulder. "Kill *you*," he said, "the most valiant of my good men? I would sooner cut out my own heart. No, Colonel Villa, there will be no killing among this band of brothers. We are all bound by loyalty to the Revolution. Go now, and prepare your brave boys to finish up our work."

From that day on, Urbina said, Villa regarded Madero as nothing less than one of heaven's own saints. That was true. How many times in the next couple of years would I hear Pancho blab on and on about the infinite goodness of Señor Madero! Listen, I saw Madero in Monterrey, I heard him speak, and I never did understand the pipsqueak's pull on people—though I never said so to Villa, not in so many words. I'd argue with Pancho about almost anything, but I never wasted my breath arguing with him about Madero. He couldn't be reasonable on the subject, so why bother? As far as Pancho was concerned, Madero's only imperfection was his tendency to trust untrustworthy men—like Orozco, whom Villa would hate forevermore for having gulled him into mutiny against the little saint.

And like Victoriano Huerta, who blew Madero's brains out.

————

It had to happen. Madero had too many serious enemies right from the start—on both sides of him. The Díaz people of course hated him, but even some of his own supporters broke away from him pretty quickly when he didn't change things fast enough to suit them. Like Emiliano Zapata down in Morelos, who wanted his people's ancient lands returned to them and he meant right *now*.

Madero had been president only a few months when Pascual Orozco rebelled. Orozco had the backing of the northern *hacendados*, who naturally detested Madero for his intention to confiscate their lands and distribute them to the peons. They made sure the Colorados were well armed and fully supplied. Orozco's boys routed the federals in their first engagements and quickly got control of most of Chihuahua. Madero was desperate for a tough federal general to fight the rebels, so he turned to Huerta.

He couldn't have picked a tougher—or a more treacherous—son of a bitch. Huerta was a Huichol Indian with a bullet head. He wore smoky amber spectacles and drank brandy day and night, yet rarely seemed drunk. He'd made a name for himself killing Mayas in the Yucatán for Díaz. Of the many mistakes Madero made as president, the biggest was letting so many Díaz men like the bullethead continue in their government offices or their commands in the federal army. They all looked on Madero with contempt, and anybody with a grain of sense could have told him they would try to get rid of him the first chance they got. Actually, a lot of his friends did tell him, but he just waved off the warnings. He really believed the Porfiristas had accepted their defeat in the field and at the ballot box. Jesus.

Villa once told me that life's worst perversion was an educated man using his learning for unjust purpose. "Sure," I said, "it's almost as perverse as an educated man having no common sense." Like Madero, I meant, and he knew it. He gave me one of those thin yellow looks that always scared the shit out of others—but I just gave him a look right back and we let the subject drop.

Whatever else Huerta was, he was a damn good general. All summer long he beat the Colorados in one fight after another. He steadily pushed them north until he drove what was left of them—including Orozco himself—across the river and out of the country. When he got back to Mexico City, the newspapers were calling him a hero.

Madero they were calling an incompetent fool. Every day he was ridiculed in editorials and cartoons. Even before Huerta ended the Colorado rebellion, the press was demanding that the little saint resign from office. The Porfiristas in the government were also pushing him to quit, but Madero absolutely refused. He said he was president by the will of the people and swore he wouldn't leave office unless he was voted out or killed. I don't think his enemies had too much trouble choosing which of those two ways they preferred to see him go.

They got him that winter, and you have to take your hat off to how they did it. With the help of a few insiders, a couple of die-hard Porfirista generals broke out of their prison cells, retook command of their troops, and declared rebellion against Madero. The whole thing was actually part of a plot hatched by Huerta, who was still professing loyalty to the president. For the next ten days his troops made a phony defense of the Maderista government against a phony assault by the rebels. But the shells and bullets weren't phony, and the two sides turned Mexico City into a slaughterhouse of civilian casualties without doing any real damage to each other. For a long time afterward the people of the capital would talk in dark tones of horror about those ten tragic days. Artillery duels rocked the streets. Gunfire cracked and richocheted day and night. The dead bloated on the sidewalks until they were thrown in piles and burned. The city's water and electricity were cut off. The only light at night was from the flames of the cremations and the burning buildings.

Huerta knew exactly what he was doing. The carnage in the capital's streets terrified the citizens so thoroughly they were

willing to accept any resolution to put an end to it. Huerta's
resolution was to arrest Madero as the cause of all the trouble
and offer him a choice: resign and go into exile, or else. Madero
resigned. So did his vice president. By law, their resignations
boosted the foreign minister—some nobody—to the presidency. President Nobody held office for barely half an hour—just
long enough to appoint Huerta as the new minister—before he
resigned too. The legal sham made Huerta the new president of
Mexico.

Three days later, as Madero was being transferred in
the middle of the night from the National Palace to the city
penitentiary—for his own safety, they said, which is pretty damn
funny when you think about it—he was shot dead. His escort of
rurales claimed they'd been attacked by gunmen intent on freeing Madero and he'd been killed in the shoot-out. What bullshit.
Everybody knew it was assassination—and that no matter who
had pulled the trigger, the turned-down thumb was Huerta's.

Madero's brother Gustavo was killed by Huerta's thugs too. A
mob of them got hold of him in the street and in their frenzy they
tore him to pieces. Somebody took his glass eye as a trophy. They
say there wasn't enough left of him to bother burying.

Huerta had the federal army and the rich on his side, plus
the support of foreign business interests—plus Orozco and his
bastard Colorados, who wasted no time joining sides with their
former enemy. But the opposition to him was quick to form up
too. The governor of Coahuila, a white-bearded old fox named
Venustiano Carranza, refused to recognize the bullethead as
president. He formed the Constitutionalist Party with himself
as its "first chief." He pledged to restore legal constitutional government to Mexico and he called for an army to fight against the
usurper. All the Maderistas who'd fought against Díaz rushed to

join him—including Villa, who was a prison escapee living in El Paso when he heard about the little saint's murder.

———>●<———

Villa was lucky he'd gone to jail, considering that before he got locked up he'd been put up against a wall in front of a firing squad.

During the Orozco rebellion, Pancho and his cavalry had been under Huerta's command and did much of the hardest fighting, but the bullethead and his friends looked on Villa and his troops as ignorant, poorly disciplined trash. They liked to joke in Pancho's presence about the raggedly comic look of his boys in contrast to their own nattily uniformed soldiers. When Huerta wasn't insulting him he simply ignored him, except to order his cavalry to lead the toughest attacks on Colorado positions. Such orders are what led to Pancho's real trouble with Huerta.

The bullethead insisted that field officers follow his battlefield strategy exactly as planned, but Villa's way was to improvise as a battle progressed, to change tactics to suit the moment. When he did that against the Colorados at Parral, Huerta was livid with him for deviating from the plan of attack. Villa couldn't understand the reason for the bullethead's anger. He'd *won* at Parral, hadn't he? What was the problem?

The problem was that Huerta hated him and wanted him gone. Two nights later Villa was in bed with a fever in a Jiménez hotel room when he was arrested on charges of insubordination. He was taken directly to headquarters, given a ten-minute trial, and sentenced to be shot at dawn.

Next morning they stood him in front of a wall and he gave his pocketwatch and money to the soldiers assigned to shoot him. But when the rifles were raised, he dropped to his knees, cursing Huerta and weeping with outrage, loudly refusing to cooperate with what he called the injustice of his execution. The captain of the squad pleaded with him to get to his feet, but Pancho only flung dirt at him. Some have said he was not brave enough to die like a man. Believe what you will, but I know a few things about men's fear of death, and I know Villa was no coward, ever. He would later explain to me that he had been playing for time. He knew a report of Huerta's order had been telegraphed to the capital during the night, and he was certain Madero would countermand it. But when Huerta finally threatened to shoot him on his knees, Pancho got to his feet and put his back to the wall. The rifle sights were set on his heart when a telegrapher came running from headquarters, yelling that Madero's order of reprieve had arrived. In the presence of so many witnesses, Huerta had to halt the execution and, as instructed by Madero's wire, remand Villa to prison to await an official trial.

Villa was the only man I ever knew who'd stood in front of a firing squad and lived to tell the tale. "I looked the Mother of Bones right in the eyes," he said when he told me about it. I asked him what he'd seen there and what it had felt like. "The biggest fucking desert you can imagine," he said, "and like lips of ice on your throat."

His imprisonment in Mexico City wasn't the roughest I ever heard of. He bought a comfortable bed for his cell and had his meals brought to him from the outside. He'd always been good at rope tricks, and now he practiced until he was a wizard. He got regular visits from a girl named Rosita, and whenever he spoke of her in later days it was always with misty affection. (I never ceased to be amazed by how well he could recall the smallest details about the women he'd made love to—from the light in their eyes to the smell of their hair to the way they kissed or laughed or cried. Me, I hardly ever remembered their names.)

He learned to read and write from a Zapatista cellmate who had once been a schoolteacher in Morelos. The Zapatista's primer was a ragged copy of *Don Quixote*, and Villa was tickled to learn that Cervantes had written his great book in prison. He was a champion of education for the rest of his life, and he built more schools in the next ten years than Don Porfirio ever did. But he could damn near bore a man to death whenever he got started on the subject. Urbina—who amused me with the perverse pride he took in his own illiteracy—always chuckled at Pancho's high-toned pronouncements on the wonders of education. He once interrupted Villa's discourse to remark that he himself had many times heard it said ignorance was bliss. "Yes, clearly, for some it must be," Villa said, glaring at him. "It would certainly explain why *you're* the happiest asshole in the world!" Tomás just laughed with delight and affected to shine his fingernails on his shirtfront. Nobody could bandy with Villa's temper as expertly as Tomás, or get away with it so easily.

Villa's faith in Madero never wavered, not even after he'd been in prison six months without a trial. Then rumors began to snake through the penitentiary that Huerta and a gang of old Díaz generals were plotting against the little saint. Villa was sure the threat was more serious than Madero realized. His suspicions were confirmed when another prisoner, a former porfirista general, told him Madero would not be president much longer and advised Pancho to join the usurpers while he still had the chance. Pancho said he'd think it over, then immediately began to plan his escape. He talked a young prison clerk into slipping him a file and arranging for a disguise and a getaway car.

On Christmas Day of 1912, Villa squeezed through the opening he'd cut in the bars of his cell and put on his disguise—a bowler hat, dark glasses, and a Spanish cape. The night before, he'd shaved off his mustache. Then he and the clerk walked out the front gate side by side, waving adios to the guards as Villa complained loudly about that bastard Madero and how the sooner he was gotten rid of the better for everyone.

They went directly to a waiting car at the end of the street. The clerk drove like a madman through the night and all next day, until they reached the coast at Manzanillo. They took a boat to Mazatlán, then went by train to Nogales, then slipped across the border and borrowed a couple of horses from a poorly watched stable. In another few days they were in a hotel in El Paso.

Villa sent word to Don Abraham Gonzalez, his old friend in Chihuahua, warning him about the plot against Madero and pledging his service against the conspirators. Gonzalez advised him to stay in Texas until he got further instructions. Villa busied himself rounding up the few friends he could find in El Paso and outfitting them with guns and horses. Other than that, all he could do was wait.

Then came the report of Madero's murder. They say Pancho cried like a child when he was told. He wept again a few days later when he got the news that Don Abraham had been arrested, put aboard a train, taken deep into the desert, and shoved under the moving wheels.

The following day, with only eight men in his company, he crossed the river into Mexico, heading for war against Huerta.

━━━➤●◄━━━

Six months later, when I arrived in Jimenez with Urbina's boys, he was General Francisco Villa, commander of the powerful Division of the North, and his might and reputation were growing greater by the day.

THREE

"I hear you're a real killer." That was the first thing Villa ever said to me. It wasn't a question so I didn't say anything back. Urbina had called me over to the railcar serving as division headquarters and introduced us.

He was big-chested and tall for a Mexican, but I was taller—and handsomer, if the truth be told. Although he was affecting casualness, his eyes were wary as a wolf's. I accepted the cup of mescal Urbina poured. Villa was having none—he said he never drank. "Just imagine," he said, "if Pancho Villa drank. Ay! What a terrible man he would be!" He smiled and shook his head as though amused by the idea that he might ever conduct himself as anything other than the amiable man of the moment. I already knew he was a tee-totaler, and that he rarely smoked, and that his only real vice was women—if a vice they can be called. They said he could outdance any man alive. But I'd also heard he had a temper that could slip its leash without warning like a crazy red dog.

"A real killer," he repeated looking me over carefully, "that's what I hear."

"You should have *seen* the serious headache he gave Borunda!" Urbina said, holding a fist to the side of his head and flicking his fingers open wide to convey the effect of my bullet.

Villa laughed. "Borunda? That bigmouth who liked to be called El Matador? Hell, that guy was scared shitless somebody was going to shoot *him*."

Urbina shrugged and said all he knew was that Borunda wasn't scared of anything anymore.

"Listen," Villa said to me, "killing a guy like Borunda is nothing to brag about. Come with me."

I followed him outside and across the railyard, then around behind the depot, where a dozen federal officers sat listlessly under guard in a stock pen. When they caught sight of Villa, they jumped to their feet, their eyes suddenly wide and white. The roused smell of their fear carried to me like a thin spicy smoke.

Villa signaled one of the guards to bring out a young officer who was trying to hide behind the others. The guard prodded the captain out of the pen with his rifle and Villa grasped the prisoner by the collar. "Easy, little brother," he said. "Be brave." The captain's eyes looked like they were trying to escape from his head. "Please, my general," he said, "I beg you, please."

"The Revolution demands many things of us," Villa said to me, grinning as he drew his pistol. "The hardest is to do this." He shoved the gun muzzle into the captain's mouth and blasted off the back of his head in a bright red spray. The dead man dropped like a sack of cornmeal.

Villa reholstered the pistol and walked over to me, no longer grinning. "It's easy to kill a man you hate personally," he said, "but not so easy to kill a man you don't know—not when you have to look into his face and see his fear, not when he's begging you for his life and telling you about his poor mother and his wife and little children. And they *do* have wives and children, these men. They *do* have mothers."

He gestured toward the prisoners in the pen, who were now even more terrified. "Look at them. What harm can they do now, eh? But we *must* kill these men, amigo. We must kill them even as we look into their frightened eyes. Because their eyes were not so frightened when they were ordering their soldiers to kill *our* boys and make widows of *our* women. Even the first chief knows this. His order is to shoot all officers. He has made it our *duty* to shoot them." He clapped a hand on my shoulder and smiled again. "Of course, such a revolutionary duty comes more easily to some men than to others, eh, amigo?"

We exchanged a long look. Feeling cheerful in a way I'd never felt before, I stepped away from Villa and beckoned the three prisoners nearest the pen gate to come to me. They came out hesitantly, one with his hands laced in front of him in supplication. The smoky scent of fear was stronger now, as heady as perfume.

"Don't be scared, boys," I said—but if they hadn't been, the proceeding would have been robbed of much of its pleasure. I stood them tightly together, the one in the middle with his chest against the back of the man in front and with his back against the chest of the man behind. They were all of nearly equal height, so there was no need for anybody to bend his knees to assure a proper alignment. One of the pistols I was carrying was a Colt .45 Peacemaker with a special fourteen-inch barrel. It had once belonged to an old Yankee cavalryman who used it to shoot Indians at long range. I stepped behind the three huddled federals, drew the gun, aimed carefully, and shot all three through the heart with the same bullet.

Villa was laughing. "A executioner with a sense of thrift!" he said, and slapped me on the back like a longtime comrade. He made me a colonel and put me in charge of the division's railway operations.

———◦———

We hammered Torreón for three days before the federals abandoned the town and retreated in the night across the Nazas River. Our booty was bountiful: a dozen artillery pieces, a thousand rifles, countless cases of cartridges, hundreds of hand grenades, six machine guns—and, best of all, *forty* locomotives and hundreds of boxcars to go with them. From now on the entire Division of the North would travel by rail. I'd already equipped one entire train for the single purpose of maintaining all the others and repairing destroyed track. Villa himself had come up with the idea of a hospital train. It consisted of thirty cars with big blue crosses on their sides and carried a team of more than forty doctors, about half of them gringos. Each car had enameled floors and was outfitted with the most modern surgical equipment. No other army in Mexico—probably in the world—had a train like it.

The richest people in Torreón—as everywhere in the country—were of course the goddamn Spaniards, who'd been the curse of Mexico since the day Cortés set foot on it. Villa ordered the confiscation of their property in the name of the Revolution and ordered every one of them to get out of town within twenty-four hours—and out of Mexico within three days—or be shot.

The Chinese he didn't give a choice. They were shot on sight and their shacks were burned to the ground. They were the yellow cockroaches of Mexico and everybody hated them, but Villa's hatred of them went deeper than most. "They are too ashamed to be poor in their own damned country," he once told me, "so they come *here* to be poor. Who the hell do they think they are to insult Mexico like that?"

We killed over 800 federals in the assault on Torreón, and took 120 prisoners. Thirty-two were officers. I was in charge of the executions but at Villa's request I permitted Maclovio Herrera a few turns at commanding the firing squad. Villa always did have a special fondness for Herrera—who knows why. I liked Maclovio all right, but I had a hunch he couldn't be trusted. When I mentioned it to Villa, he glowered at me and said I was too damn suspicious of everybody, which was why I had no friends. Christ, he was nobody to talk about being suspicious. Every night he went off into the darkness with his blanket, and in the morning he'd come back into camp from another direction. Nobody was going to shoot *him* in his sleep. Or poison him, either: his usual way of eating was to go out among the boys and have some beans from one man's plate, some meat from another's, a tortilla from still another's. But he did have friends he trusted, and, except for him, I didn't—that was certainly true. On the other hand, I never had my trust betrayed—not by Maclovio Herrera or any other man—and Villa sure as hell couldn't say that, not later on.

I won't deny that Herrera was a good field commander— and as tough as they come, which was to be expected of anybody who could survive years of slavery in the silver mines. They were the worst reaches of hell. Maclovio had been sent down into the Lampaca Mines of Durango when he was only thirteen. Every morning before sunrise the miners had to descend narrow ladders hundreds of feet into a blackness so great it seemed to swallow the light of the shaft lamps. They didn't come back out again until long after sundown. They worked naked in the smothering heat, swinging a pick against the mine wall. Every time a man filled a sack with ore, he'd labor up the ladder with the two-hundred-pound load hanging on his back by a rawhide strap around his forehead. Maclovio's scar from that strap looked like somebody had run a branding iron around his skull. At the trolley tier, still a hundred feet underground, the miner would dump his load of ore into a mule cart and go down to his pick again. Every so often a man went crazy for lack of air and would have to be subdued with ropes. Gradual blindness was a common affliction. Lungs were ruined by the thick dust in the shafts, and once a miner began coughing up blood, he'd do it till he finally drowned in it. Every day men fell to their death from the ladders. Bodies too difficult to extricate were left to rot in the pit bottoms, and Herrera said the stench could not be described. On the day Villa's boys attacked the Lampaca operation, Maclovio and the other miners came scrabbling up out of the shafts like uncaged demons. They raced straight to the main house and caught the *hacendado* just as he was about to make his escape. They crucified him against the huge mahogany gate of the *casa grande* and put a torch to his balls. Maclovio used to say the Revolution had pulled him out of the deepest grave in Mexico.

———⟫⟪———

Villa got married twice before we left Torreón. The first time was to a seamstress named Juana whom he met in a tailor shop. "Her tits are the most magnificent you've ever seen!" he told me and Urbina the next day. When Tomás said he doubted very much that they were the best *he'd* seen, Pancho insisted we come up to his wedding suite and have a look for ourselves, so we did. They were damn fine breasts, all right. But Tomás thought they didn't have quite enough sag to be perfect, and I felt obliged to admit I preferred darker nipples than hers. The girl rolled her eyes and said, "Paaanncho!" Villa flung the sheet back over her and told us to go to hell. "You jackasses don't know tits from tin cans."

The next day a girl of about sixteen stood out in the street in front of our headquarters building and cursed Villa at the top of her voice. She was waving a skinning knife and calling him a murderer because our boys had killed her brothers. Villa took a look through the window and gave a low whistle. He went out and stood in front of her, ripped open his shirt, and said if she truly believed that he, Pancho Villa, a patriot fighting for Mexico's liberty, was a murderer, then his life was not worth living and she could go ahead and plunge the blade into his heart. He moved fast enough to avoid being killed on the spot, although she managed to open a good-sized gash along his ribs. He accidentally broke her wrist in taking the knife from her. With blood running down his side and soaking his waistband, he set her broken arm and applied the splint himself, all the while whispering endearments to her and pausing to kiss the inner crook of her elbow. A doctor then bandaged his wound while a priest was summoned. Ten minutes later Pancho was making love to his new wife in a hotel across the street from the one where his bride of the day before was still ensconced.

According to Urbina, Villa already had at least a dozen "wives" throughout the states of Durango, Chihuahua, and Coahuila. "Most guys fuck a woman and that's that," Tomás said. "Maybe give her a few pesos to buy a new dress. That's natural, no? But Pancho, he insists on marrying them. He figures what the hell, a church marriage isn't legal anyway, but it makes the woman feel respected, and feeling respected makes her happy, and a happy woman gives a man a better time in bed. So, he marries them. I asked him one time how happy it made them when they found out they were not the only wife of Pancho Villa, and he said I should become a newspaper reporter instead of a revolutionary if I was going to go around asking a lot of stupid questions."

FOUR

O n our way north to attack Juarez we got lucky and intercepted a coal train bound south from the federal garrison. At a small wayside station, Villa forced the conductor to send a telegram back to headquarters saying that the rail line to Chihuahua had been destroyed and the train could not proceed. As we expected, the federal commander at Juárez wired back curses and ordered the train to return to the garrison immediately, before it could be captured by Constitutionalist rebels. In the flickering lamplight I grinned at Pancho and nodded my admiration for his plan. We quickly emptied all the coal from the cars and packed them with our troops. With a pistol pressed to his ear, the conductor wired reports of the train's safe progress from every station on the way back

We rolled into Juárez in the middle of the night without arousing suspicion, then slipped into the garrison as quiet as cats. Most of the government troops were sleeping or drunk, and our rifles were in their faces before they realized what was happening. "Viva Villa!" the boys hollered, and couldn't stop laughing at the dumfounded federals. I led a sweep of the garrison, and we made short work of the few fools who tried to fight. Villa sent Herrera's bunch into town to clean out the gambling halls. Juárez had dozens of them, and at that hour they were doing their heaviest business. In the name of the Revolution we confiscated every peso and Yankee dollar showing on the tables.

In the officers' quarters I found a dead-drunk colonel snoring loudly in bed with a big-titted blonde. I rolled him off the bed and took his pistol. For a moment the blonde gave me a narrow look—then she smiled and threw the covers off the musky whiteness of herself. At some point in the course of things I found out she was a German opera singer. When I left her at dawn I could hardly walk upright. I never should have told Villa about her: for weeks afterward he kept pestering me for details about that night.

We'd taken Juárez without losing a man. The gringo papers loved the whole thing. "The Trojan train" they called Villa's trick, and now Pancho was more famous than ever. Wherever he went in Juárez or El Paso, reporters flocked about him like cattlebirds in a bull pasture. Some of the gringo reporters were irritated at having to use translators to interview him, and one asked if he could speak any English at all. Villa grinned and said, "Sí, claro. Fuck you goddamn son of a bitch." That was about all the English most of us knew. The only one who didn't laugh was the guy who asked the question.

Even the mayor of El Paso, an Irishman named Kelly, met with Villa. His big concern was that when the federals tried to retake Juárez—which everybody knew they were sure to do—the good citizens of his town would be endangered by bullets and artillery shells straying across the river.

The mayor had reason to worry. Two years earlier, although their own people had warned them to stay under cover when the Maderistas attacked the federal forces at Juárez, the good people of El Paso had packed the rooftops to watch the spectacle of

Mexican warfare while sipping their tea and whiskey. They spread picnic blankets on the hillsides, even on the riverbank. Folks came from miles around to see the big show. Then the shooting started and bullets flew every which way, and naturally some of the spectators got killed by their entertainment. The U.S. government growled at Madero about the gringo casualties, but let it go at that. A few weeks earlier the U.S. Cavalry had crossed into Agua Prieta and put an end to a battle between federals and rebels after some of the spectators across the border in Douglas, Arizona, had been killed by stray fire.

Villa patted the Irishman's shoulder and assured him he had nothing to worry about. He told him we would engage the federals far enough to the south that the good people of El Paso would be safe even from the dust we raised. Hell, he didn't care if the good people of El Paso all dropped dead in the next five minutes. He was just trying to please some of his new American friends— people he thought might be useful in keeping us supplied with U.S. arms or in good favor with the Yankee government.

One such new friend was a grizzled general named Hugh Scott, who was then commanding the fort in El Paso. He was burly and short-haired, wore a white mustache and wire-rimmed eyeglasses, and spoke damn good Spanish for a Yankee. He came to Villa as an emissary from President Wilson, and they took a true liking to each other. When Villa introduced us, Scott said, "Fierro, eh? The man of iron." He smiled at the meaning of my name, but I knew he'd heard of me and could see he meant no disrespect.

He told Villa that although President Wilson was very much in sympathy with our cause, he was greatly concerned with our practice of shooting prisoners. Every time we executed captives, Scott said, we harmed our cause in the eyes of the American public. "Our people get all upset when they read in the papers that you boys shoot unarmed men," he said. "It goes contrary to the American sense of humanitarianism and fair play. So they complain to their congressmen, who complain to the President, who complains to those of us he's made his representatives to you. You see?"

Villa said he was surprised there was so much complaining north of the border. "I always heard the United States was a *happy* country," he said. Anyhow, we didn't shoot *everybody* we captured, he told Scott. All officers, yes, because they were often educated men who ought to know better than to serve the oppressors of the poor—and even if they weren't educated, they were the givers of orders and had to be held to account. And all Colorados, yes, because they were mostly peons like ourselves, and no peon would fight against the Revolution unless he was basically an evil man—and who could argue against killing an evil man? But captured enlisted men who were not Colorados were always given the choice of joining us in our fight for democracy and justice for all. Any of them who refused this generous offer was either one more evil man or simply too stupid to do the right thing, and we could hardly be held responsible for any man's self-destructive stupidity.

Nevertheless, to prove to Scott that he, General Francisco Villa, was as much of a humanitarian as the next man, Pancho promised him that he would give the federal officers we'd captured in Juárez the choice of taking asylum across the border or joining the Division of the North against Huerta the Jackal. Scott was so heartened by this—"Choice is the very bedrock of democracy, General," he said—that Pancho went even further and swore that from now on he'd give *all* our prisoners a choice other than facing a firing squad.

"Even the Colorados?" Scott asked.

"Yes, of course, certainly." Pancho said.

Scott smiled like a happy grandfather. He said President Wilson would be very pleased to hear of our newly enlightened policy toward prisoners of war. Villa shook the general's hand and smiled right back and said few things gave him as much satisfaction as pleasing President Wilson.

As soon as Scott was gone, Villa took me aside and said, "So now we give the bastards a choice, eh?"

I doubted it. At times he could do tricks with logic as prettily as he could twirl a rope, and I figured this was one of those times. So I just shrugged and let him get to it.

"But now, I ask you," he said, "did you hear me say *what* choices besides a firing squad, what choices *exactly*, we would give them?"

I said no, now that he mentioned it, I had not heard him state any specific alternatives.

"Well," he said, "are there not many, *many* choices a man might be given other than to be stood against a wall?"

I said yes, that was true, there were many choices indeed.

"Well then, amigo," he said, grinning whitely, "you just be sure to give the bastards *some* kind of choice from now on, you hear? After all, choice is the bedrock of democracy, you know."

⸺⊰◆⊱⸺

They cried, they pleaded for mercy, they whimpered, they prayed aloud to the Holy Virgin, they sang all the sweet songs of fear.

Shameful Colorado sons of bitches. Not one of them had the balls to curse me even now, at the hour of his death. These were men who cut the soles off their prisoners' feet, who raped little girls who had not yet had their first blood, who tied old men to pairs of horses and tore them apart. The Colorados were

despicable bastards, far worse than Huerta the traitor, who at
least always fought like a soldier and behaved like a man. (It was
said he had himself shaved every morning by a young barber
whose father he had shot in public as a rebel sympathizer.) But
these whoresons lacked all sense of honor. They thought there
was as much triumph in the slaughter of old men and little boys
as in victory over warriors. They thought it was as much a show
of power to terrify a woman as to make a man afraid. A man cannot get more contemptible than that. But now *they* were crying
like women, now *they* were as frightened as children—because I,
Fierro, had just announced that I was going to shoot them.

I raised my hands and patted down the volume of their wailing. "But you have a *choice*," I told them, "and I want you to listen
to it very carefully."

There were 302 of them. I had several counts made to be sure.
This would be an act of legend, and as with all legends its details
would change with telling over time. But I wanted that particular
detail fixed firmly, so there would never be any doubt of it: 302.

They were penned in a corral on one side of a large stable-
yard surrounded by adobe walls. The walls were eight feet high,
and the one directly across from the corral gate stood about thirty
yards away over open ground. I explained that I was going to sit
by the water trough a few feet from the gate with a pistol in each
hand. At my signal, ten prisoners at a time would be released
from the corral. "Anybody who can make it over that far wall can
go free," I told them. "You have my word."

Against the sudden chorus of confused hope, I again had to
gesture for quiet. "Your choice is this," I said. "You can try to make
it over the wall before I shoot you, or you can refuse to try, in
which case one of the boys up on the wall behind you will shoot
you where you stand."

Their protests rose like a flock of alarmed blackbirds.

"Hey, boys," I said, "*ten* at a time? I bet half of you guys will be laughing at me from the other side of that wall." I'm not about to deny I was enjoying myself.

I sat with my back against the trough and instructed Ignacio, my orderly, to sit beside me with a case of ammunition and a third revolver. "I shoot and you load," I said. "And listen, brother: if any of these shitheads gets away because I don't have a loaded pistol in my hand, I'll send *you* running for that wall, understand?"

The late afternoon was beautiful: chilly, the blue sky clear, the sunlight as smooth and bright as a polished cartridge. Of the first ten to come out the gate, two ran straight at me and met their bullet head-on. Some dropped to their knees and begged for their lives. Some tried hiding behind others as they went for the wall. Some ran in a straight line, some in a zigzag route. One of them flapped his arms as he ran, like he was hoping to fly out of there. I shot them all and signaled for ten more.

Each time I emptied a pistol, I dropped it in Ignacio's lap and continued firing with the other as he handed me a freshly loaded one. I never missed. My gunfire mingled with the cheers of the boys watching from the rear wall, with the cries and moans of the dying. An occasional rifle shot finished off the twitching among the fallen. Each shot kicked in my hand like a heartbeat.

I worked steadily, pausing only once to smoke a cigarette. A pair of vultures showed up and sailed in lazy circles overhead. Beside me, Ignacio was soaked with sweat and stinking like a goat. The layer of bodies scattered between the wall and the corral grew thicker and made footing more difficult for each successive group. By sunset the air was cold and blue, fragrant with gunsmoke and the coppery smell of blood.

I let the last twelve make their run together. Six fell as I emptied the first revolver, then I switched to the other and dropped five more. I held my aim on the last man, my gun sight following him to the wall, rising with him as he leaped and grabbed hold and pulled himself up. As he swung one leg over the top, I heard Ignacio whisper fiercely, "Shoot, chief, *shoot!*"

But I didn't, and the Colorado dropped out of sight. I had intended to spare the first one out of the pen: I wanted the others to see him clear the wall and thus be inspired to their best effort to gain it. But when the first one came right at me, I'd had to let him have it in the teeth. So I'd decided on the last one.

Ignacio gave me a worried glance, then quickly busied himself gathering the spent cartridge casings. But some of the boys thought the prisoner had got away because I'd run out of bullets, and they rushed to the spot where he'd gone over. "I'll get him, Chief!" one yelled, and aimed his Mauser into the gathering gloom. He fired twice and cursed loudly. The others jeered him for his lousy marksmanship. "He's into the chaparral, Chief!" somebody hollered. "That's it, he's gone!"

"Hey, you!" I yelled up at the corporal who had fired at the fleeing Colorado. "If that's the best you can do, maybe we ought to get rid of you too while we're at it." I raised the pistol at him. He dropped his rifle and put out his palms as if they could shield him. I aimed and fired—putting the round close enough to his ear to let him hear the buzz. Then I grinned at him and said, "Hell, boy, I guess we're *both* too tired to shoot straight anymore today." It broke the boys up. Even the corporal managed a smile. Later I was told he'd shit his pants.

Not till I gave the pistols to Ignacio to be cleaned did I feel the pain in my hands. Both index fingers were swollen. I knew most of the boys were still watching me, fixing me and the moment in their memories, me and 302 glass-eyed dead men lying in twisted piles. They would remember this day and my hands with the swollen trigger fingers. They would describe them to others, to their children—I knew that. They would always tell this tale of Fierro the Butcher.

"Ignacio," I said, holding up my sore fingers, "before some sweet *muchacha* massages anything else on me tonight, she's going to massage these."

"Hard work, Chief!" he shouted. His features were obscured by the closing darkness, but I could see the pale slash of his grin—and feel the heat of his great throbbing pleasure in simply being alive.

FIVE

To slow down the federal advance along the Central Railroad, Villa sent me and a few of the boys about forty-five miles south of Juárez to blow up the tracks. We were still planting the dynamite when the federals got within artillery range and opened fire on us. I laughed at the boys for jumping in fright at the shell bursts all around us. "Don't worry, compadres," I told them. "As long as we're standing on the tracks, we're safe. They don't want to destroy the rails with their own goddamn cannonfire."

As he hurriedly dug a small niche to hold a dynamite stick under the rail, one of the boys, a likable fellow named Calixto, shouted that he wouldn't be half as worried if the federals *were* trying to hit us. He reminded me of the many times I'd ridiculed federal marksmanship. It was because they *weren't* trying to hit us that he was sure a shell was going to land square on his head. He jumped a foot off the ground as a round blasted within twenty yards of us—and I laughed even harder.

"Don't be so scared, boys!" I yelled. "It's a fiesta! Listen to it! Dance, little brothers, dance to the music of those cannons."

Whenever I carried on like that in the middle of fusillades and artillery fire, the boys looked at me like I had horns and a pointed tail. But they also worked more surely and fought more bravely, certain that they were safe with me because I, Fierro, was indestructible.

And I was. It had been so decreed by the witchwoman who presided at my birth. As soon as the *bruja* pulled me from my mother's womb, she held me over the cook fire in the hut, blood dripping off her hands and sizzling in the coals. She blew on the fire to raise a flame and lowered me to it. Her hands smoked, but I made no outcry. "This one," she told my mother, "will never die by the hand of man."

We engaged the federals just outside of Tierra Blanca and were getting our asses kicked until Villa countered with his favorite battlefield tactic, *un golpe tremendo*—one tremendous blow: a mass charge by the cavalry, with the infantry running up right behind. As always, it succeeded. The federals piled into their trains and fled back toward their main garrison in Chihuahua City. We rolled over Tierra Blanca just as the last train was pulling away. I put the spurs to my horse and caught up to the engine. The two guards stared at me in astonishment when they should have been firing at me. I shot them both, then jumped aboard, kicked off the engineer and released the brake cylinder. The great wheels locked against the rails and shrieked like the end of the world until the train came to a halt. The federals came out of the cars with their hands up high. "Short trip, shitheads!" our boys hollered at them. "You'll never get to fuck your mothers again, but don't worry, we'll take care of that!"

Because we were in a hurry to move on, Urbina helped me with the prisoners. We lined them up along the train and then made our way quickly down the track, from engine to caboose.

"You know what I like?" Tomás said, reloading while I took my turn with the shooting. "The way the little red holes pop out so bright on those white uniforms."

Villa was jubilant to have possession of yet another train. He gave me a huge hug and put me in command of the Dorados— the Golden Ones—his elite new cavalry force. Three squadrons of one hundred men each, they were the best horsemen and most fearsome fighters in the Division of the North. They struck hard and fast and killed without quarter. Every Dorado wore a splendid special uniform and a Stetson hat embroidered with gold; each was issued two superb horses, a carbine, and a pair of Colt revolvers. The rest of the division held us in awe, and the federals came to fear us like the devil's own legion.

⎯⎯⎯⎯⎯

A month later we took Ojinaga in the same bold fashion. Most of the federals fled across the river into Presidio, Texas, where the Yankee troops took them into custody and interned them in a huge corral next to their fort. Villa met with the gringo commander on the river bridge and assured him we would not pursue any of the federals into U.S. territory or even shoot into Texas at them.

"I think it is very gallant of you, my general," Villa said, "to accommodate those noble enemies of mine who choose to cross the river to safety rather than stay and fight like men." The interpreter didn't have to translate his sarcasm.

The gringo gave Villa a tight little smile and said, "Well, General, the way I figure it, if I send them back to you, the only accommodation you're likely to give them would be about six feet deep."

They both laughed real big over that, but not me. I could see that this gringo was not a man of true humor, not at all like our friend Scott. He laughed only with his mouth, while his eyes studied Pancho as carefully as an undertaker's measuring for a coffin. I knew he was no friend of ours and never would be.

"You think I didn't see the falseness in his face?" Pancho said later. "But who cares what he really thinks. He's one more gringo big shot who thinks he's dealing with just another stupid Mexican. As long as I smile and nod at everything he says, he feels happy and superior and doesn't take us seriously. And that means the border stays loose and we don't have trouble selling cows and buying guns on the other side."

Villa later accepted an invitation from that same general to tour Fort Bliss in El Paso, and once again Pancho played the impressed and slow-witted warlord. But I don't think the lean gringo general with the little iron mustache was ever really fooled. I think he knew Villa was truly as shrewd and capable as his reputation held. I think he was letting Villa fool himself. Despite Villa's casual dismissal of him, I could see this gringo was no toy soldier. His name was John Pershing. They said he was called Black Jack because one of his regiments was composed of Negroes. Two years later his soldiers would be hunting for us all over Chihuahua with orders to kill us.

At the moment, however, a far more dangerous false friend was Venustiano Carranza. Although Carranza was no soldier himself, Villa had been loyal and obedient to him right from the start of the fight against Huerta. Carranza was, after all, the founder of the Constitutionalist rebels, the party's first chief, and Villa's loyalty to the cause obliged his loyalty to its leader. But as time went by, it became obvious that Carranza's opinion of himself was as large as the Sierras ("It's that long white beard," Urbina once said. "It makes him think he's God") and that his ambitions went a lot further than just getting rid of the bullethead. His greatest yearning—probably his only one, and thus all the more consuming, for he was said to be a man of no fleshly appetites—was to be the next president of Mexico.

As soon as they'd met, Villa knew Carranza was not the proper successor to Madero. "He never once looked me directly in the eyes through his little blue spectacles," Pancho said. "He used a lot of big words he knew damn well I didn't understand. He enjoyed showing everybody how much better educated than me he was. I was angry of course, but I didn't show it. More than anything, I felt sorrow. I was sad to see that he was just one more double-talking politician. But what else should I have expected from a rich landowner? Señor Madero was the only rich man who had a good heart. God rest his soul."

Still, for the sake of revolutionary unity, Villa had remained loyal to Carranza, although his distrust of him continued to grow. It was pretty clear, too, that Carranza was afraid of Pancho—and afraid he was getting too powerful. He was a man consumed by suspicions and jealousies, and he did everything he could to hold back the Division of the North, to keep us from getting stronger. The only help we ever really got from him was Felipe Angeles, who was the man Villa came to respect most after the little saint.

Angeles was a nobleman, a hidalgo who'd been educated in Paris and trained in the best military colleges. He was refined, restrained, impeccable in manners, a man of sober reflection— everything, in other words, that most of us were not and never would be. He was reputed to be the best soldier in Mexico, though I wouldn't say *that*. He'd been absolutely loyal to Madero, and when he joined the Constitutionalist cause against Huerta, Carranza had appointed him his secretary of war. Just after we took

Ojinaga and drove the last of the federals out of Chihuahua, Villa received a wire from Angeles expressing admiration for his leadership and saying he would be honored to serve with him at some time in the future. Like everybody else, Villa had heard of the great Felipe Angeles, and he was flattered as a schoolgirl to get such respectful attention from him. When he requested that Angeles be assigned to the Division of the North, he never expected the whitebeard to do it, but he did. It turned out that many of Carranza's officers resented Angeles's superiority and wanted to get rid of him; they were as much given to their military jealousies as the whitebeard was to his political ones. In any case, Angeles was a keen advantage to us. There was no greater master of artillery— *that* I will say—and Villa gave him command of our big guns.

One cold and windy evening an old gringo showed up at the officers' fire in our main camp. He was looking for General Villa, but Pancho was in Chihuahua City a few miles away, visiting a lady friend, so the gringo had been directed to Urbina.

Gringos were always showing up out of nowhere, many of them in response to the recruiting poster Villa was circulating throughout the borderland. "Attention gringo," it said in English. "For gold and glory, come south of the border and ride with Pancho Villa, el libertador of Mexico. Weekly payments in gold to dynamiters, machinegunners, and railroaders. Enlistments taken in Juárez, Mexico. Viva Villa! Viva la revolución!"

Some of the gringos we'd enlisted were experienced professional mercenaries, but most were just wild young men looking for adventure or on the run from Yankee law. But this hollow-eyed old fellow looked like a whiskered skeleton hung with rags. His skin was gray as his beard. He wore a blue military cap from the days of the Americans' civil war and lugged a Gladstone bag. The old Remington .44 in his waistband looked like a small cannon and weighted his pants down comically on his hips. If Death had been a clown, this old-timer would have been its picture. He claimed to be a writer of tales, a man of some literary reputation in his own country. His Spanish was stiffly formal, as though he'd learned it well in school.

"Hey, gringo," Calixto said, "you should write about me. The mouths of your American readers will hang open—like this— when they read about my bravery and all the sons of whores I've killed and all the beautiful girls I have made love to. I have lived a particularly fascinating—"

"Oh shut up, Calixto," Urbina said. "Nobody wants to hear your bullshit." Tomás's rheumatism had been flaring up and he was in a touchy mood. Calixto shrugged and grinned at our laughter. He'd told plenty of bullshit stories to newspapermen. All the boys had. The gringo reporters, especially, had an insatiable thirst for stories of what they called "the horrors of war." But they also wanted small and touching proofs of human decency and nobility worked into the tales. In addition to the killing, they wanted to hear about women lighting candles in the churches every day for the safe return of their sweethearts and husbands and sons. They wanted to hear about orphans rescued from devastated towns and removed to new and loving families, far from the war. They wanted to hear about men giving up their own lives in order to save those of their comrades, to hear about love letters found in the pockets of men killed in battle. The Yankee reporters said their readers liked war stories that were sweetened with such sentimental illusions.

Calixto was one of the best at concocting such tales. I once heard him tell a reporter he had paused in the middle of a battle to help a comrade deliver his woman's child even as the artillery shells were exploding all around them. He said they'd washed the infant with canteen water and tucked it snugly to the woman's breast, then carried her and the child through the buzzing bullets until they found a protected hollow in the trees behind a hill. The comrade promised mother and child he would return to them as soon as the battle was over, and then he and Calixto left to rejoin the fighting. But the unlucky comrade was killed by one of the last bullets fired in that battle, Calixto said, and after he'd buried him, he went back for the woman and child but they were gone. He searched everywhere but couldn't find them. "To this day, señor," he told the reporter, "I search for them. I search in every town we come to, in every village, however large or small." He said he would search all of Mexico for them until the day he found them—and then he would ask the woman to marry him, and he would make the child his own. "The *family*, señor!" Calixto had intoned with powerful solemnity as the reporter smiled to himself and scribbled furiously in his little notebook, "the family is all! The family must *endure!*"

Months later, somebody came along with a yellowed clipping from the *El Paso Times* and read it to a bunch of the boys. It was Calixto's story, all right, except that his own name had been changed to Pedro and his friend's name had also been altered, and the battlefield had been moved from Chihuahua to just north of Mexico City. Calixto was thrilled to have his story in print—even though he himself could not read it—but he was outraged by its inaccuracies. "I should go to El Paso and tell the chief of that damn newspaper what a rotten reporter this bastard is! What kind of ignorant son of a bitch thinks Chihuahua is twenty miles north of the capital! What kind of reporter lies about people's *names?"* He was so angry he refused to tell reporters any more bullshit stories for almost a month.

But the old gringo said he wasn't here to write stories. He was all through writing stories. He said a writer's life could be duller than death, and the combination of such a dull occupation and the undeniable advances of old age had become more than he could bear. He was here to join Villa.

"I seek the rediscovery of adventure, my friends," he said. "It has been too long since I last knew the excitement of imminent mortal threat."

Urbina snorted. "Another fucking gringo looking for thrills among the Mexicans. All these people think we're just another one of their fucking moving picture shows. They all want to be in the show and pretend they're Jesse James."

Urbina loved to tell about the time in Juárez he and a bunch of his boys went to one of the first moving picture shows in that town. The problems started at the ticket stand by the front door when Cholo Martinez insisted that he should only have to pay half price because he only had one eye. The ticket seller insisted just as adamantly that Cholo had to pay the same price as everybody else. Suppose *everybody* wore a patch over his eye to avoid paying full price and then took off the patch in the theatre and watched the moving pictures with both eyes? Then who would be cheating whom? "In *that* case," Cholo said, "just make everybody with an eye patch show you what's under it." He pulled up his patch and thrust his raw and empty socket to within inches of the officious little man's face. Urbina said that the fellow nearly threw up. He allowed Cholo to go in for half-price.

Then the movie started and things got worse. The movie was about the famous gringo bandit Jesse James, and the moment the James Gang rode onto the screen, whooping and shooting, many of the spectators dove for cover under the benches. A moment later a posse of lawmen was in pursuit of the bandits across the white sheet tacked to the wall, and in the spirit of outlaw brotherhood somebody in the audience joined Jesse in shooting at them. In the next instant the whole movie house was engaged in a gunfight. More than a dozen men were killed, including the projectionist, who knocked the projector over as he fell dead—and who, as it turned out, was the only one in town who knew how to operate the machine. Thus, even after the smoke cleared and the dead and wounded were removed from the theater, the survivors were denied the satisfaction of seeing the remainder of the film. They would have shot the movie house manager in protest if he had not already been taken away with a bullet in the leg. "One thing about the moving picture shows," Urbina would always say in the tone of a schoolteacher. "They are not an entertainment suitable for everyone. Only those with strong nerves should be permitted to look at them."

"What about your family, old one?" somebody asked the graybeard gringo. "Aren't they worried about Grandpa coming to Mexico to be a revolutionary?" There were snickers all around, but the old man didn't seem to mind.

"I've said all my farewells," he said. "Henceforth my future shall be decided by the fortunes of war."

We exchanged looks around the fire. *The fortunes of war?* Those were the words of a writer, all right—or of a goddamn stage actor—of anybody but a real person. Urbina was right: the Revolution was no different from a moving picture show to these people. They came to play a role in some picture show in their heads, just like in that movie Urbina had seen in Juárez. Christ! They were so full of self-deception, these gringos. They had such false illusions of the world and such heroic fantasies of themselves.

Sitting cross-legged near the campfire, Urbina squirmed in irritation with the old fool. "So you've come to Mexico to find . . . what did you say . . . *adventure?*"

"These are adventurous times in your country, my general," the old man said.

"And the risk of being killed?" Urbina said. "Does that not disturb you even a little?"

"Better death by a bullet," the old man said, "'than to droop with decay until one falls like a withered flower drained of all color.'"

"Oh, *I* see," Urbina said. "What you really want is to avoid the humiliations of old age. No pissing in the bed in the middle of the night, no spit hanging from your chin at the supper table, no sad memories of the last hard-on you ever had. I understand." His voice had an edge. The old goat had really nettled him.

The gringo was startled by Urbina's tone. He seemed unsure what to say.

"I'll tell you what else I understand, you damn scarecrow," Tomás said. "You're ready to die, all right, but you're too damn much of a coward to just go off in the desert and do it. You want somebody to pull the trigger on you. *That's* why you're here."

Now the old gringo tried to look offended, but the truth of Urbina's words was in his eyes. "You misjudge me, my friend," he said stiffly. "I'm here to fight for General Villa. Yes, I meant what I said about yearning for the excitement of my soldiering youth, but more important than my yearning is the cause of your revolution. Liberty is imagination's most prized possession, and my imagination bows to no man's."

"Bullshit!" Urbina said. "You *want* to die, old man. You have the look, you have the smell. But you won't be satisfied to just die—no, you've got to die like a hero in a song or a poem. You want to get it on the battlefield from a Mexican bullet. Well, to hell with you! Why should any Mexican do the job for you? We're not your goddamn servants. Go home, you cowardly old bastard! Go home and die in the stink of your oldness!"

Tomás had worked himself into a genuine rage. He tried to get up, but the rheumatism had him tight in its jaws, and he grunted and sat back down hard. His face gleamed with the sweat of his pain.

"You do me an injustice, sir," the old gringo said. "I am no coward."

"What?" Urbina said. "*What?*"

"I resent your accusation, sir. I am *not* rushing to that house of indifference we call the tomb, although I assure you I have no fear of—"

"Oh goddamn it, *here!*" Urbina yanked out his pistol and shot the old man squarely through the forehead before he even had a chance to look surprised.

"*Fucking* gringos!" Tomás said. "They always have to have their way, *always.*"

———————

When Villa got back the next morning and learned that Tomás had killed an American, he was not pleased. He figured that if the old man was really as well known as he claimed to be, the gringo newspapers would probably make a big story of his death and the American government might decide to crack down on our weapons suppliers north of the border. He gave the matter a moment's thought, then ordered Tomás to get rid of the body far out in the desert. "Tell your boys to bury him deep and be sure to leave no sign of a grave."

And that's what Tomás did.

SIX

O ne I didn't shoot but should have was the Scotsman, William Benton. Our troubles with him came shortly after we set up a military government in Chihuahua State. Villa had put some of our boys on police duty in the state capital and assigned others to operate the city's basic services—the streetcars and waterworks and electric plant, the flour mills and slaughterhouses and so on. He also prohibited confiscation of private property anywhere in the state except on his signed authorization. All in all, we'd made life a hell of a lot better for the people of Chihuahua—except of course the rich ones.

The Scotsman owned a ranch called Los Remedios, 150,000 acres near Santa Isabel. The local population knew him as *el inglés turbulento*—the Anglo of the terrible temper. When he came barging into our Juárez headquarters one day, complaining that our boys had been cutting his fences and stealing cows from his herds, Villa could at first only stare at him in wonder: the old fellow's Spanish sounded like a barrel of frogs. "What the hell kind of accent is *that?*" Pancho finally said.

"German!" Urbina shouted, glassy-eyed with tequila. "This is an old growling German tiger we got here!"

"I'm a *Scot*, you ignorant half-castes!" Benton thundered, looking straight at Villa—and I knew right then and there he was also a dead man. But he bulled right ahead, either blind or indifferent to the sudden storm on Villa's face: "I've lived in this rock pile of a country for thirty years—thirty years!—and I've never seen—*never*, I say!—a worse plague of brigands than you and your band of riffraff. Well, I want this bloody thievery stopped, you hear? I don't mean please and I don't mean maybe, and I want it stopped *today*." His accent ripped the air like a wood saw.

Villa's eyes were red slits. I could almost hear that "half-castes" rolling around in his brain like a bullet. I don't know if the old guy was brave or just stupid, talking to Villa like that, jabbing his finger at him, spraying spit on the table where Villa sat with his advisors, but now everybody was looking at Pancho to see what he would do.

"Tell me, Señor Inglés," Villa said softly, "how many of your cows did my men take from you?"

"How many?" the old Scot repeated. "What bloody difference does that make? One thousand or one dozen, they're my cows, and I won't stand for losing even one more, do you hear? *Not one more!*"

"You own more cows than my whole army could eat in a year," Villa said, his voice rising. "But you lose a dozen of them and you feel cheated. You own more of Mexico's land than most Mexicans will cross in a lifetime, but *you* are the victim and *they* are the thieves because they take a few cows from your herd. Tell me, Señor Inglés, with so damn many cows, how can you know when even one hundred are missing, much less one dozen?"

Veins were bulging on the Scotsman's forehead. He slammed a fist on the table and shouted, "Don't you lecture *me*, Mr. God-damn General! I'm telling *you*: keep your rabble off my land. I'll shoot the next bloody beaner who so much as touches my fence!"

He spun around and started for the door, but Villa snapped his fingers and several of the boys cut him off. Benton was fifty-three years old but he was no scarecrow: the boys had to work hard to get him under control. I thought it was funny, but Villa didn't seem too amused by the spectacle of four Dorados wrestling themselves into a sweat against one old man. In the struggle, Benton's pistol slipped out of its holster and fell on the floor. One of the boys handed it over to Villa.

"You should not have drawn your gun on the governor of Chihuahua, señor," Villa told Benton when the old Scot had at last been subdued and was held fast by a Dorado on each arm. "Trying to shoot the governor is not only bad manners, it is a capital offense."

The Scotsman was out of breath but even more furious than before. "*Governor!* A brute like you couldn't govern a proper whorehouse! And you can shove your 'capital offense' up your thieving arse!"

"I have heard more eloquent last words," Villa said. Then: "Fierro!"

"Chief." I stepped forward.

"The legal government of the state of Chihuahua has found this son of a bitch Inglés guilty of attempting to assassinate the legal governor. The sentence is death. Do it."

"Done, my chief," I said.

As we led Benton away, he put his hands to his mouth and nose and imitated the piercing notes of a bagpipe. I bit my lip to keep from laughing out loud. Urbina later told me Villa's face had been something to see.

We put the Scotsman on a horse and headed south into the desert. Daylight faded as we rode. The moon, fat and silver, hung low over the mountains, and the air smelled of sage and warm stone. A coyote called in the distance. The dying of day was always my favorite time. I felt the country's beauty like a caress.

Benton said nothing during the ride. Maybe he was recalling things: his last fine meal . . . the prettiest breasts he'd ever kissed . . . his unspent money in the bank. Rich son of a bitch. He could consider himself lucky: a lot of men went to their graves with nothing to remember but whores, beans, and hangovers. But who knows? Maybe all he was thinking about was the feel of the horse under him. I didn't ask.

The boys took turns helping him dig up the hard ground just under the top layer of sand. The moon was higher now and the wind had kicked up and turned cold. One of the boys offered Benton some tobacco and paper to make himself a smoke, but he shook his head and took a pipe and tin from his jacket. When he saw me grinning at the tremor in his hands as he tried to pack the bowl, he snarled and flung the pipe away and jammed his hands in his pockets. He was having a hard time keeping his eyes off his grave.

The boy digging looked up at him and laughed. "Hey, Señor Inglés," he said, "you don't feel like making no catfight music now, eh?"

The coyotes howled in the foothills. The Scotsman glanced out there, then said to the boys with the shovels, "Make it deep, damn you. I don't want those beasts digging me up and dragging me all over this miserable countryside."

I generally made it a point not to talk to a man once the process of his execution was under way: the fun was mostly in his fear, and I didn't like to distract him from it. But the Scotsman's remark caught me off guard—and without thinking, I said, "If you think this country's so miserable, you Anglo cocksucker, why have you been here the last thirty years?"

He turned to me and said, "*Why?*"—and in that instant his eyes got steadier than they'd been since we'd arrived at his grave site. I damned my big mouth and drew my pistol to remind him of his circumstance, but it was too late: I'd given him a chance to focus on something other than his fear of the grave and he wasn't about to let it pass by.

"Sweet Jesus, man," he said, "I've stayed in this pest hole strictly for the goods, why else? You ignorant half-breeds are too damned stupid to get the riches for yourselves. Any white man of average wit can make a fortune here—while you donkeys do all the work! Why, you're like monkeys living in a gold mine. You simply do not have the capacity to—"

His skull shattered under my pistol barrel. He hit the ground dead. I stood over him and cursed myself under my breath. I didn't like to lose my temper that way in front of the boys—it went against my reputation as unflappable. I turned to them with a hearty chuckle and said, "The old fool wasn't worth wasting a bullet on." I made a dismissive gesture, and they rolled him into the grave and covered him up.

By the time we got back to Juárez, Villa's spokesmen had put out the story that William Benton of Los Remedios had tried to assassinate General Francisco Villa, the provisional governor of Chihuahua, because of a misbegotten conviction that the general intended to confiscate portions of his land without just compensation. Señor Benton had been duly tried on the charge of attempted murder of a civil official. He had been found guilty, sentenced to death, and shot.

In no time at all, the news of the Scotsman's death was across the border and telegraphed over the Atlantic. Christ, what an outcry. You would have thought we'd killed the goddamn king of England. The news made outraged headlines from El Paso to New York to London. We heard it made the front pages in Paris.

The British of course had a national fit. We should have expected it—they always did think their blood was more precious than Christ Almighty's. They demanded that the U.S. take immediate steps to obtain the full details of Benton's death and deal with his murderers if murder was proved. The Americans had this obligation, the Brits said, because their Monroe Doctrine prohibited European intervention in Mexico.

"Viva la Monroe Doctrine!" Urbina cheered, raising his glass in a mock toast. We didn't see what the hell all the fuss was about. "A thousand Mexicans are shot every day," Villa said to a group of gringo reporters, "for good reasons and bad ones, and that's that. That's life, no? But here one old Anglo goes to his grave and ay, Chihuahua! the sky is falling all over the world. What's the matter? Don't people die in Great Britain?"

A gringo envoy in pinstripes came to talk to Villa. "You simply can't order the death of a British subject without legally justifiable cause, General."

Pancho told him the cause had been plenty legal and justifiable: "The old bastard tried to shoot me!" he said with such hot indignation I almost felt it myself.

The Yankee representative said he, personally, was certain that was exactly what had occurred, but unfortunately the British government was reluctant to accept our word for it. They were demanding documented proof that everything had happened just as we claimed.

Villa said that was the trouble with the British: they were too suspicious of everybody. "How is the world ever to improve itself," Pancho asked, "if people don't start learning to trust each other?"

The gringo said he couldn't answer that, but he did think Villa should keep in mind that the British navy was the most powerful in the world, a fact of no small importance in resolving various of Britain's past international disputes.

Villa rubbed his face hard and stared at him as if he couldn't see him very well. He leaned toward me and whispered loudly: "What the hell can anybody's *navy* do to me in Chihuahua?" It rankled him to be asked so damn many questions. "Goddammit, I'm the governor! A governor governs, he doesn't explain!"

When the British demanded the return of Benton's body, Villa relayed his deep regret that he could not give it to them. He said that an ancient Mexican law, unwritten but sacred since long before the arrival of the Conquistadors, prohibited certain acts of disturbance to the dead—such as the transfer of remains from one grave to another. I was surprised nobody inquired further into this "ancient law." Until the moment Pancho mentioned it, I'd never heard of it. None of us had. It was just his diplomatic way of making it clear that nobody made demands of Pancho Villa, not in northern Mexico.

But he did agree to give the Brits the full details of Benton's trial. He figured it was worth it if it would bring the matter to a close. And so we sent them everything—trial transcripts, witness depositions, court orders, and reports of every kind. Our legal people worked around the clock to produce it all. From this mass of evidence, the newspapers reconstructed Benton's trial in every aspect. Reading all about it, I was certainly convinced of the justness of the verdict and the sentence passed on the Scotsman.

But the Brits still weren't satisfied. They wanted an autopsy done on Benton, with one of their own doctors present. And because the body would go back into the same grave, the Brits argued, there would be no violation of the sacred law Villa had previously cited.

We were with our chief medical officer, discussing improvements Villa wanted to make on the hospital trains, when this latest British demand reached us. "Oh, what the hell," Villa said. "Why *not* let them dig up their compadre and look at the hole in his head? *Anything* to put an end to this goddamn business!"

"Listen," I said, "there's something you ought to know."

When he heard how Benton had actually died, he understood our problem: as soon as they dug him up they'd see that, contrary to our claim, he hadn't been killed by a bullet—and then some people were sure to think we hadn't been absolutely truthful about other details of the incident, as well.

"All right," Pancho said, "here's what we do. We dig him up, shoot him in the head, and put him back in the ground. *Then* we let them come and dig him up for their goddamn autopsy." His patience was wearing thin, and his tone dripped sarcasm as he said to me, "And listen, try not to lose your temper with him *this* time, eh?"

"Excuse me—excuse me, my general," the doctor said. He was a new man we'd recently recruited, damn good at his work but still very nervous to find himself working for Pancho Villa. He explained that Villa's solution to our problem with Benton wouldn't work. "An autopsy, my general, will show without doubt that the deceased was shot after he was already dead."

"A doctor can know *that* about a dead guy just by cutting him open and looking at his insides?" Urbina said in wonder. "Holy Mother of God. Sounds like witchcraft to me. I once knew a witch who could see the future in the eyes of dead dogs. She told me, 'I see money coming to you very soon.' She was right:

two minutes later I robbed her." He cackled loudly over this fond memory and took another drink.

Villa squinted intently at the doctor and said, "And what did *your* autopsy reveal about the damned Scotsman, Señor Doctor?"

"Pardon me, my general?" the doctor said, looking confused. "*My* autopsy, but I haven't—" His eyes widened as Villa drew his pistol and placed it on the table.

"*Your* autopsy," Villa said. "The one you did on Señor Benton just this morning."

"This morning . . . ? Ah, *yes!*" the doctor exclaimed, tapping his forehead with his palm in a theatrical manner I couldn't help smiling at. "*My* autopsy, of course! What an accursed memory I have! Just this morning, yes, and my finding—my unmistakable finding—was that Señor Benton died of a gunshot wound to the head, yes." He looked from Pancho to Tomás to me. "I mean . . . that *is* what my autopsy unmistakably revealed . . . ?"

Villa smiled and nodded, and the doctor grinned like a lunatic. "Yes! Just so! And I must apologize, my general, but I have been so busy today that I have not quite completed the autopsy report. I assure you, however, it will be in your hands within the hour."

"I know it will," Villa said.

And it was. And by the following day the British had it, together with a letter signed by Villa, stating that he hoped everything was now to their satisfaction.

It wasn't. The Brits said they had "reservations" about the validity of our report. They persisted in their demand to make their own examination of Benton's corpse.

"Those arrogant sons of bitches!" Villa shouted. "Now they don't think a Mexican doctor can perform a proper autopsy, is that it? Well, no more fucking autopsies, not by anybody! Those milk-face bastards! How many times do they want to desecrate that poor man's grave, anyway?"

The gringo envoy came to see us again, this time wearing white linen. He said we were putting his government on the spot: the Americans couldn't permit the British to take direct action against us, but they couldn't refuse to pursue their case for them, either.

"Goddamn it, General," he said after supper when he was half-crocked on brandy. "If only you boys hadn't tried to be so damn *legal* about it. The Limeys can't stand to see one of theirs get it in the neck from a foreigner. They think they're above everybody's laws but their own. If this coot Benton had been plugged by a *bandido* or some drunk in the street, everybody would've said it was a damn shame but what the hell, those things happen down Mexico way. But when they hear he was *executed*, well now, that's another story. You should've just ordered one of your men to go over to his ranch and bushwhack the old son of a bitch. Then you try one of your men as the murderer and hang him and that takes care of that—everybody's satisfied, see? Justice done and everything all nice and neat. None of this diplomatic hullabaloo."

Urbina leaned across the table and said, "You gringo fuck. You talk about hanging one of our boys like it's just another one of your goddamn *deals*."

The Yankee envoy drew back from him, his eyes suddenly bright with alarm. "Hey now, amigo," he said, "don't take it like that." He wasn't too drunk to see how deadly drunk Tomás was. His eyes jumped around to all our faces. "Listen," he said to Villa, "I'm an official representative of the United States government. You remember that."

Pancho stared at him without expression and shrugged.

"*Everything's* a deal with you people," Urbina said. "You talk about killing a man the same way you talk about business, the same way you talk about politics. Well, let's see you make a deal with *this!*" He pulled out his revolver and held the muzzle within inches of the gringo's forehead. I was wearing a new leather jacket and was going to give Tomás hell if it got splattered with blood.

The gringo pressed back into his chair, his eyes huge with fear, and raised his hands in front of his face. "Hold on now!" he said. "Wait a minute!"

Urbina cocked the gun. "Oh God *don't!*" the gringo said in English. I could see Urbina was going to do it—but then the gringo gave a loud cry and broke into tears. He covered his face and sobbed like a woman.

Urbina lowered the gun and stared at him in astonishment, as if the Yankee had just pulled a magic trick. The rest of the boys looked somewhat puzzled and a little embarrassed, and then began to exchange grins, and then they all started laughing. Urbina put away his pistol, shaking his head in disgust. "Hey, I never shot a little girl in my life," he said, "and I'm not going to start now."

Villa laughed until his face was as bright with tears as the gringo's. Then he dried his eyes with his shirtsleeve and ordered a couple of the boys to escort the envoy back to the border. "And listen," he said to the red-faced gringo as he was being led off: "Tell your chiefs I'm through with all this Benton bullshit. Tell your British cousins. Tell them all Pancho Villa said fuck you. And tell them to find you a pair of balls or give you a dress to wear."

But of course the Brits weren't about to let the matter drop, and the situation got even worse. Our headquarters was besieged by reporters, by diplomatic couriers, by new Yankee envoys trying to get Villa to permit the Brits to come into Mexico with their

own investigation team. U.S. troops were building up at the border. Villa was looking as crazy-eyed as a cornered cat. But just
when it seemed Pancho would shoot the next reporter who pes-
tered him about Benton, Venustiano Carranza, first chief of the
Constitutionalist alliance, stepped in and got us out of the mess.

Until now, Carranza had said nothing at all about the Benton business, and we figured the old goat was smiling through
his whiskers about Pancho's troubles with the Brits and Americans. Some of Villa's political advisors believed Carranza actually wanted to see Pancho provoke the gringos into sending their
troops across the river: if Villa was killed in a fight with U.S. soldiers, it would put an end to everybody's problems with him—
Carranza's as well as the Brits'. Such talk only made Villa more
irritable.

The situation being what it was, we were all surprised by
the arrival of the first chief's directive from Nogales saying that,
above all, Mexican sovereignty was to be protected, and he was
therefore officially denying permission for British investigators
to enter the country. The orders also specified that Villa was to
make no more statements about the Benton incident to anyone
representing a foreign government or publication. The directive
concluded with instructions to inform "all interested parties" that
any further questions pertaining to the Benton matter should be
addressed to the headquarters of the first chief of the Constitutionalist alliance.

"He's jealous!" Urbina yelped when the orders were read
to him. "The old bastard can't stand to see Pancho getting so
much attention from the newspapers and all these gringos in
suits." I thought so too. It must have chafed Carranza's sense
of importance to see so many reporters and diplomats address-
ing Villa as if *he* was the head of the revolutionary alliance. The

whitebeard's orders were meant to remind everybody who the first chief really was.

That was just fine with Villa. These were orders he was happy to obey. He ordered the regimental commanders to muster the troops aboard the trains and start heading south. To avoid the hordes of reporters on the lookout for him, he waited until the streets were jammed with our boys heading for the railyard, and then he and Tomás and I slipped down the alleyway to a stable a few blocks away.

As we saddled up, one of Villa's spokesmen was reading a statement to the mob of reporters and emissaries gathered in front of the headquarters building. He was telling them that General Villa regretted he could not stand before them in person, but he had just received orders to move immediately to engage federal forces massing to the south. Nevertheless, although the war against tyranny demanded his full attention, General Villa continued to share the desire of all interested parties to obtain complete clarification of the legally prescribed and fully sanctioned proceedings against Señor William Benton of Los Remedios. However, all further inquiries pertaining to that matter should be directed to the headquarters of the first chief in Nogales.

Even from the stable, we could hear the clamor of the frustrated reporters. "Just listen to that," Urbina said. He grunted with the pain of his rheumatism as he mounted up. "Like dogs under a cat in a tree. I don't know why you guys took the trouble to learn to read. What can people like that write that anybody would want to know?"

"Shut up, Tomás," Villa said. He was still a little testy from the recent strains of press conferences and international diplomacy. He kept shooting me hard looks while he cinched his saddle.

As we rode out of town, he suddenly reined over beside me and smacked me with his Texas hat. "Goddamn it, Rudy!" he said. "No more hitting them on the head, you hear me! From now on you do like always and you *shoot* the bastards!"

Laughing like hell, we rode back to the kind of warfare we could understand.

PART TWO

The Rich Smells of Triumph

"The Revolution was not the work of saints
but of men of flesh and blood, men of passions
and many defects."

—Francisco L. Urquizo

SEVEN

While we'd been busy in northern Chihuahua, the federals had once again occupied Torreón. In the early spring we retook it. This time the region was defended by some of Huerta's best troops, and the fighting was the roughest we'd seen yet. The ground we gained in the mornings they took back in the afternoons. Our cavalries charged and countercharged; our infantries shoved each other back and forth over the bloody cottonfields. The nights shook with cannonfire and flashed with small arms. The dust never settled, the war cries never stopped, the smell of gunsmoke and burned flesh carried on the wind. At last, Angeles's artillery blasted an opening for us and we pushed into town. The fighting was house-to-house and hand-to-hand. When the Huertistas finally waved the white flag, more than a thousand of our boys were dead and thousands more were wounded. The federal losses were of course even greater: our prisoners dug graves from dawn to dusk for more than a week before all the dead were buried.

Now only the powerful federal garrison at Zacatecas stood between us and Mexico City. With Angeles advising him closely on the plan of attack, Villa began preparing to move south. Then came orders from Carranza: he was sending somebody else to take Zacatecas and wanted us to move against Saltillo, more than 150 miles due east of Torreón. The bastard. We knew what he was up to. He was afraid that once we took Zacatecas we'd roll right on down into Mexico City, and that if Villa beat him to the capital, he'd never get to be president.

Felipe Angeles agreed with Villa that Carranza's personal ambitions and jealousies were dictating wasteful military strategy, and he sent the whitebeard a wire requesting that he reconsider his plan and let us take Zacatecas, as we were far better equipped for the assault than any other of the Constitutionalist armies. Carranza refused.

"The hell with it," Pancho said. "He's a perfumed chocolate drinker, but he's the first chief. We'll do it his way."

<hr/>

We took Saltillo with no trouble at all and did a lot of celebrating while we waited for Pablo González and his boys to arrive and take over the occupation of the town. Because they'd been told that "Jesusita de Chihuahua" was Villa's favorite song, a local band played it over and over without pause one evening just below the window of the hotel room where Pancho was taking his pleasure with some girl he'd married an hour earlier. Villa finally appeared at the window and yelled down that although he very much appreciated their intentions, he did not want to lose his love for "Jesusita" through so much rendition of her. If they played the song even one more time, he said, he would have them all shot on the charge of mutilation of music. The band quickly adjourned to a nearby cantina and did not play "Jesusita" again the whole time we were in town.

During a search of the federal garrison, the boys found a motorcycle and rolled it over to show to Villa, who was entertaining a bunch of us with his rope tricks out by the garrison stable. None of us had ever sat astride one of those things in his life, but Calixto immediately bragged that he could ride it as easily as he could a horse. It took a while for him to figure out how the clutch and gears operated, but he had no problem kick-starting the motor. He put it in gear, let out the clutch, and drove smack into a corral rail before he'd gone fifteen feet.

Now the others started making bets that they could ride the motorcycle without crashing. One after another they veered off into the crowd, scattering the spectators like chickens and running into walls, trees, bushes, water troughs. When it was his turn, Maclovio said he knew the secret. "Watch carefully, boys, and learn something from your superior." He twisted the throttle fully open, racing the motor deafeningly and pouring a thick cloud of smoke from the tailpipe, then let go of the clutch lever. The machine reared straight up in the air, went over backward, and just barely missed crushing him. Villa and Tomás and I laughed so hard our bellies ached.

"Goddamn it, let *me* on that thing!" Tomás said, and took a long pull from his bottle to steady his nerves. Not wanting to repeat Maclovio's mistake, he eased the clutch lever out *very* slowly. The motor stalled, Tomás lost his balance, and the machine fell over on him and twisted his ankle so bad he was limping for the next two weeks.

"All right, little brother," Villa said to me, "show them how simple it truly is."

"Go to hell," I said. "If it's so simple, you do it."

"You pussy. You think I won't?"

By now a photographer had set up his tripod, and Villa posed for a picture with the motorcycle—hatless, smiling, his hands on the grips, one foot up on a footrest as though it were a stirrup and he were about to mount a horse. He then straddled the machine and started it up. As smoothly as if he'd been riding motorcycles all his life, he rode that damn thing down the street and twice around the well in the central plaza. As he headed back toward us, gaining confidence and speed, he was leaning over the handlebars and grinning like an idiot child.

He spotted me standing with a few of the boys next to a pig-pen and swerved toward us to give us a scare. We all jumped out of the way—but the maneuver cost him control of the machine: it smashed through the railing and roared into the pen with a tremendous splash, sending pigs shrieking every which way as it abruptly bogged down and flung Villa headfirst into the wallow.

Steam rose off the hot motor as Pancho pulled himself to his feet, his hair plastered to his head, his suit dripping with mud and pigshit, his eyes huge and red with rage. I tried not to laugh, but I couldn't keep the grin off my face, and when he saw it he went for his gun. Everybody dashed for cover, but I just raised my hands and yelled, "Don't shoot *me*, goddamm it. *I* didn't throw you in that sty. If you have to shoot something, shoot the god-damn machine."

And damn if he didn't. He glared down at it like it had just made some foul remark about his mother, then shot it squarely in the gas tank, which had the English word "Indian" on it. He shot it in the gas tank twice, then shot it in the motor and the bullet sparked against the metal and *whump!* the thing exploded into flame and knocked Villa on his ass in the pigshit again. He crawled out of that blazing pen in one quick hurry before he caught on fire on top of everything else.

Now I really did laugh, and maybe he would have shot me if he hadn't lost his pistol in the explosion, I don't know. He looked ready to. But then his face softened and he smiled and he ambled toward me, saying, "What the hell, I guess it did look pretty funny. No hard feelings, little brother." Then he lunged and caught me in a bear hug and writhed against me, smearing me with pigshit too and cackling like a loon.

We heard Urbina laughing at us from the corner of the stable and had no trouble catching him on his sprained ankle. We dragged him to the sty and flung him in. Before that day was over, damn near everybody had either been tossed into the sty or pelted with handfuls of pigshit when they least suspected it.

The next time we found an abandoned motorcycle, Villa had it laid across the tracks and ran over it with a train.

———⟫●⟪———

By the time we got back to Torreón, Carranza had arrived in Saltillo. He telegraphed word to us that the forces he'd sent against Zacatecas were getting their asses whipped. He ordered Villa to send artillery and three thousand men to reinforce the Constitutionalist units. But Villa didn't want to split up the division; he wired back that he much preferred to take his whole army to Zacatecas. Carranza absolutely refused him permission to do that, and repeated his order. Villa argued about it as respectfully as he could, but the muscles in his jaw were twitching as he watched the telegrapher send out his response. Carranza then demanded that Villa send *half* of his artillery and *five thousand* men to Zacatecas—and send them *now*. He was signing his wires, "The First Chief of the Constitutionalist Army." The telegraph machine had been chattering faster and faster, and it wouldn't have surprised me to see smoke start coming off it. The dispatcher was running sweat as he scribbled Carranza's arrogant orders off the wire and passed them to Villa, then tapped out Pancho's angry replies.

Villa wasn't about to put any of his men under the direct command of any of the whitebeard's lackeys. When Carranza persisted, Villa's temper got the best of him: he sent a wire saying he was resigning immediately and asking who Carranza wanted him to appoint as the new commander of the Division of the North. I shook my head and gave him a look, but he ignored it. He was steaming.

The whitebeard must've been ecstatic to get Pancho's resignation so easily, though his reply was diplomatic: "I am truly pained to be obliged to accept your resignation. I thank you in the name of the nation for the important services you have rendered our cause." He told Villa to gather his top generals in the telegraph office right away: he wanted to discuss with them the choice of a successor to head the division.

When the rest of the boys read the telegrams that had gone back and forth, they all agreed that Carranza was a fool, and they refused to accept Pancho's resignation. Villa just shrugged and stared out the window. I think he already realized how damn foolish he'd been to let the old bastard get under his skin like that. Angeles sent the whitebeard a joint message from all of us, saying that we were united in our desire to retain Francisco Villa as leader of the division and urging Carranza to ignore Villa's renunciation of command.

Carranza wired back: "I am sorry to inform you that it is impossible for me to change the decision I made in accepting General Villa's resignation."

Angeles cursed softly—one of the few times I ever heard him use foul language—and replied that we were "irrevocably resolved to continue fighting as the Division of the North under the command of General Francisco Villa."

Carranza sent a reminder that he was the first chief and his decisions were the supreme authority of the Constitutionalist Army. Angeles groaned and shook his head wearily.

Herrera suddenly said, "Enough of this shit." He made the telegrapher tap out the message, "Señor Carranza, I am Maclovio Herrera and you are a son of a bitch." As soon as the words were sent, he ripped out the telegraph wires. Then he turned to a smiling Villa, and said: "Now, Panchito, *you* tell us: what do we do?"

———————————

We struck Zacatecas like a storm of blood. High in the mountains, the lovely city of silver mines stood in a narrow ravine, its little flat-roofed buildings clinging to the rock walls, its cobbled streets nearly as narrow as graves. We had the federals outnumbered, but they were well fortified and ready for us. Urbina and I led the cavalry attacks—no easy job on those rocky uplands—and Angeles tore into the federal emplacements with his artillery, as accurate with those big guns as I was with my pistols. Villa as always was everywhere, urging the boys on, shooting, singing, cursing with a crazy joy. His grace on a horse—which was always something to see (and nearly the equal of my own)—was never so spectacular as on that wonderful thunderous day when we took Zacatecas.

We overpowered them in a three-sided assault, then machine-gunned them in the ravines as they tried to flee the city. We'd begun the attack at ten in the morning, and by sundown Zacatecas was ours. In those few furious hours we killed eight thousand of the sons of bitches.

We had to climb over heaps of dead men to enter the town. In the exultation of victory, the first of our troops into the city severed the heads of a few dozen corpses and impaled them on iron balcony railings along the main street. The heads dripped onto the cobblestones as in the aftermath of a bloody rain. It was a sight the survivors would never forget, one that would be described to Huerta's troops everywhere, a vision of their own impending fate in the coming of Pancho Villa.

We took three thousand prisoners and gave the enlisted men a choice of joining us or going to the wall. The wounded among them were either treated at our hospital train or put out of their misery, depending on the severity of their wounds. Many of their officers tried to hide, and when we found them we shot them on the spot. At first we did the same even to those who came to us with their traitorous hands up high—but then Villa decided to permit surrendered officers to stand trial for their lives, a decision I knew he'd made simply to please Angeles. That damn *hidalgo* was always talking to Pancho about justice, calling it the fundamental goal of the Revolution and so on and so forth.

It irritated me to see the way Villa fawned on him, that *gentleman* with the French Academy manners and precise way of speaking, with his perfectly trimmed mustache and spotless uniforms. But I'd be a liar if I said he wasn't a superior commander whose tactical advice almost always proved to be correct. Despite his aristocratic air, Angeles was a true soldier and a brave fighter— which sure as hell can't be said of most of those among us who had educations and table manners: the politicians and professors and scribblers and fancy talkers, all their kind. Even a uniform couldn't disguise the truth about them: they were nothing but glorified clerks, and I found them no less contemptible for being necessary in an army the size of ours. Of course *somebody* had to write the communiqués, the letters, the records, the reports, the proclamations, the manifestos, the information bulletins for the press—all that paper shit (all that *shitpaper,* I should say). I knew that. But I didn't care: I detested them just the same, the lot of them, and they all knew it. None of them ever dared to speak to me unless I spoke to them first. Hell, none of them ever came near me.

We held the trials in the ballroom of a *casa grande* overlooking the main plaza. Every minute or so came the sound of a fusillade from the firing squad at its work. One of the officers brought before us pleaded with Villa not to be shot. He was a fat little fellow with the whitest and softest-looking hands I'd ever seen on a man. He claimed he was a professional musician—a classical pianist—who had been press-ganged into the federal army. Because he was well educated, he had been made an officer. "One day I was performing Chopin in the Teatro Nacional," he said, "and the next, as if in some horrible nightmare, I was in a military uniform and in command of a supply company for General Barrón. Me! What do *I* know about military supply? I was shipping saddles to artillery units and carloads of coal to the cavalry. General Barrón threatened to shoot me himself. For God's sake, General Villa, I'm no soldier. I'm an *artist.* I play *Mozart!*"

"*Mozart!*" Urbina hollered. He had a bottle in his fist and an arm around one of the whores who had flocked to the table. "I can play Mozart too! Listen!" He shifted in his chair and ripped a long resonant fart that made the whores squeal and pinch their noses and make a big show of fanning the air. It broke the boys up—except for Angeles, naturally, who gave Urbina such a look of disdain that Tomás laughed even louder and farted again. Angeles stood up, nodded at Villa, and left the room.

"Any federal so incompetent in his duties as you say you were," Villa said, grinning at the fat officer, "must be a revolutionary at heart. Maybe we should give you a medal for your heroic inefficiency in the service of General Barrón, eh?" He pointed to a piano in the corner of the big room. "Play something for me, Señor Mozart. Something Mexican. Play 'Jesusita de Chihuahua.' Prove to us you are what you say."

I doubt the little man ever played a piano anywhere with more heart and soul than he played that one—or played with greater dexterity, since "Jesusita de Chihuahua" had originally been composed for the barrel organ. Urbina whirled out onto the floor, dancing with two whores at once. Some of other boys grabbed themselves girls and joined in. Some began clapping and singing. "Louder!" Urbina commanded the little pianist. "Louder!"

I went out on the verandah and had a smoke while I watched the firing squad do its work in the plaza below. The wailing of widows and wounded men drifted up to mingle with the music and singing issuing from behind me. A federal major stood against the church wall and made a hasty sign of the cross a moment before the rifle volley jarred him like a cloth doll and he dropped. The captain of the squad, a tough young fellow named Candelario Cervantes, went up to him and put a pistol round in his skull—the customary coup de grâce. As a labor detail dragged away the corpse, Candelario gestured for the next man in the line of condemned to take his place at the wall.

A hatless, white-haired colonel stepped up to face the rifles. I recognized him: at his trial he had refused to speak a word in his own defense and had not even given us his name. He stood at erect attention, a soldier to the end. Candelario raised his saber and ordered, "Ready! . . . Aim! . . . Fire!" The discharge slammed the colonel against the wall and he crumpled to the ground.

As Candelario drew his pistol and took a step toward him, the fallen colonel sat up. Candelario stopped short. And then slowly, awkwardly, as the crowd of spectators gasped and started jabbering, the old man got to his feet and slumped against the wall.

The riflemen looked at one another. Candelario stared at the colonel for a long moment, then spun and stalked back to his position beside the squad. He raised his saber and yelled, *"Ready!"* I had never seen one get up before. "Aim!" The colonel pushed himself away from the wall and tried to square his shoulders, weaving slightly. "Fire!" The colonel bounced off the wall and fell in a heap.

And then raised himself up on his elbows. And then somehow managed to make it to his hands and knees.

The crowd hushed. People blessed themselves and knelt in the street. I thought: holy shit.

Candelario looked around wildly and spotted me up on the verandah. He raised his outstretched arms in an enormous shrug of incomprehension. With twelve bullets in him, the old colonel sat on his heels, his shoulder against the wall and his chin on his chest. He brushed vaguely at his sopping red tunic.

"Once more!" I called down to Candelario. "If he's still alive after the next one, we'll give him a fresh uniform and command of one of our battalions."

The old colonel was struggling to stand up when the next volley hit him and killed him. He was one of the few I never forgot. I rued not having gone down to speak with him before he took the last bullets. For a long time later the boys would joke with great respect about the tough old federal who died five pounds heavier than when he stepped up to the wall.

We spent days executing the condemned and disposing of the dead. The town was notorious for epidemics and we had to get rid of the corpses quickly. We threw thousands of them into old mine shafts. Others we loaded on flatcars and dumped out in the desert.

Some we simply piled in the plazas, soaked with gasoline, and set on fire. At the edge of one crowd watching the bodies burn, a little boy standing near me was amazed by the sight of the dead men's arms and legs jerking and kicking as the flames worked on joints and tendons. "Look, *Mamá*, look!" he cried as he tugged on the hand of the blackveiled woman clutching him. "They're dancing!"

We looted the city down to its bones. It was a town of rich sons of bitches and arrogant priests, and every grievance our boys had against the Spanish bluebloods, the wealthy, the Church, the fucking bosses—against anybody anywhere who owned anything from a silk necktie to the keys to God's kingdom—they redressed against Zacatecas. We picked the churches clean of their hordes of gold and silver. To extract the money we knew they'd hidden, we forced the rich to ransom themselves. The most despicable among them we shot anyway. (Some crimes cannot be paid for in gold.) The boys rode horses into the finest houses, grinding horseshit into parquet floors and shredding Middle Easteen carpets to rags. Into roaring salon fireplaces they threw books, ledgers, letters, paintings. Not a sculpture in town went unbroken, not a windowpane stayed intact. Our *soldaderas* paraded the streets in long silk dresses, in bridal gowns of delicate lace; they scuffed over the cobblestones in satin slippers. We stripped stores, stables, houses of everything that could be carried away. Toward our train flowed a steady stream of livestock and wagons packed with strongboxes, stoves, saddles, tools, furniture, clothes, gilt picture frames. Every automobile that still ran was driven onto the flatcars. The mules walked stiff-legged under the loads of booty. The wagons creaked with the weight of it. The trains groaned.

As we pulled out of Zacatecas, the air was thick with the odors of smoldering ash, bloody dust, putrefying flesh. The rich ripe smells of triumph.

EIGHT

Less than a month after we took Zacatecas, Huerta fled the country. He sailed for Europe on the German ship *Dresden*. I heard the news through an open window over the bed where I had been making love to a girl with a birthmark on her hip that looked like a small map of Mexico. The boys were yelling it in the streets, whooping and firing their guns in the air, starting up a grand fiesta of celebration.

But even as the bands were playing and the boys were dancing with the *soldaderas* and drinking and shouting "*Viva Villa! Viva la revolución!*" over and over again—even as I was pulling on my boots and admiring the naked ass of the girl as she leaned out the window, covering her breasts with her hands and yelling and whooping along with everyone else—even at that moment, my mouth suddenly went dry when the thought struck me that if the war against Huerta was won, then the Revolution was won. And if the Revolution was won, the country would swiftly submit to the rule of written law, to the authority of paper, to legislation, regulations, ordinances, bureaucratic policies—all that shit. Here came the managers and bosses and policemen, the courtrooms and jails.

I thought: Oh, fuck, not again.

Many of the boys had a regular life waiting for them, a place to call home, a wife, children, and they were of course eager to get back to it. And there were many among us who had no family but wanted to start making one for themselves. Naturally, they were all happy to hear the news.

But then there were the rest of us. Those of us who had no home, no wife, no little mouths to feed and care for—and no desire at all for any of those things. If the country were now to know peace, what the hell were *we* to do? That was the question. Go back to laying track for the goddamned railroad? Go back to the slow death of the silver mines? Back to swinging a sledgehammer in the rock quarries or hacking with a skinning knife in the stink and slime of the tanneries? Back to tending cattle fences or bean fields or goat herds? Were we to become mule drovers? Wranglers? Shit shovelers? Diggers of ditches? Were we to enlist in the regular army and be ruled by its petty regimentations? Those were not choices—hell, they weren't even possibilities, not to us. We had come to know such lives too well before the Revolution delivered us from them.

The Revolution had been more bountiful than we could have imagined, more generous to us than our own dreams. It gave us excellent guns and the best of horses, boots and clothes and Texas hats, all we wanted to eat and drink. It gave us run of the country. (Some of the boys in the division had never been five miles from home before they joined the fighting.) It gave us gold. And of course women. It gave us women wherever we went. But best of all, the Revolution gave us a kind of freedom most men only dream of all their lives, the very finest freedom of all: the freedom to kill our enemies, to kill the bastards who'd made our lives miserable—and those who wanted to take their place.

Having known that kind of freedom, how could we now return to any sort of subservience to weak little perfumed fools? How could we again submit to brutish labor for the enrichment of someone else? If the country now gave itself over to the rule of law books, what were *we* to do? A few among us would likely find a place for themselves as enforcers of the laws. But most of us would either be denied that chance or reject it out of hand. We would go on living as freely as the Revolution had allowed us—and the new laws of the land would put a price on our heads until it was collected.

In that long moment of staring at the naked girl standing at the window, I understood more clearly than ever that the line between a noble revolutionary and a low-down bandit was the line between war and peace. The girl turned from the window and let her hands fall from her breasts, her face bright. But then she saw my face and quit smiling.

<hr/>

I was chilly with sweat as I shoved through the raucous throngs in the street, making my way to headquarters. Dozens of others were already there, and the smoky room was a clamor of voices.

"The whitebeard wants to be president so bad you can smell it through his goddamned perfume!" somebody shouted.

"He can't be the president!" someone else hollered. "Not that cocksucker!"

"*You*, Pancho! You will be the president!"

Villa was sitting at the head of the table, his chin on his fist, his eyes moving slowly over every face in the room. When he saw me, he held his stare for a moment without expression. I looked hard at him: *What now?* But his face showed me nothing before he cut his eyes away.

"Yes, Pancho—you must now be the president!" cried a voice from the rear of the room.

"No," Villa said. "Don't be foolish. The president must be an educated man, not somebody so ignorant as me. But he must also insist on justice for *everybody* in Mexico, even the peon without a handful of dirt to call his own—and that leaves out Señor Carranza, for damn sure. It will not be easy, boys, but we must find for Mexico another Madero."

I liked the sound of things. In my panic of moments earlier I had forgotten about Carranza. Since his argument with Villa over the telegraph wires, the tensions between them had intensified to the breaking point—and following our victory at Zacatecas, the whitebeard's fear of Pancho was greater than ever. He was now diverting to other units the arms and coal shipments meant for us, claiming their need for them was more urgent than our own. I don't know who he expected to believe that bullshit. We weren't the only ones he was afraid of, either. The word from the southern state of Morelos was that Emiliano Zapata and his boys would never accept Carranza as president. The whitebeard's worst nightmare must have been that the Zapatistas would unite with us against him.

Villa already had that idea in mind. Even though he had never met Zapata, he admired him immensely, both as a guerrilla leader whose fierce army of peons had repeatedly beaten the federals in the fighting down south, and as a true revolutionary fighting for the return of his people's ancient lands, stolen from them over the years by the rich *hacendados*. "It is natural for him to fight against Carranza," Villa had said to me. "He knows the whitebeard will never return land to the peons." When I'd reminded him that Zapata had also broken with Madero because of the little saint's slow progress toward restoring Indian land, Pancho's mouth tightened for a moment; then he shrugged and said Zapata must have been misled by bad advisors. He persisted in thinking the best of him. "Did you hear what he said?" he once asked me. " 'It is better to die on our feet than to live on our knees.' What a wonderful thing to say! I think he must be a very good man!" I said I thought it was far more wonderful to live on your feet and make the other bastard die on *his* knees—or on his feet or his ass or his horse or his whore or anything else he might happen to be on at the moment. Villa didn't laugh; he just made a sour face and said I had no sense of poetry. "Maybe not," I told him, "but at least I still have a sense of humor." Christ, he could be a pain in the ass when he got into his Noble Revolutionary mood.

"That Carranza's nothing but a goat-fucking politician!" Urbina said. He was hot-faced with tequila. "He even looks like a billygoat. I bet his mother was one and that's how he learned to fuck them."

Villa smiled. "Since when do *you* object to the pleasures of goats, eh, Tomasito?"

Urbina grinned at the laughter and said, "At least I don't pay the animal. That Carranza, he tries to buy the goat's vote even as he robs it of its virtue."

Most of the boys were beginning to feel much better—and why not? It looked after all like there was no real danger of peace, not soon. Not while Carranza yearned for the president's chair—which he would for as long as he could breathe—and not while Villa was opposed to the whitebeard becoming president, as he always would be.

Then a Dorado captain said, "What about Obregón?"

Alvaro Obregón. Carranza's most able general, the commander of the powerful Army of the Northwest. We had heard much about him. It was said he had an Irish ancestor named

Michael O'Brien who changed his name to Miguel Obregón and served as a bodyguard to the last Spanish viceroy in Mexico before marrying a Mexican woman and settling in Sonora. There were a few Sonorans among us who had met Alvaro Obregón. They said he had done well for himself as a garbanzo farmer and had been elected mayor of some small Sonoran town. They said he had strange green eyes and a natural gift for using a great many words to say very little. ("He can make a half-hour speech just to tell you it looks like rain.") He was reputed to have a memory so phenomenal he could recall the exact order of every playing card in a deck after having been shown the cards but once. "Never do you want to gamble with this man," one Sonoran said. When Orozco rebelled against Madero, Obregón had organized a small army and joined the fight against the Colorados. He quickly earned a reputation as a superb field commander. They said he was calculating, cautious, almost excessively methodical—but there was no denying his battlefield success. He was now known as *El Invicto*— the Invincible—and his Army of the Northwest was almost as famous as our own. His ranks were thick with Mayo and Yaqui Indians, both tribes renown for their ferocity.

"If General Obregón is as wise as they say," Villa said, "he will see the folly of continuing to support Señor Carranza."

"What if he's not that wise?" somebody yelled.

"Then it's possible we would have to teach him some wisdom," Pancho said.

"Goddamn right!" Urbina shouted. "Piss on Obregón! He's a fucking farmer, for Christ's sake! Carrancistas, Obregonistas— we'll kick *all* their asses!"

"Easy, Tomasito, easy," Villa said with a small smile. "We don't want war with our revolutionary brothers if we can avoid it."

Revolutionary brothers? I took a look around: he was talking like there were reporters present. When I spotted Angeles across the room, I knew it was for his good regard that Villa was sounding so damned diplomatic.

"For now," Villa said, "we just want to make three things clear to everybody: that all we want is what is best for Mexico, that I myself have no ambition to be the president, and that under no conditions will we agree to Señor Carranza as the president, as that would not be best for Mexico."

"Very nice words, *compadre*," Urbina said, looking sly, "but what if the whitebeard says that is unacceptable? What if he tells us to go to hell?"

Yes, Pancho, I thought, watching him intently, what then?

Villa looked around slowly. Then shrugged. Then flashed a huge grin. "In such a sad case," he said, "we would have no choice but to assist him in accepting the unacceptable."

Urbina gave an ear-piercing victory cry as he brought his fist down on the table so hard the bottles jumped. The room exploded with cries of *"Viva Villa! Viva la revolución!"* The cheers rolled out the windows and into the celebrating crowd. They were taken up by the boys in the street and carried across town, echoing loudly: *"Viva Villa! Viva la revolución!"*

I caught the momentary mournful looks on the faces of some of the boys—the fellows whose families prayed every night for an end to the war, the boys with sweethearts waiting for them back home. I saw the sad, quick glances they exchanged, then their crooked smiles and shrugs of resignation. Too bad for them, yes. But for *us!* I grinned at Villa. He winked at me. Urbina yelped like a happy pup. *"Viva Villa!"* the boys yelled, *"Viva la revolución!"* Yes, yes, yes! Viva! *Viva! VIVA!*

While Obregón advanced toward Mexico City to claim the capital for Carranza from the few die-hard federals who still occupied
it, we continued to build our strength. We raised money by expro-
priating cattle from *hacendado* ranches and selling the animals to
gringo drovers at the border. Through our agents in El Paso we
then worked deals for arms, ammunition, dynamite, and coal.

The rains of early summer had been uncommonly heavy, and
by late July the countryside bordering Chihuahua and Durango
states was even more beautiful than usual. The high grass of the
hills was richly yellow, the trees densely green. The fields were
bursting with flowers of red and gold. The air seemed softer than
I'd ever felt it before, and sweeter, and the rivers ran fast and cold
and clear.

Near the end of that magnificent summer, Urbina invited
Villa and me to his hacienda in Durango, to attend the christening of his newborn daughter. We set out from Chihuahua with
fifty Dorados and a big band of musicians—and even took a
priest, since Tomás had shot or scared off every priest in Durango.
(His wife had made him promise to spare whichever cleric presided over their daughter's service.) Maclovio Herrera invited us
to visit his home in Parral en route to Durango, and we spent two
fine days there, celebrating with his parents and neighbors before
pushing on to Urbina's hacienda.

Tomás had expropriated the place—called Las Nieves
because of the year-round snowcaps on the looming sierras—
from some rich Spaniard. It covered more than a million acres of
mostly lush pastureland on which Urbina grazed cattle, horses,
and of course goats, the beloved stock of the true peon. The main
house was magnificently furnished with Tomás's spoils of war.
When I entered it for the first time and beheld its splendor, I
glanced at Urbina and thought of a donkey stabled in a ballroom.

He was happily drunk and swollen with pride in his beautiful home and new infant daughter. Like all of us, he'd fathered
children everywhere, but with his wife (and unlike Villa, he had
only one) he'd previously sired only boys, five of them, and he was
genuinely happy to add a daughter to the family. "She will be the
queen of Mexico one day, you'll see," he said.

Pancho cradled the baby in his arms and crooned softly to
her. I myself was never comfortable with children, especially
infants, but Villa was a fool for children of every age. In every
town, they came to him in droves, and he never failed to stop and
chat and make a big fuss over them and buy them treats.

It was a damned swell fiesta. The sky was brightly blue and
cloudless, and the sun gleamed off the mountains' snowy peaks.
There was music and singing and dancing, joking and dicing,
laughter and fistfights. The bands played without pause. There
were horse races and cockfights and roping contests. The shooting contest that drew the biggest crowd was of course the one
between me and Villa: we shot at gold pieces lined along a wall,
then at cigars clenched in the teeth of brave *compañeros*, and
finally at the heads of live chickens flung into the air. He beat me
by one chicken head. He was the only man I ever knew who could
outshoot me.

Whole pigs and goats and sides of beef roasted on slow-
turning spits, and the boys gorged themselves at patio tables
loaded with heaping platters of pork, beef, kid, and chicken, with
turkey in chile gravy, with tamales and enchiladas of every variety,
with steaming bowls of beans and chiles, and piles of tortillas.
They drank rivers of beer and tequila. They sang *corrido* after
corrido—country ballads of unpredictable love and certain death,
of doomed heroism, of Mexican history as the same bloody tale
told again and again.

At one point Urbina unsteadily stood on a table and called to Villa: "Panchito, look! Look at me! Don't I look just like a fucking Spanish don?" He struck a pose in his glittering black *charro* outfit studded with polished silver conchos: his hand thrust into the front of his jacket, his upthrust face a stern imitation of aristocratic arrogance. Everyone laughed but me. He joked too often about the might of the Spanish lords, too often mimicked their manners: I suspected he was secretly enraged that he could never steal enough gold—not even if he robbed heaven itself—to buy such blue blood for his own veins. The rest of us hated the Spanish for the good and simple reason that they had for so long oppressed our people; but I was sure Urbina's hatred of them was at least partly fired by his fury that he could never be one of them. I liked Tomás for his daring and his ready laughter in the face of hard odds—but I despised him for his secret hatred of himself and his own kind.

Later in the day he was taking a few of us for a tour of the big house when his mother—a tiny woman in a wheelchair, still wearing black eighteen years after her husband had been hanged as a horse thief—came rolling into the room and chided him for some filial transgression. Snarling an obscenity, Tomás drew his pistol and fired at her, missing by less than six inches and shattering a crystal bowl on the table beside her. In the next instant he was on his knees and hugging her lap, beseeching her forgiveness. For a few moments she wept along with him, loudly lamenting her lack of a properly respectful son. Then she relented and patted his head and gently suggested he go sleep it off. "Yes, *mamacita*, yes," Tomás said, kissing her hands, "as you command."

After he staggered away, she announced, "He loves me so very much, my little Tomasito. It makes him crazy that he cannot adequately express his love for me, so he shoots." She excused herself and left the room.

A maid informed us that it was not the first time Tomás had shot at his mother. Nor, obviously, was it the first time he had missed. Someone murmured that Tomás had to be drunker than usual, since he was normally an excellent shot even when full of tequila. A couple of the boys took immediate exception to this explanation. Candelario claimed it was a scientific fact that a man was incapable of doing physical violence to his mother, no matter how much she might deserve it or how much he wanted to in his heart. He had learned this scientific fact from a whorehouse madam who had read it in a magazine article written by a French doctor of the mind. Calixto agreed with this view because his own mother had told him the same thing. In the lively discussion that followed, the only sure fact to emerge was that none of us had ever known a man who had deliberately killed his own mother. Somebody else's mother, yes, but not his own.

Two hours later Urbina was back at the head table in the main patio, swapping stories with Villa about their bandit days. Pancho looked more relaxed than he had in months. His laughter boomed over the blaring of the band. Except for brief respites at the table to eat and reminisce a little with Tomás, he spent most of his time on the dance floor, whirling tirelessly to the raucous ranchero tunes, twirling the girls, jangling the spurs on his stomping heels. Every now and then he'd withdraw into the house with a giggling girl on his arm like a happy bird.

The fiesta abounded with pretty girls. In addition to those who lived and worked at Las Nieves, Urbina had rounded up dozens more from Durango City, and still others from the neighboring villages. Many of the peasant girls were virgins, but they couldn't pass up the offer of a week of luxury at Las Nieves. It was a rare chance for them to escape the dull grind of their usual lives, if only for a week—an opportunity for which they were quite ready to surrender their virtue. Tomás had given each girl's father a small sack of gold to assuage the man's shame and outrage. One of them flung the gold back in Urbina's face, bloodying his mouth, and Tomás shot him. To the widow he then gave *two* sacks of gold.

Although many of the village girls were nervous and clumsy, all of them were hot-eyed with excitement and eager to please. It was clear that the city women among them—some of whom were Durango's most talented prostitutes—had taught them a few things in the days preceding the fiesta. Of course I indulged myself. They were all a pleasure—all thrillingly different, yet all wonderfully the same. They came to my room and closed the door behind them, let their dresses fall and stepped boldly into my embrace, moist mouths open. Their hips were urgent as engines, their laughter low in their throats. They all knew who I was, and the knowledge seemed to inflame their desire.

On the second evening of the fiesta, as I was about to go in my room with a Papago girl off the dance floor, I spotted a particularly pretty thing watching me from under a torch-lit tree. She wore a simple shift of white cotton and a silver ribbon in her blue-black hair. Her stare was too intense to ignore. "Hey, bold-eyes," I said, and beckoned her as I pushed away the Papago. The fiesta lasted another two days, and we spent nearly every hour of it in bed.

She was from a little pueblo south of Parral and had several months ago come to Las Nieves with her sweetheart Rafael, who had come to join the Division of the North. Except for the Dorados, who had to travel fast and live without encumbrance, Villa permitted our boys to take their women with them wherever we went, and the roofs of our trains were always packed with *soldaderas*. The accompaniment of women was an excellent morale booster which most army commanders allowed. But Rafael had forbidden this lovely girl (Carlotta?) to go with him when his unit was ordered to join our main force. "He said *he* would be the soldier in the family," she told me. "He said the *soldaderas* forget how to be women, and he did not want such a thing to happen to me." So she'd stayed behind at Las Nieves when his train pulled out. Not long afterward came the news that he'd been killed at Zacatecas.

Rather than return to her little town—where she wouldn't have been welcomed anyway, not after defying her father's prohibition against leaving with Rafael—she'd stayed at Las Nieves, working in Urbina's dairy. The memory of Rafael had lingered like a sickness in her heart, and she'd endured a lot of teasing from the other girls, who told her she was destined for spinsterhood if she didn't forget the dead lover and take up with one who was still breathing. She had intended to stay away from the fiesta despite Urbina's orders that all the unmarried women of the hacienda must attend, but when she saw me come riding through the big gates of the main patio she changed her mind. "I wanted to know the man who rides the brute white horse," she said, referring to my great stallion, Balazo, "the man whose eyes the other men fear." She talked like that. She told me she had fought off the gropes and denied the entreaties of dozens of men while she maneuvered to catch my attention. Her manner of speech was constantly breathless. Her eyes were never still.

She unleashed her hair from the silver ribbon, and its dark richness tumbled over her shoulders and into my face. She tied the ribbon around my cock and cooed over the scars on my stomach and legs and chest. She ran her fingers over them, her lips, her tongue. "Each is a kiss you received from Death herself," she whispered as she traced a fingertip along a ropy cicatrix over my heart, "and still she has never won you away." I had to laugh at her romantic lunacies. I hefted her by the hips, kissed the smooth swell of her belly, burrowed my face in her sex.

She wanted stories of violent spectacle, of battles and blood and atrocity. I regaled her with such tales while we roamed each other's flesh in the candlelit bed. When I told her of the 302 Colorados I'd executed in Juarez, her nipples puckered hard and she kissed me like she was trying to breathe my soul. (What is more fearsome than the secret source of a woman's deepest thrills?) I'd never forget her (Conchita?), she who relished my tales of killing and whose flesh was such an insistent reminder of life's immense sweetness (Caterina?). That one I would dream of every night forevermore.

A few weeks later I nearly asked Urbina about her, but then I thought better of it and said nothing. He probably would have joked at my interest in one of his dairy maids, and I would have had to shoot him then and there.

NINE

In August the Carrancistas drove the last federals out of Mexico City. A couple of weeks later Alvaro Obregón proposed a meeting with Villa at our Chihuahua headquarters to try to smooth things out between Pancho and Carranza and reach some agreement on the future of the Revolution. Villa said fine.

We gave Obregón a ceremonious greeting at the train station. He was everything we'd heard—diplomatic, cautious, cool-headed. He was built much like Villa, a little shorter but about as thick through the chest and shoulders, and he wore an almost identical style of mustache. But his features were sharper, and his green eyes reflected his Irish ancestry.

The talks were surprisingly cordial. Contrary to our expectations, Obregón came across as a man with a mind of his own, not just another of the whitebeard's bootlicks. Villa spoke frankly about his mistrust of Carranza, and was delighted when Obregón agreed that revolutionary unity was far more important than the whitebeard's personal political aspirations. He also concurred with Villa that Carranza should serve only as interim president until a national election was held—an election which would exclude Carranza as a candidate. They included this suggestion among others in a joint memorandum to the whitebeard which Obregón promised to deliver personally.

They then took a train to Juárez to mediate a squabble between some of our boys and a band of Carrancistas. After settling that matter, they accepted an invitation to meet with the gringo general John Pershing at the International Bridge and receive his congratulations for their success against Huerta. Obregón wore his uniform with all the polished gold buttons, while Villa looked like some kind of salesman in his Norfolk jacket and bow tie. Pershing called Pancho "my old friend" and patted him on the shoulder as if that were what he really was. A photograph was taken of the bunch of us, with Pershing and Obregón flanking Villa in the forefront. The only one of the three who smiled was Black Jack—a smile so big and false it looked as stiff as his starched tunic.

When Pancho and Obregón said good-bye back at the Chihuahua depot, they called each other "brother," and clutched in a warm *abrazo* like dear old friends.

———— >•< ————

A month later I was at the south end of the state, attending to various matters of train transport logistics, when Obregón once again showed up in Chihuahua for a talk with Villa. Carranza had by then rejected the Villa-Obregón suggestions for the new revolutionary government—particularly the one about disqualifying himself from the presidential elections—and Pancho had come to suspect that Obregón and Carranza were in cahoots and playing him for a fool. I thought so too. By the time I got back to headquarters, their meeting had degenerated into a Villa tirade. The first thing I heard when I stepped off the train was that Pancho was about to have Obregón shot.

Urbina wore a grin as big as the moon. "*El Invicto* is about to become *El Enterrado*," he said: the Invincible was about to become the Buried. "I can't believe he was so goddamn stupid to walk right into our hands like this."

When I entered the conference room, Villa was raging about Carranza's duplicity and lust for power and so on and so forth. He accused Obregón of conspiring with Carranza from the start, of showing us a false face while spying for the whitebeard. Obregón was cool, you had to give him that. He sat at the table, watching Pancho with a look damn close to open boredom. After another minute of Villa's ranting, he abruptly stood up and said, "With your permission, General, I will retire to my quarters to await your arrangements for my return to the capital." Without waiting for a reply, he strode briskly from the room.

Villa was dumbstruck. For a long moment he stared at the door through which Obregón had exited. His eyes looked ready to explode from his head. On the advice of his doctor he had been eating less red meat in an effort to control his temper, but the prescription had had little effect. Just as he was about to bellow the order for Obregón to be dragged back into the room so he could shoot him until his pistol was empty, one of Obregón's staff officers, a colonel named Serrano, blurted, "General Villa! If you please!" and Pancho turned his attention to him with eyes like little coal fires.

Speaking calmly and carefully, Serrano said, "We came to meet in *your* headquarters, my general, in complete confidence that our safety was assured by you, personally. I need not remind you, sir, that the code of warriors prohibits doing harm to one's guest. Though a man may be one's military enemy, when he has been permitted under one's roof he is entitled to safe conduct. It has always been thus among men of honor."

"Bullshit!" Urbina shouted. "Get that double-crossing son of a bitch back out here, Pancho, and let's shoot him!"

I agreed with Tomás. I could see what that slick Serrano was trying to do. Later on I'd come to find out he'd once been a singer and piano player in a fancy Mexico City whorehouse. It figured: all his bullshit about "honor" was a pretty smooth song and dance. By luck or shrewd insight he'd come up with the one argument that might sway Villa from executing Obregón. Urbina blamed this weakness on Madero: ever since Pancho had taken up the cross for the little saint, he'd been eager to prove he was just as *honorable* as any other man in a general's uniform, as though most generals—and most everybody else, for that matter—weren't a bunch of two-faced, double-crossing, back-stabbing bastards. (Sometimes his notions of honor went beyond foolish to plain loony. Shortly after this business with Obregón, for example, he would send a wire to Carranza proposing that the two of them— Pancho and the whitebeard—meet somewhere and simultaneously commit suicide. He explained that this selfless act would remove Mexico's greatest barrier to peace: their resolute hatred of each other. He concluded with "No long-winded answer is required, señor, only a simple yes or no." Was he serious? With Villa you could never be sure—but I do believe he loved Mexico more than his life, so yes, I think he was serious. Carranza never sent a reply, which didn't surprise me, but later we heard that when he read the proposal he turned white as his beard and said, "That man's not only a barbarian, he's a *demented* barbarian!" When he was told this, Villa sighed and said, "I guess that means no, eh?")

Now I could see Serrano's desperate argument working in Villa's head like a carpenter in a hurry. I rarely gave Pancho my opinion until he asked for it, but this time I thought I'd better speak up quick. "They're trying to save their ass with talk," I said. He gave me a narrow-eyed look. "These arrogant pricks came here to tell you how things are going to be. Now they know they fucked up. Obregón's neck is in the noose and they're trying to get it out again with a lot of talk. You *got* him, Pancho. What do you think the bastard would do if he had you? You think he would want to talk about honor?"

His eyes had turned to black ice. "Anything *else*, General?" he said. I shook my head and held his stare. Too bad if he didn't like what I had to say.

"*Shoot* the fuckers!" Urbina said. "*All* of them! Goddamn it, Pancho, Rudy's right. Who the hell they think they are, coming here and telling us Carranza wants this, Carranza wants that? Man, we got that Obregón, we *got* him! This is our chance, brother. Shoot him and send his head back to the whitebeard on a stick!"

The boys around Tomás shouted their agreement. Like him—like me, like Villa—they were from the desertlands, a world in which mercy was scarcer than tree shade. Where they came from, honor was a word of narrow meaning, a purely personal possession, something for a man to defend against insult, like his looks or his mother. Honor was not something to apply to the larger world, where those of property and education and political office defined it in ways that, like everything else, worked entirely to their own advantage. In our world you killed your enemy at the first opportunity, as you always expected him to do to you. And if he had his chance first and didn't take it—for whatever reason, including his sense of "honor"—that was his mistake and in no way obligated you to make the same one.

Unfortunately, we had more than a few in our ranks who believed in the larger concept of honor Serrano was talking

about—and even more unfortunately, Villa had lately been listening to them. All our goddamn schoolboys joined in the argument against shooting Obregón—Felipe Angeles, Raul Madero,
the Aguirre Benavides brothers, too damn many others. Angeles,
naturally, did the smoothest talking. "Colonel Serrano speaks the
truth, my general," he said to Villa. "Honor forbids bringing harm
to a guest, even if he is a military enemy. Indeed, honor demands
that he be protected while he is in one's house."

"Jesus Christ, we're not in Pancho's *house*!" Urbina yelled.
"This is some goddamn building! Pancho's house is on the other
side of town!"

Angeles was never one to let emotions interfere with his reason, but his contempt for Tomás was as obvious as his perfectly
trimmed mustache. "You take my meaning too literally, General,"
he said evenly. "The obligation holds under any shelter where the
guest is received."

Urbina kicked a chair and sent it rolling across the floor.
"Well, he's not going to *be* in any fucking shelter—because we're
going to take him *outside*!"

"Enough!" Villa commanded. Tomás saw the decision in his
face and cursed under his breath. I'd known his mind was made
up from the moment he asked if I had anything more to say. The
appeal to his sense of honor had struck home. And so, although
Obregón had not spoken a word on his own behalf, Pancho let
him go.

It was a terrible mistake.

———————

War with the whitebeard began to draw closer by the day. My
blood hummed with the certainty. Villa felt the same way: his eyes
brightened and danced at the talk of it. But many of the other

Constitutionalist factions wanted to avoid another civil war on the heels of the one they'd just fought against Huerta, and before things got any worse between us and the whitebeard, a convention of delegates from all the revolutionary parties was arranged in the town of Aguascalientes, to try to reconcile our differences and agree on a new government.

The convention lasted for weeks, and in that time a lot of speakers let loose a lot of hot air. I suppose many of them truly meant well, genuinely wanted to bring peace to the country and so on, but I knew all the talk would come to nothing. The bitterness between Villa and Carranza was never going to be resolved with talk, and I was amused by those who acted as though they really believed it could be. Carranza himself did not attend, but he was supported by about half the delegates who did, including of course Obregón, who read aloud a letter from the whitebeard stipulating the conditions under which he would accept the convention's resolutions. Among those conditions were that General Francisco Villa and General Emiliano Zapata would resign their military commands and, "like me," retire to private life; they would pledge not to run for any political office, and, if the convention decided that Carranza should leave the country, would also exile themselves from Mexico. When Villa heard the conditions, he said they were fine by him. "Better still," he said, "I think the convention should order both me and the whitebeard to be shot." He was serious.

Zapata's delegates, however, were outraged by Carranza's call for their leader to resign as head of the Army of the South, and some pretty good brawls broke out on the convention floor. If Carranza had been counting on a failure of accord among the delegates, he made a good bet. The Zapatistas had already angered a lot of the other representatives with their one-note argument about getting back their ancestral lands—like it was the only issue that mattered in the whole country. It was a high moment when their chief spokesman, an arrogant egghead named Soto y Gama, infuriated the whole hall during his address: he snatched up the specially designed convention flag on the podium and shook it in their faces, calling it a "rag" and saying all flags were "lies of history" and so on and so forth. He had earlier antagonized the Carrancista delegates by denouncing the whitebeard and insisting that the only truly revolutionary plan for Mexico was Zapata's. Now nearly everybody in the hall was waving a pistol at him and cursing him ("You shithead savage!" "You barbarian bastard!"), demanding that he show respect for the flag. That loony loudmouth just stood up there on the stage with his arms folded over his chest and sneered at them. He came this close to getting his brains blown out. Lucky for him cooler heads prevailed and he managed to get out of the hall with his life. I admired the crazy bastard's brass.

Villa had insisted that we would show unity with the Zapatistas, and we did: our speaker followed Soto y Gama at the podium and told the assembly we agreed with the Zapatista priority of land reform.

The convention voted in favor of the resignations of Villa and the whitebeard, but it put off a decision on the question of Zapata, and its deliberations on a choice for provisional president were full of factional rancor—the Carrancistas opposing all Villista candidates and vice-versa, and the Zapatistas opposing damn near everybody. They finally compromised on some harmless nobody named Gutierrez, then sent word to Carranza in Mexico City that his major conditions had been met and he was obliged to step aside.

Carranza's response was that the convention lacked the authority to elect a president and that it had in any case not met with all of his conditions. What's more, he claimed he'd been persuaded by "many" state governors and military generals not to resign but, for the good of the country, to press ahead with his program of governmental reform. Lying cocksucker made me laugh out loud. When he refused to honor his side of the deal, the convention declared him in rebellion and all bets were off.

And so the war was on. Us against the whitebeard, and the sides fanned up fast. Obregón stayed with Carranza, Zapata was with us.

Maclovio Herrera deserted us for the Carrancistas. He sent a note: "Forgive me, my chief, but I do not think you can win this war and I do not want to lose it." It had been only a few short months since we'd been his family's guests in Parral. They'd all given Villa great, back-patting *abrazos* and pledged eternal friendship. Maclovio had become his goddamn favorite, for Christ's sake. Through his tears Pancho swore he'd make every man of the Herrera family pay for Maclovio's treachery.

It didn't take us long to put the whitebeard on the run. With Zapata's army hammering at the capital from the south and ours bearing down steadily from the north and west, Carranza had nowhere to run but the Gulf. He took his headquarters to Veracruz. His main strength, Obregón's Army of the Northwest, was reported to have tons of weapons and supplies, but defections had reduced its ranks, and Obregón would have to recruit heavily to fill them again.

The Division of the North was now the most powerful army in the country, and Villa the most powerful man. We rolled south like thundering fate. But because they were closer to the capital to begin with, Zapata's boys got there first. When our trains reached the northern outskirts of Mexico City, Villa ordered a halt. He did not want to enter the town without first meeting with Zapata himself.

I wasn't the only one opposed to such deference to Zapata. (In their usual sensationalistic fashion, the newspapers had taken to calling him the "Attila of the South," a nickname that for some reason really rankled me.) Felipe Angeles also thought Pancho was making a wrong decision. He urged Villa not only to put a garrison of our troops in the city immediately, but also to send the main part of our army to Veracruz to crush Carranza now, while the opportunity was as ripe as it would ever be. "His forces are scattered between here and the sea, my general," Angeles said. "They're weak and disorganized. Now, *now* we should run him down and finish him."

Villa said no. Veracruz was in Zapata's sphere of operations and the honor of finishing off the whitebeard rightfully belonged to the Army of the South.

Angeles persisted. The Zapatistas were fine guerrilla fighters, he said, but they couldn't be counted on to crush the Carrancistas. He pointed out that the Army of the South had never won a battle on the scale of our victories at Torreón and Zacatecas, and that the Zapatistas rarely held on to any territory they did take. They were always in a rush to get back to their *patria chica*, their "little homeland" in Morelos.

"The fact of the matter, my general," Angeles argued, "is that while you fight for the liberation of all of Mexico, General Zapata and his people fight solely for the sake of their own little corner of the country. If you entrust them to deliver the coup de grâce to Carranza, I do not believe it will be done. General Zapata's hesitancy to venture beyond the borders of Morelos any farther than the capital will permit the whitebeard to escape from the vise in which we now have him."

Even though Angeles usually struck me as something of a priss (He washed *every* day! He always ate with knife and fork, even around the campfires!), there was no question of his loyalty to Villa, or of his honesty and his courage. His explanations of tactics were invariably clear and precise. As long as he was talking about practical military matters rather than expounding on some philosophical crap (like his concept of "honor"), he was nearly always right. Which, yes, I suppose is another reason I didn't like him. My objections to his arguments at staff meetings more often sprang from spite than from genuine disagreement. But this was no situation in which to indulge spite and I knew it. I told Villa I agreed with Angeles. "Let's finish the whitebeard while we can," I said. I no longer worried about an end to the war. I knew now that there would be war—some war, *a* war, enemies to fight—for years and years, no matter who we beat today, who we defeated tomorrow. The only thing that really mattered was not to *be* defeated.

Villa shook his head. His mind was made up and nothing was going to change it. There was nothing to do but shrug and shut up, and Angeles finally realized it too. Although Pancho was usually quick to follow Angeles's suggestions on military strategy, he was less concerned with strategy this time than with honoring the territorial rights of a brother revolutionary whom he greatly respected. He not only refused to belittle the Zapatistas' narrow revolutionary ambitions, he absolutely would not intrude into Zapatista turf without invitation, not even to finish off the whitebeard.

Another terrible mistake.

TEN

Our first meeting with Zapata was on his ground in Xochi-milco, a pretty little town a few miles south of the capital, well known for its floating gardens. We were greeted by cheering villagers bearing bouquets. The street was covered with flowers, the air heavy with their sweetness. Brass bands blatted tunes of the Revolution. Zapata was waiting for us in the company of his advisors at the municipal schoolhouse. He wore a tight fancy outfit and was lean as a lariat. The ends of his large mustache drooped past the corners of his mouth.

The meeting started out stiffly, uncomfortably. Villa was at an uncharacteristic loss for words, smiling tightly at Zapata, who sat mutely and stared around at all of us with eyes like black fires in a stone face. The clamor of the crowd outside, the loud music, and the incessant barking of dogs poured in through the windows. At last somebody mentioned Carranza—and they both started talking at once about how much they hated that perfumed, chocolate-drinking, blue-spectacled, white-bearded son of a bitch. That's all it took to loosen their tongues, and they conversed easily from then on.

They pledged an alliance against the Carrancistas and discussed plans for redistributing the land to the poor when the war was won. I got bored with the discussion pretty quickly: all their talk of how things would be after the war sounded a lot like the talk of priests on the way things will be after the end of the world. It all sounded silly and unreal. My ears didn't prick up again until they started making deals for certain of each other's prisoners, picking and choosing from among them the ones they wanted their own boys to kill.

To celebrate their pact, Zapata called for brandy. The glasses were brought and he handed one to Villa. "Thank you, little brother," Villa said, "but I don't drink."

"Of course not," Zapata said. "Neither do I." It was the only time I ever saw him smile. He thought Pancho was joking. He held his glass out in a toast. "The Revolution!" he said, and took the drink in one swallow.

Villa gave his drink an uneasy look, then said, "The Revolution!" and tossed off the brandy as Zapata had done. Instantly he began coughing and choking. I quickly gestured for one of the boys to take him a cup of water. Villa accepted it with a grateful nod—but even then, still fighting for breath and with tears rolling down his face, he first held the cup toward Zapata and gasped, "Would you care for some, amigo?" Zapata shook his head, frantically waving away the offer, and Pancho gulped down the water like a drowning man, sloshing some down his chin and on his sweater.

Nobody was so stupid as to laugh, not at the time. (Later, whenever I wanted to get Villa tight and red in the face, all I had to do was recall the moment for him and chuckle about it.) And even though Zapata's amazement was all over his face, he was

sufficiently quickwitted—and well mannered—to divert attention from Pancho's embarrassment by calling for the bands to play
louder and for everyone to dance.

⸺⬦⬦⬦⸺

Two days later we paraded into Mexico City. Together with the
Army of the South we were fifty thousand strong. Villa rode at the
head of an endless column of cavalry and marching troops, Zapata
on his right, me on his left, Urbina directly behind. All along our
route, from the outskirts of the city to the National Palace, people
were lined a dozen deep on both sides of the streets. We moved
through a steady rain of flowers, a thunderous cheering that nearly
drowned out the music of the bands and the clopping of the horses.

I thought Villa's face would burst from the force of his grin.
He looked at me and showed me his fist. I nodded and laughed.
"*Look* at us!" Urbina said. "The kings of Mexico!"

Villa looked splendid in his dark blue uniform flashing with
braiding and buttons of gold—but Zapata, that dandy, was spectacular in an enormous silver-studded sombrero and a charro suit
of deerskin with golden thread. Urbina had encased himself in a
stiffly starched, high-collared khaki uniform and a pith helmet
he had appropriated from a German civil engineer in Durango.
I myself looked wonderful in my new business suit from Chi-
cago and a bright necktie of pure silk, my Texas hat cocked over
one eye, my polished gold watch chain hanging just so from a
coat pocket. Although the city's cheers were chiefly for Villa and
Zapata, I knew that the deepest yearnings of the women in the
crowd were for me. I could feel the heat of their eyes on me as
Balazo, the only white horse in sight, pranced majestically down
the capital's wide boulevards.

A few hours later we were in the National Palace, posing for photographs. One of the most famous taken on that occasion shows Villa sitting in the presidential chair, the gold eagle embossed on its high back blazing over his head like a pagan halo. At first he had insisted that Zapata sit in the chair—"You deserve the honor, little brother, not I"—but Zapata had absolutely refused, and so finally Pancho shrugged and eased himself into the chair slowly, like he thought it might be some kind of trap. The grin he gave then was his biggest of the day. In that picture, Urbina is seated on his right, Zapata on his left. I'm standing next to Zapata. Nearly two dozen people are packed around the presidential chair, forming a rough pyramid of faces behind the gold eagle over Pancho's head. They're bareheaded and in hats, in uniforms and suits and neckties, in bandoleers and bandanas and bandages, some staring defiantly and some grinning with delight. Directly behind Villa stands a woman all in black whom none of us later recognized (or even remembered seeing in the room) when we looked at the picture.

I do recall a woman in the room when the picture was taken—one of Zapata's *soldaderas*, a dark beauty named Valentina who they said was one of his best fighters and was often put in charge of executing prisoners. When the famous picture was taken, she was standing off to the photographer's right, and it is her I'm looking at. She was looking back at me with a hard, small smile, her arms folded under her breasts and swelling them up for my pleasure. I'll say it myself: I look like a handsome devil. Villa looks happy, relaxed, satisfied with the world. Zapata looks like a hawk on the hunt. Urbina, as always, looks drunk.

We arrested hundreds and hundreds in Mexico City. Grafting politicians and bureaucrats, profiteering shopkeepers, black marketeers, counterfeiters, thieves, rapists, bootleggers, imprudent newspapermen, loudmouth priests, everybody who even looked like a pimp. We jammed the jails with the corrupt, the crooked and the counter-revolutionary. Our military prisoners we kept in the penitentiary, and we handed over to Zapata's boys any personal enemies they wished to execute in their own way. In return they gave us those prisoners of theirs we wanted to deal with ourselves.

Our firing squads were at work every day. Some of our boys went so far as to make occasional public examples of the condemned: one morning I spotted three dead federals hanging by their feet outside a police station, each with a small sign pinned to his chest. One sign read, "This man was shot for being a thief"; the next said, "This man was shot for making false money"; and the third said, "This man was shot by mistake."

Villa chuckled when he heard about it. "It takes honesty and courage for a man to admit his blunder to the whole world like that," he said. "The boys who did it are men of character, and I'm proud of them."

The Zapatistas preferred less direct means of execution. They were inclined toward skinning knives, anthills, and slow fires. They crucified men on telephone poles. They sewed men up in wet hides and left them in the sun to be suffocated as the hides dried and constricted.

I watched them work on one fellow, a federal major who had once led an attack on a Morelos village inhabited only by women and children and very old men. They hung him upside down about a foot above a coal fire and slowly cooked his brain. The smell of his burning hair gave way to the odor of roasting flesh. He screamed till his voice was gone, but the cords in his neck continued to strain in silence as the crown of his head slowly darkened and crisped. Nearly three hours passed between his first scream and his last breath. The Zapatistas spit on his corpse and called him a pussy for dying so fast.

When I described the execution to Villa, he shook his head and looked sad. He said he'd seen men die in even worse ways than that. He did not favor torturing men to death. "It takes too damn long," he said. "The time you spend torturing a man is time you could spend dancing and making love. Besides, it makes me feel like the kind of man I hate. No—even if some men don't deserve to die like a man, I won't let them keep me from killing like one."

Our prisoners would beg us to stand them against the wall rather than turn them over to Zapata's boys.

———————

One evening I got together with the Zapatista girl named Valentina in a hotel room a few blocks from the Zócalo. She had lovely brown breasts with nipples like burnt-sugar candies, but she got morosely drunk very quickly and made love like it was a duty. I had expected fire and spice, not this sullen bitch. Even her talk about killing lacked zest—and killing was all she talked about. In less than an hour she'd lost all allure. When I thrust her clothes at her and shoved her into the hallway, she screeched like a cat and swore she was coming back to cut my throat in the night. I expected her to try but she didn't. The next day I found out she'd picked a fight with two of our *soldaderas* in a joint down the street and they'd slashed her to death with their razors.

———————

Villa tried hard to establish a democratic government in Mexico City, going so far as to permit, as Madero had, freedom of the press—for democracy, they say, cannot exist without free speech. I had given this concept much thought, and I agreed with it. I still do. A man should have the right to say any damn thing he pleases—anytime, anywhere, about anybody.

However. If what a man chooses to say should offend another man, the offended man then has the right—under the democratic principle of equal rights for everyone, another concept with which I agree—to respond to the offense. And because a *true* democracy (the only kind I believe in) permits a man freedom of choice, the offended man may rightfully choose to respond to the offense in some way other than speech. He may, for example, prefer to respond with a fist—or, in an instance of *severe* offense, perhaps with a bullet. Thus does a true democracy impose upon its citizens the obligation to be prudent in the exercise of their rights.

Villa felt the same way, and during our occupation of the capital we occasionally had to impress upon unmindful citizens the consequences of ignoring this basic obligation. Those civic assignments most often fell to me of course, and most were so routine I barely distinguished one from another. But I never forgot the business with David Berlanga.

The whole thing started one evening when a group of our officers had dinner at a fancy place called Silvain's—owned by a Frenchman who thought he was something special because he had once been a chef for the czar of Russia (as though it takes great skill to cook a pot of beet soup). For some reason or other the boys got irked with the frog and refused to pay their bill. One of them wadded it up and tossed it across the room. But a fellow at another table got up and retrieved it and told the Frenchie—told him loudly, so that everybody in the place heard him—that he would pay it. When one of our boys asked him who the hell he thought he was, he answered, "A supporter of the Revolution who hates to see its principles dishonored by rabble like you."

Naturally our boys wanted to deal with the insulting bastard on the spot, but they reminded each other of Villa's order against abusing civilians in public disputes. Any complaints our boys had against a citizen were to be reported to headquarters—just as we'd instructed the local citizenry to do with any problems they had with our troops. We had recently executed one of our boys for killing an Avenida Juárez shopkeeper in an argument over the price of some bauble. Another man, a cavalry captain, had been stripped of his rank and reassigned to the gravediggers' squad for making a loud proclamation of desire to a passing young lady of good family, who took offense. The boys knew Villa was serious about this.

"If only there hadn't been so many witnesses," one of the boys in the group told me privately. "Bigmouth made us look like assholes and we couldn't do shit about it."

The bigmouth was David Berlanga. He was a newspaperman who claimed allegiance to the Revolution, but in several recent articles he had criticized many of Villa's government policies and strongly berated our troops for their public rowdiness. Villa had been shown the articles and had been irritated by them, but he'd managed to shrug off his displeasure with some halfhearted remark about the rights of a free press in a free society and blah blah blah. Because Villa's moods were as variable and quick to change as a sierra wind, it had been Berlanga's good luck that every time Pancho had seen one of the critical pieces he'd been in a mellow frame of mind.

But the report of the restaurant incident reached Villa on a morning when he was angry and confused about another matter: the night before he had been spurned by a beautiful woman he had spotted coming out of a church. The widow of a federal officer, she told him she would rather drink rat poison than permit him to touch her.

"How can it be?" he asked me a half-dozen times on the way to the staff meeting. "How can a woman say no to Francisco Villa? And the hatred in her eyes, Rudy, it was *real*." He sat at the table with his head in his hands as an adjutant read through a list of matters to be dealt with. The last item on the list was the complaint about David Berlanga.

There was a momentary silence when the adjutant finished reading—and then Villa exploded: "That son of a bitch! I've had enough of that little dog and his constant yapping! All that shit he writes about me and my boys! Enough! I want him shut up!"

"But, my general," one of the advisors said, "the man is a journalist. What of his right to freedom of expression?" Before the Revolution the advisor had been a university professor, one of those guys who's read hundreds of books full of big words and big ideas—but who can't read the handwriting on the wall. "Only a few days ago we released an official proclamation permitting the free expression of any—"

"Yes, yes, yes!" Villa shouted. "I know! Everybody's got a right to say whatever the fuck he wants—including me, goddamnit! *Fierro!*"

I stepped out of the shadows in the rear of the room. "Chief."

"Under my right of freedom of speech, I freely say to you: go shut that fucker's mouth!"

"Done, my chief."

I found him at Silvain's. He was sitting with friends and unwrapping a cigar as I approached the table. They all knew who I was—everybody in town knew who I was—and I smiled at the sudden fright on their faces. Only Berlanga did not look afraid. He stared at me with curiosity.

"You," I said, "come with me."

"May I ask why?" His voice was steady, his tone polite.

"Because you have been convicted as an enemy of the Revolution and sentenced to be shot, and it should be done in its proper place." I always liked giving it to them like that, quick and direct, and watching their faces as the news raced around in their heads like a trapped rat.

The others at the table reacted with all the usual theater—gasps, widened eyes, horrified glances all around. But not Berlanga. His eyes simply went cold for a moment, then he shrugged and smiled. "Convicted, you say? So I must have been given a trial. Strange that I don't recall it, especially since my lawyer so obviously did a poor job in my defense." He looked around at the others. "Remind me to fire him, whoever he was."

It was a good show of coolness, but I wasn't greatly impressed. Others before him had affected indifference when I came for them. But once they reached the moment of truth—once they arrived at the wall or looked down into their grave or heard the hammer draw back on my pistol—all of them, in one way or another, showed their fear. Some were despicable in their terror: they pissed their pants, they kissed my boots, they cried as hysterically as women. Some prayed to me to spare them, beseeching me as though I were a saint on a church wall. Even the bravest of them showed some sign of fear at the end—a tremor in the hands, a facial tic, jackrabbit eyes, something. I knew this one would too.

His friends all began jabbering at once: "But why, *why* . . . ?" and "David, what will you *do*?" and "David, they cannot *do* this to you, they must present a warrant, you must demand a proper trial, you must *demand* that they—" I swung my attention to the one yammering about "demanding," and he bit off the rest of his words and hastily dropped his eyes to the cappuccino cooling in front of him.

Berlanga stood and carefully pushed his chair in against the table. He smiled at his companions and said, "Was it not Everyman who said, 'O Death, thou comest when I had thee least in mind'?" To see the careful way he adjusted his tie and set his hat on his head, you would have thought he was preparing to pay a call on a woman. "Well," he said, "*I've* had him in mind ever since I saw him ride into town on his tall pale horse." He turned to me, his eyes still cool and steady, and said, "After you, señor," gesturing toward the door. I had to hand it to him: although I never thought it took exceptional courage for a man to put on a good show while his friends were looking on, it was a hell of a lot more than most could do.

The execution wall was at the San Cosme barracks, only a few blocks away, so we walked. The street was uncrowded and bright with late morning sunlight. The fragrance of flowers melded with the spicy aromas of lunch grills. A pair of guitars were being strummed lazily in the open-doored darkness of a cantina. I had expected him to start talking as soon as we were outside and away from his friends, to offer me money, to tell me the names of all the important men he knew, to talk faster and faster about courtrooms and lawyers and judges, to resort to all those things these educated ones think are as real as earth and fire. But he didn't. He strolled beside me with his hands in his pockets and his unlit cigar in the corner of his mouth, looking as casual as if he was with an old buddy on the way to have a plate of enchiladas and a couple of beers. He hopped over a pile of horse droppings on the sidewalk, and he smiled and tipped his hat to every young lady and *dueña* we passed.

He didn't say a word until we were almost to the wide double gate of the barracks courtyard. He paused under a tall cypress and said, "Excuse me, señor."

I stopped and turned, smiling, thinking that now it would begin, the pleading for his life. But he simply held up his cigar and asked, "Do you have a match?"

The look on my face must have told him what I'd expected, and he seemed amused. The son of a bitch. For an instant I felt like knocking him down, kicking him in his smiling mouth and smashing his cool facade with a storm of pain. But the impulse passed as quickly as it came. He suddenly reminded me of Felipe Angeles. They probably could have been fast friends. They could have discussed art and philosophy over brandy and cigars in the mansions of wealthy acquaintances. Goddamn rich schoolboys. But it was hard not to admire those among them who had guts as well as a sense of style.

I dug a match out of my vest pocket and handed it to him, and he made a busy ritual of lighting the cigar. Once he had it burning evenly, be said, "Thank you. The last one of the day has always been my most enjoyable." He took a few deep puffs and we entered the courtyard.

The boys were already there with their rifles, standing around telling jokes and smoking. They'd been at work since sunrise. When they caught sight of us, they threw away their cigarettes and fell into a loose line facing the wall. Without hesitation Berlanga went straight to the stained patch of ground in front of the pocked wall and turned toward the squad.

"My last request," he said to me, "is permission to finish my cigar." He held it up and I saw that its ash was unbroken and more than a half-inch long. He took another long puff and exhaled luxuriously. His hand was steady as stone. He continued to smoke, watching me, smiling at me around the cigar. I couldn't keep my eyes off the ash. We stood in silence while he puffed and regarded the sky, then the ground under his feet, then met my eyes again, still smiling, still puffing, the ash growing longer.

Finally he said, "Ready?" and took his deepest draw yet, the burning tip flaring redly. He expelled a long, thin plume of smoke and brandished the cigar for my consideration: the ash was intact, cylindrical and nearly four inches long. I had seen dead men with less control of their hands.

"*I'm* ready," he said, and dropped the cigar and crushed it under his heel.

A minute later they were dragging his corpse off to the burial pit.

That evening I sat alone in a cantina, puffing the same sort of cigar he'd been smoking, but the ash always broke off at a shorter length than his had. The best I could do was a little less than three inches.

I couldn't figure out his trick. It had to have been a trick because there were only two other explanations possible, and I could accept neither of them. One was that he was crazy, someone properly belonging in a madhouse or a monastery. But I had studied Berlanga's eyes carefully and there had been no madness there. I wished there had been, because insanity is not courage, and the only other explanation possible (other than a trick) was that he had been courageous, and that notion disturbed me.

The power of men like me does not come solely from our ability to kill—which is no small talent in itself, true, but neither has it ever been as rare as gold. No, the true source of our power is so obvious it sometimes goes unnoticed for what it is: our power comes from other men's lack of courage. There is even less courage in this world than there is talent for killing. Men like me rule because most men are faint of heart in the shadow of death. But a man brave enough to control his fear of being killed, control it so well that no tremor reaches his fingers and no sign shows in his eyes . . . well. Such a man cannot be ruled, he can only be killed. I refused to believe such fearlessness could exist in any man who, like Berlanga, was not himself a killer. I could no more accept such a notion than a priest could accept the idea of a godless universe.

I knew Berlanga had used some trick—I just never figured out what it was.

ELEVEN

We stayed in the capital a month before moving out to drive encroaching Carrancistas from our northern territories. Our boys up there were running low on ammunition and supplies. We'd also got word that Obregón had received enormous shipments of arms and had recruited thousands of fresh troops, including many more Yaquis. He looked ready to move against Mexico City again. We left it to Zapata's boys to hold the town— but as Angeles had predicted, as soon as we left they withdrew to Morelos, and toward the end of January Obregón retook the capital.

We heard he came back in a flaming fury. He'd been humiliated by having to abandon the city in the first place, and he was outraged that so many of its citizens had accepted our occupation without resistance. So he turned his boys loose in the streets to do as they wished—and that's when the people of Mexico City came to realize just how restrained our own boys had been during our stay.

Our troops had committed a few random abuses while we were in town, I don't deny that. Our boys did a little stealing and hurt some people they shouldn't have and frightened damn near everybody. But Villa also kept a degree of order and policed our boys fairly well, all things considered. We respected the rights of honest citizens as much as possible under the circumstances, and we preserved at least a portion of the civil amenities. Under our occupation the capital had law, food, medicine, and reason to hope things would get better. But still most of the capitalinos had complained bitterly about us and were happy to see us go.

Then Obregón and his boys came back to town and taught them the true meaning of hard times. That garbanzo farmer was their worst green-eyed nightmare. He skinned the city to a bloody carcass.

⟶⦁⟵

In the following months things changed fast: Under the constant strain of conflicting ambitions, the convention alliance became a futile joke, and we broke from it and went our own way. So did most of the other convention armies, each one now fighting for no cause greater than its own survival. Thus the Division of the North was now a sovereign power, and as its commander, Villa answered to nobody. Pancho finally admitted how right Angeles had been about Zapata: that Morelense wouldn't fight anywhere—or for anything—but his own goddamn bean fields. Some ally.

We headed north to regroup and re-arm—and Obregón, feeling ready and cocky as hell, came after us. He'd looted the capital to its last centavo. He'd sacked the churches and forced the archdiocese to hand over a "contribution" of more than $100,000 in gold to "alleviate the suffering of the citizens"—though we heard it mostly went to alleviate the suffering of his own pockets. He'd imposed a heavy tax on every business still in operation—including those owned by foreigners—and threatened to shoot

anybody who didn't pay up. He built up his store of medical supplies by cleaning out the hospitals of what remained of theirs.
When he pulled out to come get us, he left the capital writhing
with smallpox and typhus, dying of disease and starvation. They
were said to be selling rat meat in the markets.

Once Obregón's army left town, the capital became noman's-
land, now belonging to this army, now to that one, now to
another, round and round and raped by everybody. They said the
city stank of rot and ruin and total despair.

As Obregón drew nearer to us, Villa's eyes narrowed and glinted
with a keen anticipation of the fight. He had come to despise
that bastard even more than he hated Carranza: "The whitebeard
couldn't stand if this Sonoran son of a bitch wasn't holding him
up!" Every day we received reports of how much nearer Obregón
had advanced, and at each report Pancho would smile tightly and
look off to the south and say, "Good, good. Keep coming, little
Invicto. Come to me."

In early spring Obregón reached Celaya—and there he
stopped.

"He's come all this way," Villa said, "and now he's so close, he's
afraid to get any closer." He laughed without humor. "Well, it's too
bad and too late. Now we'll give him the fight he came for."

Angeles argued for greater caution. He was on crutches with
a broken ankle after his horse had recently been shot out from
under him. "Be patient, my general," he counseled. "Pull our units
farther back and force him to put even more distance between
himself and his supply sources. Then *we'll* have the advantage of
position, cover, reinforcement routes, supply lines, everything."

I thought Angeles was right again—damn him!—but Villa was beyond the reach of reason on the subject of *El Invicto*. He could smell Obregón's nearness on the fine May breezes off the plains, and he couldn't wait to destroy him in spectacular fashion, in the way he knew best—by attacking with everything he had, all at once, and crushing him completely with one tremendous blow.

"Out there on those open fields," he told Angeles, "it will be like rolling beer barrels over frogs in the street." He dismissed all further argument.

Maybe if we had known that Obregón had with him a handful of German army officers, including a certain Colonel Maximillian Kloss, Angeles could have argued more persuasively against Villa's plan. He could have warned Pancho about Kloss's style of warfare, could have told him that the German was fresh from the battlefields of the Great War taking place in Europe and was an expert in the tactics of trenches. It was a sort of fighting that had proved especially effective against cavalry attack, and the irrigation ditches of Celaya were perfect for it. Under Kloss's guidance, Obregón would position his riflemen in the wide ditches fronted by rolls of barbed wire and flanked by coordinated machine gun emplacements. Obregón's Yaquis would add a touch of their own to the trenches: long, wooden stakes sharpened to fine, tapering points and angled toward heaven.

But we didn't know about Kloss and the other Germans— and even if we had known, I doubt it would have influenced Villa in the least. He was determined to smash *El Invicto* then and there, and nothing could have swayed him from the attempt.

And so we attacked.

And so we were slaughtered.

In the shudder and abrupt tilts of the earth, under the rolling drifts of smoke and the deep tides of dust, I heard us dying by the thousands in the blasts and bursts of artillery, the incessant chatter of machine guns and the cracking of rifles, the rumble of hooves and the high shrilling of horses, the war cries, the screaming.

Our foot soldiers got caught on the rolls of barbed wire and were annihilated by the machine guns. Our cavalry was gunned down as it searched for a break in the wire—and when we did find a break and got behind the wire and tried to jump the trenches, the horses were impaled on the wooden stakes. The animals' screams melded with those of their riders, who were run through by Yaqui bayonets. The boys fell around me like fruit from a shaking tree. It was a wonder Villa himself wasn't killed. He was everywhere, firing his big pistols and shouting encouragement: "At them, boys, at them! Up, up, little brothers! Kill the sons of bitches before they get us all!"

I lost my beautiful Balazo in the ditches of Celaya. He died with a stake through his white belly, his hooves kicking against the trench boards like gunshots, and blood raging from his mouth in bright gouts. I shot every Yaqui son of a whore in that ditch, never feeling the bullets I took in the back and leg until after we'd made our retreat, all of us bloody, Villa in tears, weeping for his thousands of dead boys.

"They killed us, Rudy!" He wiped at his eyes and streaked his face with blood. "Oh, Goddamn them, how they killed us!"

Our hospital trains howled with the wounded, the crippled, the dying.

Obregón captured hundreds of our boys. On his orders they were packed into goat pens and then machine-gunned, all of them.

We'd been savaged but not broken, not yet. Villa repaired to Agauascalientes to regroup his forces. Angeles had missed the battle because of his bad leg, and he blanched when he heard how badly things had gone. Villa's sorrow had transformed to rage: "I would rather have lost to a goddamn *Chinaman* than to that fucking Obregón!" He was sure we had traitors in our midst. When somebody pointed out that one of our infantry commanders had an uncle serving in Obregón's army, Villa sent for him to be brought to the headquarters railcar. He took a close look into the man's face and said, "It's true—it's in your eyes. You are a traitor." He shot him before that fellow could say a word in his own defense. Others came under suspicion too, and also were executed.

He made plans for another showdown with Obregón, this time in León, midway between Aguascalientes and Celaya. Again Angeles remonstrated, making the same argument he'd made before the horror at Celaya: Villa should dig in at Aguascalientes and let Obregón come to us. "Make him extend *his* supply line, my general. Make *him* run all the risks of an attack."

Villa gave him a look that was a cross between irritation and sorrow. "My general," he said, "I have the greatest respect possible for your advice. You are without doubt the finest military mind in the world. But, my general, I am Francisco Villa, and I was born to attack. *To attack!* If I was beaten by attacking today, I will win once again by attacking tomorrow." End of argument.

The battle at León lasted forty days and nights and its destruction was as biblical as its duration.

This time we dug trenches too. And we introduced hand grenades to the war. And an airplane: Villa had recruited some wild-
ass gringo pilot and his flying machine from God-knows-where
and sent him to fly over Obregón's position to scout for us. It was
a brilliant idea—but on his first reconnaissance, the gringo flew
too low and Obregón's boys shot him down and that was the last
we saw of that Yankee.

We'd charge their trenches, then they'd charge ours. The summer heat was like hell's own furnace. It drove men crazy. Every
now and then, somebody—sometimes from our lines, sometimes
from theirs—would jump out of a trench and run, screaming
madly, into the open field between us and be gunned down.

Every day saw a doubling of the dead men in the fields. The
dusty stench was indescribable. The storm of flies could be heard
a half mile away. The rats—a massive, squirming army of their
own—feasted on the corpses in broad daylight.

And once more we got our asses kicked raw.

The only good thing that happened at León was that
Obregón got half his right arm blown off by an artillery blast. It
says everything to me about that man that he tried to kill himself
to end his pain. He later admitted it: he claimed his agony had
been so great he tried to shoot himself in the heart with his own
pistol, right there on the battlefield. Think of it: we were trying
to kill him, and he was trying to kill himself. How in hell did we
ever lose to that candy-ass, to that hairless pussy! And *damn* the
orderly who forgot to reload Obregón's gun after cleaning it the
night before!

(I do like the tale they told of how Obregón's arm was recov-
ered from the field of carnage. It seems he had a reputation as
something of a skinflint, so one of his aides went walking through
the field of dead, holding out a ten peso gold piece—and as he

passed by the arm, it flew up and grabbed at the coin. I heard
that one of Obregón's generals put the arm in a jar of alcohol and
kept it for a souvenir. Good Christ. And years later, when he was
campaigning for the presidency, Obregón would make the lack of
an arm seem a virtue: he'd tell an interviewer that everyone knew
all politicians were thieves, but the people would vote for him
because he could only steal with one hand.)

Our defeats at Celaya and León were mortal wounds: the great
Division of the North was dying in bloody rags. In less than three
months we'd lost tens of thousands of men. We'd lost rail lines,
artillery, ammunition, supplies of every sort, much of everything.

We continued to fight, of course. What else were we to
do? But now defeat followed defeat. We lost at Aguascalientes,
Zacatecas, Torreón. It was a terrible reversal of our triumphant
route toward Mexico City just the year before. Down south, the
Zapatistas fought the same battle over and over again—giving up
a portion of their damned *patria chica* to the Carrancistas one day
and then taking it back the next. We no longer even talked of getting any help from those useless fucks.

Although Villa always preferred to keep me and my Dorados
close to hand, his desperation to turn things around decided him
on setting me loose with my boys and a regiment of cavalry to
do whatever damage I could. I'd been champing for that chance,
and my boys were raging to go. We tore south through one Carrancista force after another, like a furious rolling storm. We took
Irapuato, then Silao, then Salamanca. We retook Celaya, me and
my boys. We took Querétaro. But—goddammit, *but!*—I didn't
have enough troops to spare to post defensive garrisons in the
towns we captured, and Villa had no reinforcements to send. All

I could do at each place was drive out the Carrancista unit, blow up the tracks behind us, and keep going. But then—goddammit, *but then, but then!*— they'd move right back in as soon as we were gone, and they repaired the railways almost as fast as we destroyed them.

When we routed two thousand of Carranza's troops in Tula and found ourselves within fifty miles of the capital, we felt more like losers then victors: we didn't have the manpower or artillery to push our way in. We could only look at the capital like a prize for the taking which we lacked the muscle to lift. Besides, our lightning advances, all-out assaults, and quick getaways had taken their toll: we were worn and in need of rest. We had no choice but to head back north for sanctuary. In the meantime, Obregón had organized a huge fresh counterforce specifically to send against us, and he set a trap at Jerécuaro. The knowledge that we would be passing through there he could only have learned from one of the cowardly fucks who deserted us in the night. The ambush caught us good and they smashed us like a water jug.

I had started out with more than four thousand men. By the time I rejoined Villa in Chihuahua, I had fewer than six hundred. When Pancho saw us, he wept.

That night we sat together out in the desert and fired our pistols at the moon.

TWELVE

By the middle of that sorrowful summer of 1915 many of
our old *compañeros* were dead. Many others were cripples.
Still others had been taken prisoner and, if they had not yet been
shot, were rotting in captivity somewhere. Some had lost heart in
the cause and fled to the mountains or to refuge across the border.

Felipe Angeles was in Washington trying to get Yankee support for our cause, but he was not having much luck. Neither was
Villa's old gringo friend General Hugh Scott, who'd been doing
all he could to keep President Wilson's sympathies with our side.
The gringo government tries never to bet except on the side that's
winning, and every defeat we'd suffered that summer had moved
them closer to recognizing Carranza as Mexico's legal head of
state. "The goddamned gringos," Villa growled, "have less honor
than whores!"

But his greatest bitterness—like mine—was for the turncoats. It was one thing for a man to desert to the hills or the other
side of the river. When we caught up with them, we simply gave
them a bullet in the head, or, in special cases, let them live and
serve as shitworkers—repairing rail tracks, digging graves or
burning the dead, shoveling coal, things like that. But those who

jumped to the Carrancistas were outright traitors, and Villa no longer objected too strongly if our boys taught them a few special pains before killing them.

Yet when he heard that Maclovio Herrera had been killed near Nuevo Laredo, he cried. Maclovio's desertion to Carranza the year before had turned in his heart like a knife. He'd sworn to avenge the betrayal on all of Maclovio's grown male relatives and still meant to keep that vow. But that had nothing to do with his grief for dead Maclovio.

Worse heartbreak followed. He had dispatched Tomás with a company of cavalry and a chest of gold bullion to meet with some gringo dealers bringing several wagonloads of munitions to the border. When Tomás did not come back as scheduled, Villa was afraid the Carrancistas had intercepted him. That wasn't what happened. He had absconded with the gold to his hacienda and fortified the place. We got word that he was negotiating a deal with Carranza.

The news left Villa looking like he'd lost his mind. He couldn't talk about it without his eyes filling with tears. "We've ridden together since we were boys," he told me a thousand times.

"Listen, Pancho," I said, "we can sit around here and cry about it while he makes a deal with the whitebeard and gets fat off our gold, or we can go down there right now and show him the error of his ways."

We picked a hundred Dorados, loaded our horses on a train, and rolled off to the south. We stared out at the passing desert lit white by the moon. Tumbleweeds bounded in a gusting wind. The mountains were black and sharp. Just north of the Río Ramos the tracks had been dynamited, and the twisted rails looked like crippled things. We saddled up and moved on. An hour before daybreak we were overlooking the Hacienda de Las

Nieves, counting the guards along the main wall and forming our
plan of attack.

"So this is what it comes to, the glorious Revolution," Pancho
whispered in the chilly darkness. "Now I make plans to attack my
oldest friend, my little *compañero*."

I hated it when he wallowed in sentiment that way. Except
in him—and in some women who seemed to get aroused by
their own indulgence in it—I never had much tolerance for sen-
timentality. Villa most often got that way when he was remi-
niscing about his gang of the old days. I usually just gritted my
teeth against it, or claimed duties to attend to and went away. But
that wasn't the case now. We had things to do and we had to do
them right. There wasn't time for any of his raining-in-my-heart
self-pity.

"Hey, man," I said, "you're not the first guy to ever get shit
upon by a friend. Better hearts than his have turned crooked as a
corkscrew."

For a moment he looked like he might take a swing at me.
Then he just walked away and sat by himself until it was time.

———⟶•◆•⟵———

We hit the hacienda at sunrise, charging down from the east to
have the sun blazing at our backs. We picked off the wall guards
like bottles on a fence. We blew apart the front gates with a pack
of dynamite, then rode into the main courtyard shooting everything that moved—men, pigs, dogs, the astonished stableboy
whose wide-open mouth admitted my bullet to remove the back
of his skull an instant before I recognized him. He had been
a shy simpleton who'd presented a handful of wildflowers to a
pretty girl with a silver ribbon in her hair and her arm linked
in mine at the fiesta for the christening of Urbina's daughter.

(Consuelo? Carina?) The memory came to me as abruptly as a finger snap—and the sight of the boy lying in the bloody spill of his dull brain filled me with such fury I ignored the cries of "We surrender! We surrender!" from the three house guards coming out through the side door and I shot all three with their hands up high.

Urbina came dashing out the front door with a pistol in each hand, firing wildly and running in a crouch toward the stable. A slug knocked a leg from under him and he did a neat little flip in the air, landing hard on the courtyard cobblestones.

"Cease fire!" Villa yelled. "Cease fire, goddammit!" He vaulted off his horse and hurried to Tomás. He helped him up and gingerly assisted him to a stone bench under a cypress tree.

"As if I didn't have enough trouble getting around with this fucking rheumatism," Urbina said through his teeth as Villa examined the wound. "What hit me, a Sharps?"

The round had taken a good-sized chunk out of his calf. It was messy but not fatal. Pancho tied it off with a bandanna, then sat beside him on the bench and waved me away. "See to things," he said.

I walked through the house as the boys went at it like wolves on a wounded cow, stripping it of whatever they could carry off in their saddlebags or tied across their horses. I couldn't help wondering how many times these things had been stolen before, how many different men had called themselves their owners. Some of the intricate gold figures going into the boys' pockets had been fashioned by the Aztecs.

A Dorado captain came out of the kitchen, chewing on a chicken leg, and informed me they'd found the women and children of the house hiding in the cellar. Urbina's wife and kids were not among them. They were mostly maids and their daughters, but there were also a few whose dresses and pampered hands made it clear they were not part of the housekeeping help.

"I recognized one from the fiesta last year," the captain said, grinning. "I guess some of those girls found themselves a home, eh?"

"General Urbina likes his pleasures close at hand," I said.

A woman's scream, partly muffled, came up from the cellar. The captain gave me a fearful glance and started for the kitchen. He knew what Villa and I thought about rape. I'd shot more than one man for violating Pancho's order against assaulting women. But before he was through the door, I called out, "Captain!" and he stopped and looked at me. "Let the boys have some fun," I said.

His face brightened. "Truly, Chief?"

I nodded. He grinned and rushed out of the room.

Why the hell not? A defeated but honorable enemy deserved certain amenities of respect—such as protection for the women under his roof. But a traitor deserved no such considerations. To the contrary, nothing of his—property, women, reputation, life, *nothing*—should be spared. I continued searching the house, but his wife and children were gone. He had known we would come.

In a small parlor I found one of our boys with a woman pinned under him on a sofa. He was straddling her hips, fumbling with the buttons of his trousers and fighting to keep his balance as she gasped and struggled to throw him off. Her dress was ripped open to the waist and her breasts quivered with her efforts.

A few feet away a dead man in an expensive-looking suit lay on the floor, blood still running from an empty eye socket. A representative from the whitebeard, most likely.

When he caught sight of me, the *compañero* froze. I shrugged to let him know I didn't give a damn, not today, and he smiled, still jouncing as the girl kept trying to wrest herself from under him. He pointed at the dead man and said, "I got that fucker there, Chief." The girl bucked hard and almost unseated him. He backhanded her across the mouth and grinned at me. "And I got me a real bronco here."

"Watch out she doesn't throw you and break your ass," I said as I turned away.

I was stepping through the door when I heard "Rudy?" It was said so low that for a moment I thought I had imagined it, as I had imagined it so many times since that fiesta of a year ago. So long ago.

I turned back and looked closely and saw that it was her. (Caridad? Consuelo?)

"Rudy." She said it like releasing a held breath. Maybe she hadn't been sure till just then either. "Rudy, stop him. *Please.*"

The puzzled *compañero* hesitated, with his pants flapped open and his hard-on jutting up. "You *know* this one, Chief?"

Her torn dress was made of silk. The fine necklace holding an ivory brooch was gold. Her lips and eyes were painted, and even through the *compañero's* musk I could smell the sweetness of her perfume.

The dress she'd dropped at my feet had been cotton, her only adornment a silver ribbon in her hair.

"Listen, Chief, if you know this one, well, I—"

My bullet took him through the heart. He bounced off the wall and tumbled in a heap next to the well-dressed corpse on the floor.

For a moment neither of us moved. The thin gunsmoke drifted to the ceiling as the ringing in my ears slowly eased.

She sat up and reached out to me. "*Rudy,*" she said, beckoning with all her fingers. Her breast tips looked like pink stones.

I shot her through the left one. She died with her eyes wide open and her lips formed as if for a kiss.

In my continuing dreams of her I would see her as I always had: stepping from the pooled white dress, freeing her hair into my face, listening like an enraptured child to my stories of war and death, holding my face in her hands as she kissed me with her heart's hot tongue.

Who *this* whore was I neither knew nor cared.

Out in the courtyard Urbina still sat on the bench, Villa standing beside him with a hand on his shoulder.

"I bound up his leg a little better," Pancho told me as I approached, his voice high and tight, the way it always got when he was in a state. "It's not bleeding so bad now. We'll take him to a doctor in Durango. He'll be all right, you'll see."

"Fuck him," I said.

"*Hey!*" Pancho said, stepping up to me fast, trying to hide his confusion with anger. "This is *Tomás*, goddammit—our *compañero*. We don't say fuck *him*."

"Where's our gold, you son of a bitch," I asked Urbina. He wouldn't even look up at me.

"The *gold*—shit, the boys found the gold," Pancho said, gesturing vaguely toward the other end of the courtyard. "Some of it. Down in the well. The *well*—can you believe it?" He tried to laugh but it came out a high groan.

He looked down at Tomás, who smiled up at him and shrugged. "That's no place to hide gold, you dummy," Villa said. "That's the first place anybody looks."

"Where's the rest of it?" I said, giving Urbina a shove on the shoulder. He refused to meet my eyes. He just shrugged and stared at the ground.

"What, did you spend it already?" Villa said with a weak grin, still trying to make light of the situation. "You gave it to some good-looking *chica* with a great ass? You bury it someplace, hide it for your old age? Ay, Tamasito!" He shook his head at Urbina like an exasperated father, then turned to me and said, "What the hell's it matter, anyway? Goddamn gold. We can always get more gold, eh?"

I stared hard at him.

"Goddammit, Rudy," he said, "this is *Tomás*."

"*Tomás?*" I echoed. "No it isn't. I don't see Tomás anywhere around here. Tomás was our brother. This"—and I quickly stepped up and kicked Urbina in the ribs so hard I nearly knocked him off the bench—"*this* is a bag of shit!"

Villa jumped between us, looking wild. "Rudy, Rudy listen . . ."

"He *stole* from you!" I shouted.

"So what—so what!" Pancho yelled, his hands on my chest, pushing me away. "He's our *friend*!"

"Bullshit! He *stole* from us! He stole from the *Revolution*!"

His face folded in agony and the strength seemed to drain from his push. "Fuck the Revolution," he said in a choked voice, nearly whispering. "He's my friend." His hands dropped off my chest.

"Yes," I said, "your friend. And your *friend* betrayed you. He *betrayed* you, Pancho! What crime is greater—what crime!"

He knew I was right, of course. That wasn't the argument. No, what he wanted was my complicity. He wanted to pardon Tomás for an unpardonable crime, and he wanted me to go along with it. But I wasn't about to. I would not conspire against the only . . . what? . . . understanding? unwritten law? code?— different men call it different things if they call it anything at all— but it is the only thing in the life of men like us that has absolute value, the only thing, finally, that counts.

God damn it, the compact of comrades is all that separates men like us from the rough beasts of the earth, that makes us something more than another random catastrophe of nature like earthquake and fire. Villa knew that. He'd always known it. Urbina knew it too, which is why he couldn't look me in the eye. He had violated the compact, had deliberately betrayed his friends. He *had* to be punished. For him it would be penance. For me and Villa it would be fidelity. I was saddened by Pancho's weakness in the face of that truth.

Villa's eyes continued to plead with me, but I shook my head. Finally he looked away.

He wiped his nose with his shirtsleeve, dried his eyes on his cuffs. He smiled at Urbina, and Tomás smiled back, crookedly, like a guilty boy. "My little *compadre*," Pancho said softly, and affectionately ran his hand through Urbina's hair.

Then he stepped away, looked off toward the sierras, and said, "Shoot him."

He went straight to his horse and mounted up. And without once looking back, he rode away.

I ordered the boys left with me to set torches to the house. Soon flames were leaping from the roof and bursting through the windows. Smoke rolled skyward in towering gray plumes. Looking at his burning house, Urbina shook his head as sadly as any rich man pained by his loss of property.

"I suppose you wonder why I did it," he said, finally raising his face to me—only to see my pistol pointed at him in implacable judgment.

"No," I said, "I don't."

I blasted away his left kneecap. He tumbled off the bench, howling and writhing on the ground. The remainder of his side of the proceeding was conducted in screams and spasms. I shot his feet and ankles, then an elbow, then a shoulder. I shot his thieving hands, the other knee, and the points of both hipbones, tearing flesh and smashing bone but sparing the big arteries. I shot the other elbow, then blew off an ear. I pressed the bore of the gun against the side of his nose and shot the whole thing off his face. I went through three reloads, then paused to piss on him, then clapped my hand over his mouth to cut his moaning while I whispered into his good ear: "You'll never rest in peace, Tomás, never. Not you."

I gave him the last one in the belly, then sat in front of him and watched the light fade slowly from his eyes.

When we caught up to the rest of the boys near the Durango border, Villa was entertaining them around a campfire with Tomás Urbina stories. I'd been a part of some of those stories, and I'd heard almost all the others, plenty of times. But on this night they seemed funnier than ever before, and I laughed along with the boys at every story Pancho told.

Like Villa, I believed that even though some men did not deserve to go on living, they still deserved to be remembered at their best.

PART THREE

Dead
or
Alive

"All the men of the Mexican Revolution were,
without a single exception, inferior to its demands."
—Daniel Cosío Villegas

THIRTEEN

Early that fall the United States recognized Carranza's Constitutionalist Party as the "de facto" government of Mexico. Other countries immediately followed the Yankee lead and did the same. To make things worse for us, the gringos placed an embargo on all arms shipments into the country except those going to Carranza. Bastards.

Our immediate problem was figuring a way around the embargo. Villa sent me with a half dozen Dorados to search out new entry points along the border for arms shipments from renegade gringo dealers and new routes for transporting the munitions down to our Chihuahua territories.

"Find some good spots for getting the guns across," Pancho told me. "A few places where we won't be surprised in the middle of things. Safe places."

"*Safe* places?" I had to laugh. "Hell, brother, you're talking about our graves."

During the next couple of weeks we found a few good transfer points along the border west of Palomas, then began charting a shipment trail south. We were making our slow way through the swamplands just north of Casas Grandes one chilly morning when we came up against a long, foul-smelling lake dotted with sandbars. We were at about its midpoint, so we had to either ford it or swing a long way around.

The lake looked shallow enough to cross easily on horseback—some of the sandbars stood more than a foot above the waterline. But the boys said they wanted to ride around it. It wasn't only that most of them didn't know how to swim: they'd all heard bad stories about the place. The local Indians claimed the lake was evil, that its bottom was littered with the bones of men who'd drowned in it, that if a man so much as got both feet wet with its tainted water ill fortune would plague him for the rest of his life.

Well, hell, I couldn't swim either. But it's one thing to be afraid of a stinking yellow lake because you might drown in it, and it's something else to be scared away from it by a lot of Indian mumbo-jumbo. The boys were already in pretty low spirits from the ass-kickings Obregón had given us lately—I wasn't about to let them be whipped by Indian superstition too.

"Listen," I told them, "we're going *through* this pisshole, all of us! Don't be so worried about getting your pussies wet. Your main worry better be not to cross *me*. Anybody want to argue about it?"

Nobody did.

"Good," I said. "Now, I can see how scared you girlies are, so I'll go first. Anybody who doesn't cross over after I do is going to see me come back to say good-bye to him. Understood? All right then, girls: watch me, then follow the route I take."

I was mounted on Sangria, a brawny but high-strung bay stallion as reluctant to ford the lake as the boys were. I had to spur him into the water. He sagged under me as he sank into the soft mud, but then he found firm footing and moved forward briskly when I put the spurs to him again. As he high-stepped awkwardly through the muck, his hooves stirred up the bottom and brought up a thick, gagging stench of sulfur and rotten meat.

We were about thirty yards from shore, in water to Sangria's belly, when he abruptly sank to his withers. He panicked and lurched sideways, trying to kick free of the mucky bottom, then lost his balance and fell over with a high shriek. I slid out of the saddle fast enough to keep from getting pinned under him as we both went under. But as the big bastard rolled, he kicked wildly with a free hoof and drove it into my right shin, snapping it like a stick.

A surge of hot vomit rose to my throat. I took it down with a searing gulp of rancid water as I floundered desperately, finally gaining a vague foothold on my good leg and pushing myself upright. I bit huge gasping gulps of air, my throat and lungs on fire.

A few feet away, Sangria was thrashing madly, his muscular neck straining to keep his head up. He was screaming through his enormous teeth, his eyes crazy with terror. My Texas hat bobbed beside him.

Then I understood the trouble: I felt the quicksand's enveloping yield under my good leg. I tried to push off the soft bottom with my broken leg but the pain flared like white fire behind my eyes and I heard myself cry out.

Sangria's terrible shrieks were suddenly cut off as he went under again, his great weight pressing him deeper into the quicksand. The water over him shook queerly for a moment and then went still.

I sank to my chin, my mustache. Snorting and choking, I turned my face up to the clouded sun—and as the yellow lake closed over me, I thought: so *this* is how you die . . .

I did and I didn't.

I opened my eyes to a white ceiling brilliant with lights. Then a dark figure loomed over me and slowly shaped itself into Villa's broad familiar face. He was hatless and smiling gently. Not until he put his hand on my arm was I sure I was really alive. I was vaguely conscious of a soreness in the joints of my arms and legs. There was the gentle smell of fresh cotton sheets and the hard odors of disinfectants and medicines, the clatter of metal, the light rumble of a cart rolling over a wooden floor, a clinking of dishware, soft voices far and near. I felt, rather than heard, Villa speaking to me, and I eased back into the sweet soft darkness.

The next time I came awake, Pancho told me Calixto Contreras had saved me. Calixto was the only one of the Dorados with me who could swim. When he saw Sangria suddenly sag under me, he knew we were in quicksand. He wound the end of his lariat around his saddle horn, kicked off his boots, threw off his bandoleers, and splashed out to me with the other end of the rope in his teeth. Only my hands were above the surface when he got to me. He looped the rope around my arms and pulled it tight, then signaled the boys to lash his horse away from shore.

They said I came bursting out of the water like a fish on a line. The suction pulled off my boots and pants. I wasn't breathing when I was dragged on shore, they said, and I looked like I was made of clay. My lower leg was bent in a sharp awkward angle where the shinbone had broken in two, but although one of the jagged ends jutted from the ripped flesh, there wasn't much blood. They were sure I was dead, and who could blame them?

They figured the only thing to do was take my body back to Villa. But when they heaved me on my belly over a horse, a hard stream of yellow water gushed from my mouth—and I gasped and started coughing. They yanked me off the horse, but I slipped from their grasp and my leg doubled under me, twisting the broken bone and tearing the wound open even wider.

They sat me under a tree and pounded me on the back to help me disgorge more water. They said my bloodshot eyes came open for a moment and I cursed them for hitting me, then passed out again. My leg was pouring blood now, the bone ends completely exposed. They tied off the bleeding with a strip of rawhide tight above the wound, and a couple of the boys went to the nearest village to get a wagon to put me in. The best they could find was a cumbersome solid-wheeled oxcart.

It took almost three days to get me to the doctors at the Mormon settlement at Colonia Dublán. I was unconscious for most of the trip and later had no recollection of the few times I came to and accepted water from a canteen and cursed everybody in sight.

By the time we got to Colonia Dublán my lower leg was black and bloated larger than my thigh, and the wound was smelling of rot. The surgeon cut it off just below the knee.

"They wouldn't have done it if I'd been there, little brother," Pancho said. "I would have shot the bastard who raised the knife to your leg, you know that. I got here as fast as I could but it was too late to stop them."

He wanted to punish somebody, everybody—the boys who'd knotted the tourniquet so tightly and didn't know enough to loosen it every now and then, the doctor who'd done the cutting, his assistant.

I said no, let them be, they all only did what they thought best. Pancho wiped his tears and looked at me strangely, but he spared them all.

The boys who brought me to the Mormons had at least been quick-witted enough not to tell them my true name. It was too well known. The news that I was laid up with a missing leg would

surely have brought the federals on us in a hurry. Calixto told
the Mormons I was Ramón Contreras, his older brother. And to
mislead any Carranza spies in the region who might have heard
rumors of what happened, Villa put out the story that I, Fierro,
the Butcher himself, had drowned in Lake Guzmán (a good sixty
miles northeast of the Mormon settlement) when my horse gave
out under me.

Naturally the story took on embellishments the more it was
circulated. The most popular account became the one claiming
that I could have saved myself if I hadn't been wearing a money
belt loaded with gold. I liked that touch. It amused me to think of
mothers giving their children moral instruction through the story
of my death. "You see?" they would say. "You see how a man can be
drowned by his own greed?"

The proclamation of my death struck me as quite proper.
Why not? In a way, I truly *was* dead. Rodolfo Fierro was no
cripple and never could be. The man I'd been would never wear a
wooden leg. That man was no more. Not that I got melancholic
about it; what happens happens, and to hell with it.

After a night of thinking things over I told Villa, "Listen, no
more Fierro. Let's leave that sad son of a bitch in the lake. Now
I'm Ramón Contreras, the fucker with one leg."

Villa squinted at me and scratched his head and said he won-
dered if my brain had been damaged by all the water that got in
it. Then he shrugged and grinned. "But hey," he said, "you want to
be Ramón Contreras, fine with me. We'll call you Benito Juárez,
Napoleon, Jorge Washington, any damn name you want. What's
it matter, a name?" (He never called me Fierro again, but he continued to call me Rudy.)

He chuckled and said, "You know, the boys are telling jokes
about how poorly you would now do in an asskicking contest."

"We'll see how much they joke when I get off my ass," I said. "When I get back on my foot."

Villa groaned and rolled his eyes, and we both burst out laughing. What the hell.

So . . . I died but I didn't.

As soon as I could be moved, Villa had me put in a wagon and we went to a haven in the western foothills. One of the Mormon doctors came with us at Villa's pointed request—to tend to my wound and fit me with a wooden leg when I was ready for it.

The air was turning cooler now, and every evening the shadows came sooner and got a little longer. Over the next few weeks, Villa often took some of the boys and went out to rustle cattle from the nearest *hacendado* herds. They'd drive the steers to the border, sell them and use the money to buy munitions. While he was doing that, I got fitted with my new leg and kept busy learning to walk with it. Following the doctor's specifications, our best woodworker fashioned the leg, and the local blacksmith made the harness to attach it. With the smithy's help, I designed a special stirrup for it, one I could easily attach to any saddle.

The hardest part about riding again was having to sit differently on the horse to balance myself properly, especially at a gallop. In the first few days back in the saddle I fell off twice before I started to get the hang of it. Christ. *Fierro* had been the best horseman in Mexico. (Villa thought different, naturally, but I think in his heart he knew which of us was truly the best.) My angry shame made me a little thin-skinned: the first time I fell, a couple of the boys laughed out loud as they rode by and I shot their horses out from under them. I hobbled over faster than I would have thought I could and shoved my pistol in their scared faces and asked if they felt like laughing some more. I put the horses out of their misery, then went back to my riding practice. For the first time in my life I felt like a bully. That evening in the cantina I bought each of the two boys a bottle and told them to pick out a couple of good mounts for themselves from the Dorados' special remuda.

Villa was doing most of his arms business with a pair of Jewish brothers named Sam and Louis Ravel in Colombus, New Mexico, just across the border from Palomas. They always insisted on payment in advance, and then two or three weeks later they'd deliver the goods to our man in Palomas. Their chief source of munitions, however, was somewhere farther west, and the Ravels told Villa we could get faster delivery after payment if we had a transfer point on the Arizona border. Agua Prieta was a perfect spot, but it was under the control of the federal army. Villa told the brothers we'd take Agua Prieta within the next two weeks.

He'd never given up the idea of rebuilding our army and going back to open war with the whitebeard. Carranza was claiming to have control of seven-eighths of the country, which was bullshit, but he did control enough of the key parts of it to have won the gringos to his side—which of course was what now made him tough to beat. Just the same, nobody was fool enough to think the war was over, not while there were still so many rebels holding out in the hills and mountains—and for damn sure not while one of them was Pancho Villa. In the meantime, Carranza had officially declared us bandits to be shot on sight—us and every other rebel still resisting him, including Zapata, who we heard was giving the government a worse time than ever down in Morelos.

Felipe Angeles was still in the picture too—and still in the United States, even though all his diplomatic efforts to keep the Yankees from siding with Carranza had come to nothing. He wired Villa that he was ready to rejoin us whenever he got the order, but Pancho told him to stay put. He didn't want Angeles at risk in Mexico, not yet, not until we once again had a full army.

Villa's confidence was higher than it had been in months. As our stock of armaments had grown in recent weeks, so had our ranks. Pancho's name was still magic in northern Mexico, and boys as young as thirteen came out of their pueblos to join us. When our ranks grew to six thousand, Pancho was champing at the bit to move against a Carrancista garrison. Agua Prieta was his choice—and not only because it gave us control of a border point. "The town's in full view of the gringos on the border," Pancho said. "When they see us take it, they'll know Pancho Villa's still the toughest bull in the plaza. They'll think again about having sided with the whitebeard, you watch. We'll soon be getting visits again from gringos in pinstriped suits."

I wasn't so sure. Besides, Angeles had warned him to hold off making any large-scale advance until we were even stronger. But Villa had only laughed and said, "Hell, when I went to war against Huerta, had eight men with me. Eight!"

We hadn't counted on the sudden early winter. We were high in the sierras when it fell on us like a bombardment of ice and snow. Horses and pack mules slipped on the icy rock trails and broke their legs. Wagons overturned. The wind howled into the passes and cut through our clothes. The earth was a frozen white blur. Fires were hard to start and keep burning in the blowing drifts. Ears, fingers, toes turned black with frostbite.

"At least you only have one fucking foot to freeze," Villa said through his chattering teeth as our mounts labored through the snow.

"I've always been lucky," I said.

Some of our boys froze to death in their sleep. That hard crossing cost us nearly a thousand men and a good portion of our supplies before we at last descended the western slope into Sonora. Many of those who made it were sick. All of us were exhausted. We rested for a few days, killed and ate some of our remaining scrawny beeves, then pushed on to Agua Prieta, where we ran into more bad surprises.

———⪢⪡———

The Carrancista commander in Agua Prieta was Plutarco Elías Calles, one of Obregón's closest friends, a big hard-faced bastard everyone called the Turk, mainly because he was as treacherous as one. He had been tipped we were coming and had somehow received thousands of reinforcements without our scouts having spotted them. And he'd prepared for us in the fashion of his good friend Obregón: miles of barbed wire strung in front of camouflaged machine gun nests. Villa wasn't dissuaded. He believed his old tactic of a massive cavalry charge would succeed if we did it under cover of night. He ordered me to stay back with a small troop to guard against any attempt at a cavalry countercharge, then he and Pablo López, a young firebrand who'd won our admiration with his fearlessness and command of men, led the attack.

But as they closed in on Agua Prieta at a gallop, shrieking with war cries, the protective darkness suddenly vanished in a white glaring flood of searchlights—and a massive storm of machine gun fire hit them head-on. It was the latest trick Obregón and his boys had learned from their German military advisors. Our boys were perfect targets—all lit up and blinded by the lights. They panicked, broke every which way, and got gunned down like rabbits in a pen. We made it out of there with hardly more than a thousand men.

Villa's sorrow for his slaughtered boys was as great as his fury at the gringos. We were certain that the searchlights had come at us from their side of the border. A short time later—at about the same time that the Ravel brothers failed to deliver a shipment of arms we had already paid for, further feeding our suspicion that they had been the ones to inform Calles the Turk of when we were planning to attack Agua Prieta—we found out the gringo army had permitted Calles's reinforcements to get to him by rail on the American side. They'd boarded a train in Texas and ridden the rails to Douglas, Arizona, across the line from Agua Prieta.

Pancho nearly choked on his rage. "Those bastard sons of whores!" Villa ranted. "All of them! Tell the boys, Rudy: we shoot all gringos from now on—all of them!"

But there were only about four hundred of the boys left to tell. He had dismissed the rest of them and told them to go home. He'd finally faced the fact that too many of our fellow Mexicans were in support of Carranza—most of them in the mistaken belief that U.S. support of the whitebeard would bring peace to the country.

Even though his Yankee support made him too tough for us to beat in open warfare, we knew Carranza couldn't last. Already there were rumors of bad friction between him and Obregón, without whose allegiance he'd sure as hell lose hold of the country—and maybe even the gringos' support. If Obregón broke from him, we'd all be back at war in a hurry. In the meantime, all we could do was take to the hills and fight as guerrillas—striking

suddenly, retreating quickly, moving fast and often to evade our
pursuers.

———————

Thus were we reduced from being "the kings of Mexico," as Urbina
had called us, to being a gang of a few hundred outlaws with a
price on our heads. But at least we were still alive and on the loose
and hoping for better days. That was more than could be said
for a lot of other revolutionaries, including our two old enemies,
Victoriano Huerta and Pascual Orozco, whose paths had come
together again during the past terrible summer.

Huerta had been living in Barcelona, Spain, since sailing out
of Mexico the year before. The way we heard it, the Germans
went to him in the spring and offered him a deal. They promised
to back him with arms and money if he'd return to Mexico and
lead a coup against Carranza. The gringo president, Wilson, had
always disliked the bullethead, and the Germans figured Huerta
could keep the U.S. too distracted with its own border to join
the Allies against them in the European war. Huerta's side of the
deal was a promise to cause Wilson that distraction. It was said
the Germans opened a Havana bank account for him containing
more than five million pesos, that in St. Louis they'd bought thousands of rifles and millions of rounds of ammunition for the army
he would raise. They got him a passport and booked his passage
to the U.S.

But the gringos got word he was on his way to the States and
had agents watching his every move from the minute he disem-
barked in New York. Carranza had been tipped off too, and had
his own men tailing Huerta and his boys all over the city. Rumors
of his deal with the Germans were everywhere. Carranza wanted
the U.S. to extradite him to Mexico, but the Yankees knew the

whitebeard would shoot Huerta the minute he got his hands on him, and they sure as hell didn't want to get involved in that sort of diplomatic mess. The war in Europe was giving them plenty enough to worry over and argue about.

We heard Huerta rented a big house on Long Island, where he was joined by his family. Somebody sent Villa a photograph clipped from a New York newspaper showing the bullethead with his shirtsleeves rolled up and pushing a lawn mower, trying ridiculously to look like Señor Good Citizen. He told reporters he was a simple family man now and had no political ambitions whatsoever. Villa stuck the picture on a tree and used it for target practice till not an inch of paper was left intact. He talked about going to New York and shooting the son of a bitch right on his well-trimmed lawn.

"Maybe I'll stake him to the ground and run that grasscutting machine over him until he's in a thousand pieces," he said. "That's what Zapata would do."

"Bullshit," I said. "Zapata wouldn't leave Morelos to go after the rapist of his own mother."

In June, Huerta and a group of friends boarded a train for San Francisco. He told the newspapers he was going to visit the Panama-Pacific Exposition, but in Kansas City he changed trains and headed south. He got off at a little station just a few miles north of El Paso, where a motorcar was waiting for him. In the car was Pascual Orozco. The word was, they'd been in contact for weeks.

By then the gringos were sure Huerta was bent on stirring up new troubles in Mexico, and a band of customs agents backed by soldiers arrested him and Orozco in their El Paso hotel. They were charged with violation of Yankee neutrality laws and locked up in jail.

But the bullethead had friends in El Paso, including one of its former mayors, a man named Lea, who acted as his lawyer and was able to get a friendly judge to set bail. Huerta put up the money for himself and Orozco and they were released. The gringo authorities kept them under close watch, however, and a few days later, when it looked like they were about to cross into Mexico, they were taken back into custody.

Or rather Huerta was. He submitted peacefully, probably thinking it wouldn't be any problem for his lawyer to free him again. But Orozco had other ideas. He went out the back window of his hotel room just minutes before lawmen kicked down the door. He overpowered the guard assigned to watch the alley, stole a horse, and rode like hell into the desert to the east. He must've been figuring to cut south for the border when he was well clear of El Paso.

A telegraphed call for assistance in the pursuit of Orozco was picked up by a detachment of Texas Rangers passing through Van Horn, and they set out to intercept him. A couple of days later they spotted him near a mesa just south of the Sierra Diablos. They boxed him in and ordered him to surrender or die. When he came out of the rocks with his hands up high, a half dozen carbines opened fire. They brought his corpse back to El Paso and put it on public display, then buried it in the local cemetery. Huerta sent an enormous wreath of flowers for his grave.

They imprisoned the bullethead at Fort Bliss for months. We heard he was under round-the-clock guard by government agents, that he was suffering greatly from his lack of brandy. In one newspaper report he said the water they were serving him in the fort was "a little weak." His wife rented a house in El Paso and visited him every day, but he had so little to do he took up the study of English.

Villa was pleased to hear of Huerta's hard times. His hatred of the bullethead as the murderer of his beloved Señor Madero—and as the man who damn near had him shot at the wall—would never lessen even a little. I didn't feel that way about him myself. Hell, an enemy was *supposed* to try to kill you. We would have killed him if we could. Enemies were just like other men—there were brave ones among them who deserved respect and cowardly ones who did not. I always thought that Huerta was a truer soldier and more of a man than most you'd ever meet. I never said so to Villa—why get into a senseless argument with him about it?—but I hated the idea of Huerta as a Yankee prisoner. It was no fit circumstance for a brave Mexican.

When we got word that Huerta had fallen seriously ill, I wasn't surprised. They said his sickness had given him the color and smell of piss. Now the gringos got nervous about the diplomatic problems that might crop up if he died in their custody, so they allowed him to be moved from the fort to the house Señora Huerta had taken on Stanton Street. Even then, they kept an armed guard at his bedside until the bullethead went into a coma. A few days later—just a couple of weeks into the new year of 1916—he was dead.

FOURTEEN

Around the time of the bullethead's death, Pablo López held up a train carrying a party of gringo mining engineers from El Paso to the Cusi Mines, about fifty miles southwest of Chihuahua City. We'd gotten word that the company manager would be on board with a satchel containing $10,000 in gold and American currency, and Villa sent Pablo and a few dozen boys to get it.

Pablo stopped the train near Santa Isabel, and the boys searched it from one end to the other. They found the satchel wrapped in an overcoat and stuffed behind a coach seat where the manager had tried to hide it. Pablo ordered the gringos to empty their pockets into a passed hat, but one of them refused to hand over his watch, so a couple of the boys wrested it from him.

Inside the watch lid was a small photograph of a woman. Pablo asked if the woman was his wife, but the gringo didn't understand Spanish and angrily snarled something in English. Pablo told him the woman was ugly as a cockroach and said, "This is what we do to cockroaches in Mexico." He dropped the watch on the floor and crushed it under his boot heel. The gringo lunged at him, shouting, "You greaser son of a bitch!"—but was held back by a couple of his pals. Pablo didn't speak English but he well enough understood "greaser" and "son of a bitch." He pressed his pistol against the gringo's forehead and blew his brains all over the rear wall of the coach.

Some of them tried to make a run for it, dashing for the front and rear doors, and were killed right there in the car. Others jumped from the windows and were shot down as they ran for the river. Most of them threw their hands up and stayed where they were, no doubt hoping—as the stupid always do—that they would be spared if they behaved like sheep. They were pulled off the train and made to stand in line against the coach.

When Pablo called for three volunteers to do the shooting, a fight almost broke out among the boys over which of them would be on the execution squad. Five minutes later all seventeen gringos who'd been on the train were dead and the boys were hightailing it back to our camp in the sierras. Everybody else on board had been Mexican, and Pablo did not harm or rob any of them. Only the gringos. I never knew anybody who hated gringos as much as Pablo López, not even me—not even Villa, who now hated them so much he only shrugged when Pablo told him what he had done.

Naturally there was an uproar on the other side of the border. When the miners' bodies arrived back in El Paso, an angry mob tried to burn down the Mexican quarter. The police had to be reinforced by troops from Fort Bliss, and martial law was declared. Mexicans were shot on sight every day along the borderline and the Rio Bravo.

For the next couple of weeks the border was full of talk of sending U.S. troops into Mexico to protect Yankee interests. But even though the Texas politicians in Washington—as well as a lot of gringo newspapers around the country—were calling for armed intervention, nothing came of it, partly because Carranza made plenty of loud apologies for Villa's "acts of murder" and promised Washington that federal troops would soon capture and punish every one of the killers involved in the Santa Isabel "massacre."

A few days later he announced that eleven of the Villistas responsible for the killings had been captured and executed. He even ordered their bodies put on public display in Cuidad Juárez, so that any Americans who wished to do so could view the corpses for themselves. When we heard about it, we could only wonder who the poor devils were that the federals had killed, since none of them belonged to us.

More than anything, Carranza wanted to keep Yankee troops out of Mexico. *We* didn't have a goddamn thing to lose if the Americans charged across the border swinging their swords, but the whitebeard sure did. He'd been bragging to the Americans that he had the country under control and because he'd assured them Pancho Villa was no longer a threat to life and property, the gringo engineers had felt safe enough to take the train into Chihuahua. Yankee intervention would be proof that the whitebeard was weaker than he claimed to be—and it would surely make things tougher for him while he was trying to organize a government and get a campaign going for his formal election to the presidency. The whole country would be infuriated if the gringos trespassed into the fatherland—just as it had been infuriated by every other instance of Yankee intervention (the most recent having been at Veracruz only a year-and-a-half before, an invasion that began over some stupid incident involving U.S. Navy sailors and led to an occupation lasting seven months.) Even the whitebeard's friends would demand that he either do something about a gringo invasion or step aside for somebody who would. The old bastard sure as hell didn't want those kinds of troubles.

While we lay low during the following weeks, Villa was often moody and subdued, nursing his bitterness toward the Yankees for having helped Calles defend Agua Prieta against us. And he was still fuming at the Ravel brothers for having cheated us— and for having very likely passed information to Calles about our plans of attack.

Then one evening, during a rambling discussion around a campfire, one of the boys said he'd been told that the United States had never been invaded, not by anybody—at least not since it had become the United States. Villa didn't say anything, but when he turned to look at me he was beaming.

———→»•«———

Columbus, New Mexico, is a few miles north of the frontier and a long way from the nearest gringo town. Sun-bleached, dusty, without trees—a typical little pueblo of the western border. We'd been there before, Villa and I, back when we were buying much of our munitions from the Ravel brothers—back when we believed they were our friends. We'd stayed in the Commercial Hotel and bought supplies in their general store and had a drink or two in their club. The business district was on the north side of a set of railroad tracks running east to El Paso and west to Douglas. On the south side of the tracks was Camp Furlong, headquarters of the U.S. 13th Cavalry Regiment. The gringo soldiers often joked that Columbus was the sort of place every man ought to visit in order to improve his appreciation of everywhere else.

We weren't too concerned about the soldiers. There were about three hundred of them, but our spies told us that few of them had ever been shot at. They were a shabby bunch who spent much of their free time in El Paso, riding there and back on a daily train called the "Drunkards' Special." Their armory, however, was full of rifles and machine guns and ammunition, and their stables held plenty of good horses and mules. We wanted those munitions and stock.

We also intended to repay the Ravel brothers for their theft and their treachery. Villa was looking forward to hanging them side by side from the sign over their hotel entrance.

But best of all, Villa said, the Yankees would have to rewrite their histories. "From now on their books will have to say, 'Nobody ever invaded the United States except for Francisco Villa, the magnificent Mexican patriot who tried so hard to be our friend but who we treated so shamefully because we are such stupid sons of bitches and have no honor.'"

Our spy line relayed a steady stream of information to our sierra camp from Columbus. Every day a different pair of our boys would loiter around the railroad station, from where they had a clear view into Camp Furlong. They counted soldiers and memorized the patrol routines, learned the layout of the camp— where the barracks were, the stables, the guard posts. We had spies wandering about town too, making note of the houses where the married officers lived, of the stores with the best supplies. We soon had a good map of the place and were thoroughly familiar with its ways and habits.

We made our plans and went over them again and again. Near the end of February we came down from the hills and headed north, all four hundred of us.

<hr />

We traveled by night, moving fast and quiet, and camped by day, cooking on small smokeless fires. Villa was in high spirits, as he always was when we were on our way to make an attack, and his exuberance was infectious. For the first time in ages he told stories of his bandit days before the Revolution.

One time, he said, he and Urbina had robbed a small herd of cattle from the Terrazas hacienda but hadn't got very far with it before a patrol of *rurales*—the mounted police—came riding up behind them, closing fast. They abandoned the herd and headed into the Durango sierra, the *rurales* hard on their heels.

They rode through the night and all the next day and through the night after that. Pancho and Tomás knew that sierra as well as they knew their own smells, but they couldn't lose their pursuers. A few times they thought they had, and dismounted to rest—but each time, within minutes, the mounties suddenly galloped into view on the trail behind them, and they had to leap to the saddle and hightail it again.

Another day and night went by. Their horses were in a constant lather, white-eyed and long-tongued. Villa and Urbina were ready to drop from the saddle for lack of sleep. They couldn't understand how the *rurales* could keep on coming so steadily. Didn't *they* need sleep? Maybe one band of them was being relieved by another as they came along. Whatever the case, the *rurales* never stopped coming. Pancho and Tomás could only keep riding and riding, climbing higher and higher into the wilder reaches of the mountains.

On the fifth morning of the chase, when Villa was sure their horses would buckle under them, they lost the *rurales*. He and Tomás had gone through a lot of heavy thicket in the night and at dawn found themselves on a ridge overlooking the entire mountainside. There was no sign of the mounties. They had either been slowed down or given up the chase. To reach the spot where Villa and Urbina now were would have taken anybody at least two hours from the time they came into view on the trail below. At last they could get some rest. There was a stream close by and plenty of grass for the horses. But even as tired as he was, Villa was uneasy and suggested that they take turns sleeping while the other kept watch. Urbina said fine, you be the first guard, and he was asleep in an instant.

Barely an hour later the tiny single-file figures of the *rurales* appeared far down on the narrow trail. Villa shook Urbina but Tomás would not wake up. Pancho shook him and slapped him and yelled in his face, but Tomás slept on as if in a coma. "It was frightening," Pancho said, "the way he was sleeping, like he was both dead and alive."

He saddled the horses, then tried again to wake Tomás. He kicked him in the ribs, pulled on his ears, even splashed water in his face, but nothing worked. Tomás would not rouse from his deep sleep. Pancho was desperate. Abandoning all caution, he screamed in Tomás's ear. He even fired his pistol beside his head. But Tomás did not stir. Pancho finally picked him up and draped him face down over his horse. He tied his hands to his feet under the animal's belly so he wouldn't slip off, then mounted up and led Urbina's horse by the reins into the higher sierra.

He said the next few hours were the worst of his life. Every time he stopped to scan the trail behind him, the *rurales* had drawn closer. Urbina still could not be awakened by any means. The brush was denser now, and the trail got steeper and rockier, the horses' footing more unsure. Then, on a particularly steep rise, Villa's mount suddenly slipped and keeled over sideways. Pancho barely avoided getting crushed under the animal. He was sure the *rurales* had them now. He could hear the hooves of their horses clacking on the stony trail, their saber scabbards clinking against their silver-studded saddles.

A rifle shot ricocheted off the side of an outcropping over his head. That's when he noticed a small clump of boulders at the lip of the outcropping. He grabbed up a fallen tree branch, scrabbled up the rocky incline, and wedged the end of the branch under the rocks as a lever. He said he nearly busted a gut heaving on that branch—but the boulders finally gave and went tumbling down the mountainside, crashing through trees and brush, bounding down the trail, knocking loose more rocks and pulling them along behind. Villa heard the screams of horses and the horrified shrieks of their riders as the rockslide rumbled down into them.

His horse was all right. Pancho remounted and led Tomás's horse on over the summit of the mountain and down into a misty forest of heavy pine. Every once in a while he stopped to listen, but he heard no sound of anyone coming behind them. "By the middle of the day, even *I* didn't know where we were," Pancho said.

He made camp in a grassy clearing beside a rock spring. When he pulled Urbina off his horse, Tomás's face was darkly purple from all the blood that had settled into his head—but he continued sleeping soundly. Villa picketed the horses, took a long drink from the spring, then fell asleep too.

"When I woke up the next morning, that goddamn Tomás was *still* sleeping!" Villa said. "I kicked him in the leg and he sat up real fast, blinking like an owl and grabbing for his pistol. He says, 'What? What? Are they coming? Let's ride, Panchito, let's ride!' He looks all around and sees everything's all right, so he shrugs and gives a big yawn. Then he stretches and gets a little look of pain and says, 'Damn, I must've slept the wrong way last night—my ribs are sore.' He never even asked how the hell we'd gotten from where he fell asleep to where he woke up, and the whole thing was so damn scary I never told him."

———

Two days from Columbus we came across a herd of cattle being driven by four cowboys. The cows belonged to the Palomas Land and Cattle Company, which was owned by gringos. Naturally we took the cows. Villa picked out some boys to drive them to a ranch near Colonia Dublán, whose owner would buy them with no questions asked. One of the Palomas cowboys was Mexican, so we let him join us. The other three were loud, tough-talking gringos who said their chief was quick to hang rustlers. "This is Mexico, amigo," Villa said. "*You're* the goddamn rustlers."

We hanged all three.

We cut through the border fence about three miles west of Palomas and crossed into the United States. We had a small remuda with us, in case we should need the extra mounts to make our getaway. Villa and Pablo López took half the boys and headed east. I kept going north with the rest of the boys and the remuda. The plan was for me to hit the town from the west and shoot up the place, drawing as many soldiers as we could out of the camp and to the north side of the tracks. I would also seek out the Ravel brothers and prove to them the folly of treating us unfairly. As soon as Villa heard the shooting, his boys would charge into the camp from the rear, one bunch of them attacking the barracks while the rest cleared out the stables and raided the armory.

At about four in the morning we reached a hill at the southwest end of town which provided cover for our approach and was a good spot to leave a boy with the remuda. But as we came around the hill and started toward town, a voice in the darkness demanded, "Halt! Who goes there!"

The sentry had been hunkered down at his post, hidden by a creosote shrub, but he then made the great mistake of standing up and presenting a vague silhouette of himself against the white sand. I shot him squarely in the face and let out with a war cry—and the attack was on.

We rode in yelling "Viva Villa!" and howling like hell's own devils, circling through the streets of town, shooting at everything. A man came running out of a lighted house and several of us fired on him at the same time, sending him spinning back through the door in a spray of blood as bullets shattered the windows on either side of him.

A huge slavering dog came bounding from the darkness, and as he rode by it, one of the boys slashed it nearly in two with a machete.

I heard Villa's boys charging into the army camp on the other side of the tracks, shooting and shouting. The camp was bursting awake in a panicked confusion of outcries and wild commands and sporadic return fire.

While some of the boys attacked the married officers' houses scattered around town—their job was to keep those officers pinned down and out of the fight—I dismounted and hobbled into the Ravels' general store, followed by a dozen men. According to our spies, the brothers' living quarters were in the back rooms. A light was burning in the front section of the store and I went in with both pistols cocked but found nobody there. I rushed to the rear rooms and saw that they were living quarters all right, but no one was there either. As soon as they heard us ride in, they must've flown out the back door. I shot up their beds and mirrors for the hell of it, then went back to the front room. The boys were looting the place and loading it on a pair of mule-drawn wagons they'd pulled up out front.

Just as I stepped out on the sidewalk, a gunshot blasted from my left and one of the boys in the wagon grunted and pitched into the street. I whirled and fired twice and killed the shooter—a soldier hunkering at the corner of the building. I stripped him of his .45 automatic and his pistol belt and magazine pouches, then headed for the Commercial Hotel to look for the Ravels, taking a few of the boys with me. The others went on plundering the stores and shooting at every window that showed light.

Several men watched us from the windows of the lighted lobby as we approached. One of them opened fire with a rifle and took down the boy on my right. We charged through the doors shooting and killed the rifleman and another man beside him—both of them in nightshirts. We shot at the others as they scrambled out the back doors, but none of them dropped. A man in a vest appeared on the second-floor landing, blasting at us with an old-fashioned cap-and-ball Colt and hitting one of the boys in the neck. Somebody shot him in the stomach and he fell on his ass. I finished him with three quick shots as I clumped up the stairs. I marveled at the .45's smooth action. The first one I'd ever seen was Urbina's, but it was constantly jamming on him, so I hadn't been too impressed. This one was a work of art.

We went down the hallway, breaking open the doors to the rooms, terrifying the occupants, but found no sign of the Ravels. One man came at me swinging a water pitcher, so I gave him a bullet in the eye. A woman in the bed screamed and screamed, and I was tempted to shoot her too, just to shut her up, but one of the boys backhanded her across the mouth and that did the job. He gave her tit a squeeze and laughed at the look on her face.

When I got back downstairs, the hotel was on fire. So were several other buildings on the street. Villa had given orders not to set any fires till we began our retreat—fire would illuminate us and make us better targets—but some of the boys got all caught up in the thrill of the raid and just had to begin burning things.

The gringos were starting to form up their defenses now. The intensity of the shooting across the tracks told me the Yankee camp was putting up a better fight than we'd expected. Some of the troopers were coming across the tracks and taking up positions along the street. Gunfire was cracking and flashing everywhere. Now a machine gun opened up on us. Horses screamed and men went down. We were stark silhouettes against the flaming buildings. I mounted up and reined my horse around just as a bullet thumped into his side and one whacked into my wooden leg. He bucked wildly and threw me, then staggered in a circle as more rounds hit him, and then his legs broke under him like straws.

A riderless horse came loping by and I tried to catch hold of its reins but I missed my grab and went sprawling again. Then a spunky little pinto trotted right up like he'd been looking for me, and I swung up on his back.

A deep rumble of hooves rose from the far end of the camp. Villa and his bunch had gotten the army horses out of the stables and were lighting out with them. Some of my boys were still loading the wagons with goods from the stores, and I hollered, "Go! Let's go!" They jumped into the wagons and lashed the mules into action, heading back the way we'd come in.

I set out behind them—but as I rode through the intersection of the main road and the railroad tracks, my pony was hit and down we went, the pinto shrieking as I rolled clear of him.

I got up fast, looking around for another horse, bullets buzzing by my head and snatching at my clothes. A wagon came clattering from behind the railroad depot, pulled by four huge, wild-eyed mules and drawing a fury of rifle fire. Pablo López was driving the team, hunkered low, popping a whip and laughing like a crazy man. He saw me and slowed the rig enough for me to grab on to the seat beside him and pull myself up as he laid into the whip again. We bounced and swayed past the custom-house with bullets hammering into the munitions cases stacked in the wagon bed.

"They cut off the camp's back road!" Pablo yelled. "Had to turn this rig around and drive it right through the middle of those fuckers!" He stood up and looked over his shoulder, grinning fiercely, then shook the whip high over his head and yelled, "Fuck your mothers, gringos! Viva Villa!"

A machine gun chattered over the cracking of the rifles, its rounds punching into the gun cases—and then Pablo cried out and collapsed into the back of the wagon.

I grabbed up the reins and whipped the team on, driving us away from the fires of Columbus and into the darkness of the open desert.

———⬥———

We flew across the border and didn't stop till the next afternoon when we got to the Mormon settlement at Colonia Dublan. There we tended the wounded and took on supplies. A posse of gringo troopers had chased us fifteen miles into Mexico—but there were only about thirty of them, and they turned and ran for home when some of our boys dropped back to give them a fight.

Our casualties were twenty-nine wounded and thirty-one missing. It turned out ten of the missing had been taken prisoner.

They would be tried for murder and hanged in a Yankee jail. The gringos lied as always and said they'd killed a hundred of us. They burned the bodies out in the desert before anyone else could make a true count. The fact is, we'd kicked their ass and they damn well knew it. We killed some twenty of them, about half of them soldiers, and we could've had a higher tally if we hadn't been a lot more interested in getting weapons and horses than in killing gringos.

Even so, we'd ridden into the United States and into the heart of a Yankee army camp and shot the hell out of them and taken three hundred rifles and dozens of boxes of ammunition. We even got a machine gun. We got eighty-five horses and twenty-five mules. And of course a whole lot of loot—blankets, tinned food, and so on.

Hell, what we'd really done was make history. *Us.* We happy bastard few. The friends of Pancho Villa. Damned right!

We headed to one of our favorite hiding places in the high sierras—a fine camping spot just west of Guerrero. We traveled by mountain routes all the way, which was slower than by the valley trails, but better for avoiding federal scouting parties or spies who might report our whereabouts to the gringos.

We had no doubts the gringos would be sending soldiers after us. Carranza wouldn't be able to talk them out of it, not this time. "Let's see how well the Yankees and their good friend Señor Whitebeard get along now," Villa said.

⟫◆⟪

Our progress on the mountain trails would have been even slower if Pablo López hadn't chosen to go his own way. He'd been hit in both legs and couldn't even stand without help. We'd stanched the bleeding, but every jolt of the wagon he lay in knotted his jaws and brought more sweat to his face. He knew he was slowing us down, and when we stopped to water the animals at the Río Santa Marta before turning west, he told Villa he wanted to go home. His family lived in a little pueblo only a dozen miles from where we were. He chose two trusted *compadres* to transport him in the wagon and promised to be healed and ready to rejoin us by the end of spring.

A few weeks later, Candelario Cervantes, one of the two *compadres* who'd gone with him, showed up at our hideout with a sad tale to tell. They'd gotten Pablo home all right, and his wounds had been cleaned and treated and properly bandaged. But to spare the villagers trouble with Carranza's federals, who were patrolling the region, Pablo had his two friends take him away to a secret cave where he'd often before hidden from pursuers. Once they got there, Pablo sent Ernesto, the other friend, back to the village for supplies.

Two days later here came Ernesto at the head of a column of federals making their way up the mountain toward the cave. Pablo ordered Candelario to make his escape while he had the chance, but Candelario refused to abandon him. Not until Pablo argued that one of them had to remain free in order to take revenge on Ernesto did Candelario agree to get away. He slipped off into the heavy brush and circled back down to the village. There he learned from Pablo's family that someone had sent word to a passing federal troop that Pablo was hiding nearby. The federals had come quickly, and when Ernesto showed up for supplies, they arrested him and threatened to shoot him if he did not lead them to Pablo's hiding place.

The man suspected of informing on Pablo, Candelario was told, was a wheelwright named Mendoza who had always hated Pablo for stealing his sweetheart from him when they were boys.

Although they weren't absolutely sure Mendoza was the one, Candelario sneaked into his house that night and cut his throat.

"Even if Mendoza wasn't the one," he told us, "I figured it was a good idea to let everyone see what happens to informers." Villa agreed and commended him for his morally instructive action.

A couple of days after leading the federals to Pablo, Ernesto returned to the village and was received by silent, angry faces. Candelario was waiting for him in the cantina. "I expected you to be here," Ernesto said, "when I saw you were gone from the cave." He said Pablo had not given him a chance to explain things and had spit in his face when the federals carried him down from his hiding place. The soldiers had taken him to Chihuahua City to stand trial as a bandit. "I had no choice, *compadre*," he told Candelario. "They would have killed me. You understand."

Candelario said he surely did understand—and then shot Ernesto five times in the heart. The villagers didn't even bury him. They threw his carcass out for the dogs to feed on in an arroyo.

By the time Candelario arrived in Chihuahua City, Pablo had been tried and convicted and sentenced to death. The next morning a huge crowd gathered in the main yard of the military garrison to watch the execution. Pablo was brought out in a wagon and helped to stand on his crutches in front of the wall. When he was asked if he had last words, he said he wanted to know if there were any gringos in the crowd. The spectators instantly pointed them out—"Here! Here's a gringo!" and "Over here! Over here!"

There were two Yankees present, and Pablo demanded that they be removed from the garrison yard. "I won't permit a gringo to watch me die!" he yelled—and the crowd cheered and applauded, crying out, "Death to all gringos!" The Yankees might have been killed by the mob, Candelario said, if the soldiers hadn't acted quickly to get them out of the yard.

When the gringos were removed from the scene, Pablo said he was ready. The captain of the firing squad ordered, "Ready! . . . Aim! . . ." and Pablo dropped his crutches, spread his arms wide, and shouted "Viva Villa!" in the instant before the rifles fired.

FIFTEEN

A week after we hit Columbus the gringos sent an army of
ten thousand men into Mexico to find us and kill us. They
called it a "punitive expedition," and their commander was the
lean general with the little iron mustache, John J. Pershing, the
one they called Black Jack. Our scouts said they were moving due
south in two columns about fifty miles apart. They were coming
on horses, wagons, motor vehicles, even on airplanes. But the flying machines were having trouble in the sandy desert winds, and
already one of them had crashed. A couple of our scouts saw it
happen, and they never got tired of describing its spectacular spi-
raling fall and fireball impact with the ground.

The Yankees posted a reward for Villa's capture. Five thousand dollars. The newspapers said it would be paid for him "dead
or alive." Pancho was astonished at the sum. "So many dollars,"
he said, "for one little head so full of ignorance. They are so rich,
those people, but they know the worth of nothing."

Naturally, Carranza had tried to talk the gringos out of intervention. The bastard actually tried to make them believe that our
raid was proof of his government's great success against us—that
the reason we'd crossed into the U.S. was to escape his troops, who

he claimed had been shooting us down like dogs all over northern Mexico. Our attack on the U.S., he said, was clearly a desperate ploy to try to "ignite friction" between the two countries and
destroy the "stability" he had brought to Mexico—as though anybody with a pair of eyes couldn't see that most of the country was
still in chaos. He promised that his army would use "the most vig-
orous tactics" to hunt down Villa and "avenge his horrible crimes."

The gringo government said, "Yes . . . certainly . . . of
course"—and sent their soldiers anyway. The whitebeard sput-
tered a lot of protests but there wasn't much he could do except
deny them the use of Mexican railroads.

The Yankees had as much chance of finding Villa in the Sierra
Madres as a blind man has of finding gold dust in a sand dune.
Pancho had grown up in these mountains and could move through
them like a cougar. The people of the region still revered him and
would be of as little help to the gringo scouts as they were to the
Carrancistas. A telegrapher in Chihuahua City told us of the local
garrison commander's frustration in searching for Villa: the general
sent a wire to the whitebeard, saying, "I have the honor to inform
you that through rigorous interrogation of the local populace I have
learned beyond doubt that the bandit Francisco Villa is most certainly dead and buried and very much alive and well, and that at
this very moment he is to be found everywhere and nowhere."

Moving fast and far and wide, we skirmished with the Carrancistas all over Chihuahua. We ambushed their patrols in the
canyons, made hit-and-run night raids on their camps, rustled
their horses and stole their arms wagons, dynamited their rail
lines, led them on wild chases across the desert and on fruitless
pursuits in the sierras. We were having a hell of a good time.

Meanwhile, the Yankee army lumbered deeper into Chihuahua with its enormous loads of supplies and equipment, its

wagons and machinery raising towers of yellow dust visible for miles. We kept watch on their convoys from our mountainside outposts. Their trucks strained mightily over the main southern road—which to begin with had been nothing but a set of wagon ruts through the dry earth—and they often bogged down in the sand.

The weather drove them to madness. The vagaries of the border climate were even harsher in Chihuahua's interior. Few of the Yankees were used to scorching days followed by nights so cold their canteen water froze. Few of them had ever before known weeks of windless heat broken only by blinding sandstorms that lasted days and blew away their tents.

The deeper they came into Mexico, the louder Carranza barked at Washington about violations of Mexican sovereignty and so forth. And the more Villa and I smiled at each other.

——————

Near the end of March we caught a Carrancista cavalry patrol by surprise a few miles outside of Guerrero and shot them up pretty good. We put down a dozen of them before the rest gave up the fight and beat a hasty retreat. As some of the boys chased after the stragglers for the fun of it and the gunfire began easing off, Villa came riding toward me, laughing and waving his pistol. Suddenly his right leg jerked sharply and his horse gave a cry and stumbled, then slowed to a limping gait. Villa reined up, yelling "Son of a bitch!" and slid out of the saddle. He tried to support himself against the horse, but the animal was in its own pain and shied out of his grasp, and he fell.

His lower leg was soaked with blood. A rifle round— large-caliber and soft lead by the look of the wound—had gone in high in the back of his calf and come out through the front of his lower shin, leaving a ragged hole big enough to hold a plum. The bullet had smashed the shinbone, and chunks of bone the size of dice were visible in the torn flesh.

Pancho's eyes were red with pain. "You never told me a shin hurts *this* much, you bastard."

"Listen to you," I said. "You didn't hear *me* complain, and mine was a lot worse than this."

"Hell no, you didn't complain—you were out cold! A man *can't* complain when he's fainted like some little girl."

I sent Calixto to Guerrero to find Dr. Gomez—who'd repaired plenty of wounds for us in the past—and take him to our nearest camp, a deserted ranch house a few miles to the south. A couple of the other boys went off and got a wagon in which to transport Villa.

Calixto and Dr. Gomez beat us to the ranch. We carried Pancho inside and laid him on a table, and Gomez got busy cutting away his bloody trousers and washing off the wound. He was a tidy, bespectacled little man with a beard and a quick, sure manner.

Villa's teeth flashed in grimaces as the doctor probed and examined, shaking his head in dismay.

"The tibia is shattered beyond the possibility of proper setting, my general," he said. "I can remove the pieces of the bullet and the larger shards of bone matter, yes, but much of the bone has been pulverized like broken glass. I could never get it all out, and what remained in the wound would certainly breed a toxic infection that would likely prove fatal. There's really nothing to be done but to amputate."

Villa pushed himself up on his elbows to better see the doctor. He shook his head. "No cutting."

"But, my general, have you not heard me? I advise you not only as a doctor, but as your friend. If I do not amputate—"

"No," Villa said. He lay back with a groan and said, "Rudy." I pulled my pistol and cocked it. Gomez looked at it sadly and sighed. Then he bent to his work.

An hour later he'd cleaned the wound of bullet fragments and as many bone chips as he could get at, swabbed it out with permanganate of potash, and bound a splint on either side of it. He gave me the rest of the potash solution and wished us luck.

⸻

We were too many to travel together as slowly as we would now have to—with Villa being carried in a mule cart—so I dismissed the boys, all but ten. I told them to disperse in bunches in every direction, and to continue giving the Carrancistas all the hell they could. They were to keep moving all over Chihuahua and keep making guerrilla attacks on the whitebeard's boys every chance they got, keep them busy, lead them on merry chases. And they were to spread the word in every town and village that Pancho Villa had been killed up in the mountains. If any of them were captured, they were to insist that it was so, that Francisco Villa was a dead man.

Pancho had made me give my word that if he should die, we would burn his body to ashes. "If the bastards never find my body," he said, "they'll never know for sure if I'm really dead, and I want them to worry that I'm not."

We sat him up in the mule cart and he gave the boys a farewell speech, telling them that if he did not die, we would all meet again on the sixth of July in San Juan Bautista, a little town on the Durango border where he had many friends. The boys all said they'd be there, and off they went.

⸻

Well supplied with sacks of beans and bags of dried beef, we took Villa deeper into the sierras. We went up into the wild country where there were few villages within fifty miles of each other, following his directions to a cavern where he and Urbina had sometimes hidden from the *rurales*. It was rough going, getting that cart up those narrow, rocky trails and through the thick thornbush. The animals fought for footing in the loose stone. The air thinned out and breath came hard. We were still a few days away from the cavern when it started to snow, lightly for the first few hours, then much harder. It covered the trail and made footing even more uncertain. I kept giving Villa handfuls of snow to cool his fevered face.

We came to a section of trail barely wide enough for the cart, flanked on one side by a precipice overlooking the blue cloud tops and on the other by sheer black rock face. The snow was several inches deep but at least had stopped falling.

I had Villa removed from the cart before letting it proceed. Pancho protested, but he was too weak to put up much of an argument. I was acting on a hunch that proved to be a good one. The cart had gone only about thirty feet along the little cliffside trail—nearly half the distance to where it widened out again— when the mule stepped into a hole hidden by the snow. Its leg buckled and the animal toppled off the precipice with a terrified bray. The driver leaped clear of the cart as it abruptly heaved sideways and went tumbling behind the mule—but he struck his head hard against the rock face, staggered backward, and stepped off the edge of the trail, too stunned even to yell as he dropped out of sight. All this spooked the horses. The one directly behind the cart reared too far back in its fright, lost its balance, and took its rider with it over the side, their screams unrolling behind them like useless ropes.

The whole thing was over in seconds. Villa muttered, "Holy shit," and gave me a grateful look. A couple of the boys went to the edge of the cliff, stared down for a moment, and made quick signs of the cross.

We cut saplings and stretched a blanket between them to form a litter for Villa, then pushed on, taking turns carrying him in teams of four. His wound was turning foul and his fever worsening. Several times we had to shake him awake and help him sit up so he could get his bearings and give us directions. We almost lost him when the litter overturned as we forded the Rio Conchos. When I dragged him up on the bank, he coughed violently and spit water at me and cursed me, accusing me of deliberately making him go through the same sorts of sufferings I had endured only a few months before.

Two days later we reached the cavern. The entrance was halfway up a steep rock slope, hidden in dense pine trees, heavy scrub brush, and tall grass. Unless you knew exactly where it was, you could have searched around there for two weeks and never found it. Only a few feet wide and two feet high, its mouth made for a tight fit when we crawled through and pulled Villa in behind us. Yet the cave itself was spacious and dry. A small, cold stream ran down its rear wall, and its upper reaches opened into several natural flumes which carried our fire smoke all the way to the other side of the mountain before dispersing it thinly into the wind. It was a perfect hiding place, everything Villa had claimed it was. From its mouth we had a clear view of the canyon trail two hundred feet below.

I ordered six of the boys to take the horses back down the way we'd come and clear the trail behind them of all traces of their passing. No need to make it easy for any trackers who might come looking for signs of us up here. Once the boys got back to the Río

Conchas, they were to spilt up in opposite directions along the river, leaving as much trail as they could without being too obvious about it. I said I'd see them again in San Juan on the sixth of July. With me and Villa I kept only Calixto and a fine boy named Rosalío Rosales.

Pancho's wound swelled and darkened and stank worse every day. He was on fire with fever and often delerious. He'd shout orders of battle and curse blackly at Huerta, Obregón, the whitebeard—then let out cries of triumph—then weep sorrowfully for his killed boys. He sometimes conversed with his wives, now whispering endearments to this one, now chuckling with that one, now cooing with pleasure at the amorous attentions of still another. He swore to them all that he loved them, and I don't think he was lying.

We took turns squeezing handfuls of pus from the blackening flesh and picking out more pieces of bone. The stench was terrific. I washed the wound every day with the potash solution but it seemed to have no effect. Gangrene seemed certain. Calixto and Rosalío didn't ask it, but I saw the question in their eyes: would I sever the leg to save him? I didn't know. He had sworn he wouldn't have let them cut mine if he'd been there to stop it.

Finally the potash was all used up. That evening Rosalío slipped out of the cave and was gone for several hours. The night was moonless and dark as a well bottom. He returned with a writhing handful of maggots he'd dug out of the meager remains of a deer carcass down by a creek The smell had told us there was something dead down there and he'd followed his nose to it. He also had a sack full of prickly pear cactus. "I had to crawl all over the goddamn mountainside like a blind man, brushing my hand over everything before I got stung good and knew I'd found some."

Rosalío put the maggots into Pancho's wound and let them eat at it for a couple of days before cleaning them out. Then he sliced the cactus ears into thin blades, peeled them, layered them carefully over the wound, and bound them gently in place with strips of bandana. We took turns staying awake through the next two days and nights and changing the cactus dressing every hour. By the third morning the wound had begun to improve. Calixto clapped Rosalío on the back, beaming at him, and said, "That ignorant goddamn Gomez should kiss your ass and beg you to teach him the true arts of medicine." From then on, we often addressed Rosalío as "Dr. Rosales."

———⇒•⇐———

The canyon walls greatly amplified sound, and we heard the horses' clattering hooves long before the Carrancista patrol came into view down on the trail. As they passed directly beneath us, we could even make out portions of conversations. One of them was bragging loudly to the others about a girl he'd managed to seduce in Guerrero. He described her in detail, right down to the double nipple on her left breast. Her name was never mentioned, but listening beside me at the cavern's mouth, Calixto cursed under his breath: "Martina Maria! Nobody else in the world has a tit like that. She swore she loved only me, the faithless bitch!"

I grinned along with Rosalío at the outrage on Calixto's face. And on his bed of pine needles, Villa smiled. His fever still lingered, but it burned much lower now, and the first crusty signs of scab were forming at the edges of the wound.

———⇒•⇐———

He was strong enough to drag himself to the cave entrance when the gringo soldiers came by a week or so later. It was a cavalry patrol of about 150 men, unburdened by supply wagons or pack mules. Like the Carrancistas, they were heading south.

"I hope they go to Parral," Pancho said. "They love me in Parral. They'll give these bastards a hell of a welcome."

The gringos were singing as they filed past. Calixto translated for us: "It's a long way to Tipperary, it's a long way to go. It's a long way to Tipperary, to the sweetest girl I know"—and so on.

A song about wanting to get back home to a girl was nothing new, but the only place it mentioned that any of us had heard of was Picadilly, which Villa announced was in England, as though nobody but him knew that. But the song said "good-bye to Picadilly," and we couldn't understand why gringos in Mexico would be saying good-bye to a place in England. It also said good-bye to other places as foreign to us as Tipperary, where the girl in the song was waiting.

Calixto said: "I don't think these damn gringos know *where* they're going."

Rosalío said: "I don't think they know where they've *been*."

Villa said: "Listen, boys, most of the time they don't even know where they *are*."

———⟶•⟵———

The gringos did go to Parral—and Pancho was right about the reception they got. We heard all about it later on. There was a Carrancista garrison in the town, and the Mexican commander, a General Lozano, rode out to warn the gringos away. Parral was full of Villista sympathizers, he told them, and the sight of Yankee troops was rousing much agitation among the townspeople. Even some of his own soldiers were muttering darkly about the gringos' arrogant intrusion into the fatherland. Besides, they'd come too far south, he informed them: Villa was reported to be in the wild country to the northwest. He offered to escort them a few miles to the north, where they could make camp for the night. But by now a mob had formed at the edge of town and was advancing on the gringos, shouting threats and curses, chanting "Viva Villa! Viva Mexico!" They ignored Lozano's orders to disperse and started pelting the Yankees with stones and horseshit. Lozano called for his troops to break up the mob, but they refused—and instead opened fire on the gringos.

There was a running battle for the next three hours. The Carrancistas chased the Yankees north more than fifteen miles, all the way back to the village of Santa Cruz, where the fight finally ended when Yankee reinforcements showed up.

A handful of gringos were killed in that skirmish, and naturally the recriminations flew hot and fast between Washington and Mexico City. Still, they agreed to meet for diplomatic talks in Juárez. As his representative Carranza sent Obregón—whom he'd made his secretary of war to try to keep him happy. The U.S. proposed a plan to pull its soldiers out of Mexico in gradual phases, but, on Carranza's orders, Obregón rejected it. Only immediate and unconditional withdrawal of the troops would satisfy the whitebeard. When the gringos refused, the talks broke off. Just the same, Washington ordered Pershing to pull his troops back up to central Chihuahua, and they never ventured so far south again.

We were happy of course to hear that Mexican soldiers had put gringo troops on the run. What Mexican wouldn't be? The bad side of it was that their success had boosted the whitebeard's popularity all over the country.

A few weeks later we got the bad news that Candelario Cervantes had been killed by the gringo soldiers. He and a couple of his boys were getting a horse shod in a little village just north

of Chihuahua City when a Yankee patrol arrived in three motor-
cars and a motorcycle equipped with a machine gun. Rather than
run for it, Candelario and his boys charged at them head-on and
killed one before they were cut down by the machine gun. Villa's
sadness gave way to outrage when he heard that the gringo officer
in charge—a young lieutenant named George Patton—had taken
the bodies back to his camp draped over the hoods of the motor-
cars like hunting trophies.

"I'd like to kill that son of a bitch and put his head on the
wall of the nearest cantina," Pancho said. "I'd put it low enough so
everybody could use it for a pisser."

His leg was healing fast now. Rosalío carved a crutch for him,
and Pancho was soon hobbling around the cave on it, exercising
for longer periods every day. Before long he was using only a cane.
He'd always been a little pigeontoed, but now was even more so,
the shin having knitted with an inward twist. He was aching to
get out into the fresh air, to feel the sun on his face again. His
plans to rebuild an army to fight the whitebeard grew steadily
more enthusiastic. I listened and nodded agreeably, enjoying his
furious confidence.

In the meantime, the gringos had ordered Pershing to pull
his troops even farther back, and he'd moved his main camp to a
spot near the Mormon colony at Colonia Dublán. Carranza took
the pullback for the sign of weakness that it was, and he got even
bolder with the Yankees. He sent Pershing a widely publicized
message telling him he was free to send his army in any direction
except east, west, or south. Any movements except to the north
would be considered hostile action calling for immediate defensive action by Mexican forces. Pershing replied that until his own
government told him otherwise, he would send his soldiers in any
damn direction he pleased.

He then ordered a cavalry patrol east to Carrizal, where the Carrancista garrison commander warned them not to enter the town. But they went in anyway—and found themselves in the biggest battle Pershing's boys would get into the whole time they were in Mexico. The Carrancistas killed twelve of them, took twenty-three prisoners, and sent the rest running for their lives.

Not even the raid on Columbus had caused such a furor in the U.S. as the beating the Yankees took at Carrizal—or worked up so many Mexicans into a patriotic lather. A lot of people on both sides of the border were howling for war. But the gringos couldn't afford a war against us—they were too close to getting pulled into the European war. And Carranza sure as hell didn't want a war with the gringos—he had too damned much to lose. After holding the Yankee prisoners for a week, he let them go as a gesture of "goodwill" toward the United States. A week after that he sent a team of representatives to the U.S. to negotiate once again about pulling their troops out of Mexico. They talked for the next six months without agreeing on anything except to stay out of war with each other.

The Yankees knew damn well by then that Black Jack was never going to catch Villa. Their main objective now was to avoid any more skirmishes with the Carrancistas. Wilson even prohibited Pershing from going any deeper into Mexico than 150 miles from the border. It was pretty obvious they were looking for a way to get the hell out of Mexico without losing face, but the white-beard, by refusing all alternatives to an immediate pullout, wasn't making things easy for them.

Meanwhile the Punitive Expedition had become a bad joke. The gringo troopers were out in the desert with nothing to do with their days but drill and curse the weather. In the evenings they could at least go into the nearby pueblos and drink and whore and fight each other. They were a miserable lot of soldiers, as much the butts of ridicule with some of their own countrymen as they were with us. For the people of the local region, however, those six months were the most lucrative they ever knew.

The negotiations over the pullout of the gringo troops stretched out for so long that both sides were finally able to claim they'd made their point: the gringos could say they didn't pull out of Mexico until they were good and ready, and Carranza could say he'd never weakened in his refusal to accept any resolution but unconditional withdrawal. The pullout began at the end of January, and the last gringo troops crossed the border into Columbus on the fifth of February, 1917—eleven months after they'd come charging into Mexico to put an end to Pancho Villa.

Long before the Yankees took their soldiers out of Mexico, Villa twisted their tail by letting everybody know he was very much alive and still a force to reckon with. By early June he was back in the saddle and directing an ambush of a Carrancista patrol near San Javier. He let the prisoners we took have a good close look at him, then set them free with orders to "Tell them all—the gringos and the whitebeard and all the oppressors of Mexico—tell them Francisco Villa lives! Tell them they will never be safe from the wrath of Pancho Villa until true justice prevails in the fatherland. Go! Tell them!"

Around that time, Felipe Angeles sent us this item from the *Kansas City Journal* of 1 July 1916:

Since General Pershing was sent out to capture him, Villa has been mortally wounded in the leg and died in a lonely cave. He was assassinated by one of his own band

and his grave was identified by a Carranza follower who hoped for a suitable reward from President Wilson. Villa was likewise killed in a brawl at a ranch house where he was engaged in the gentle diversion of burning men and women at the stake. He was also shot on a wild ride and his body cremated. Yet through all these experiences which, it must be confessed, would have impaired the health of any ordinary man, Villa has not only retained the vital spark of life but has renewed his youth and strength. He seems all the better for his vacation, strenuous though it must have been.

At the bottom of the clipping, Angeles had written: "Your recuperative powers are most enviable, my general."

Pancho loved it. He laughed uproariously when it was translated aloud by Miguel Trillo, a smart little fat guy who'd recently joined us and won Villa's affection as well as a job as his secretary. I lost count of how many times in the next few years he had Trillo take out the clipping and read it for somebody's amusement.

We reunited with our boys in San Juan Bautista on the sixth of July as we'd planned. As the word spread through northern Mexico that Villa still lived, his legend grew greater than ever. Eager young boys flocked to join us. On September 16, Independence Day, we sneaked into Chihuahua City in the dead of night, took the Carrancista garrison by surprise, and got control of the town in quick order. We freed dozens of old *compañeros* from the prison. Hundreds of the Carrancistas threw off their uniforms and joined us too. Villa made a speech from the balcony of the governor's palace, pledging that he would never stop fighting for Mexico's liberty and true justice for all. He grinned at me through the rousing cries of "Viva Villa!" We left Chihuahua City with

twenty automobiles loaded with loot, with chests of gold and silver, with cases of rifles for our boys.

We would never again be the army we'd once been. The
mighty Division of the North was but a memory. But we were
still the people of Pancho Villa. We moved fast and struck hard,
and if we were too few to hold the towns we captured, we were
also too quick and elusive to get caught. And as long as we were
armed and saddled and on the move, the Revolution still lived.

SIXTEEN

I n March Carranza got what he'd always wanted: he was elected
president. He took the oath of office on the first of May and
announced that the Revolution was over, that its goals had been
won, that national peace was at hand.

Nobody believed him. How could the Revolution be over
when Villa was still raising so much hell in the north and Zapata
was still making war in Morelos? To add to the whitebeard's troubles, Obregón loudly condemned the new government as being
even more corrupt than the Porfiriato at its worst. He resigned as
secretary of war and returned to Sonora, claiming he wished to
live as a private citizen the rest of his life. Nobody believed him
either. The next election would be held in three years and everybody knew damn well that Old One-Arm would be the top man
in the running.

But three years was a long time down the road. The whitebeard's main concern between then and now was us—us and
the Zapatistas. Until he did something about both Pancho and
Zapata, he knew he'd never convince anybody that he had the
country under control. He made a lot of speeches about the
"plague of reactionary bandit forces" still "infecting" the country,

and promised to use the full might of the federal army to bring an end to them.

The commanding general of the Carrancista forces in Chihuahua was Francisco Murguía. Over the next three years we fought dozens of battles against him, winning about as often as we lost—although even when we won we always had to pull back, since there were never enough of us to hold any town we took. Murguía was a tough son of a bitch, but he was a big bullshitter too. He went around bragging that he could finish us off whenever he wanted, but he didn't want to because then his boys wouldn't have anybody to fight. It was a good line, and a lot of people believed it, but it was bullshit just the same. Murguía's boys were good soldiers, yes, but we were still the best. There just weren't enough of us.

Like most men named Francisco, Murguía went by the nickname Pancho, but in Chihuahua they called him Pancho the Noose to distinguish him from Villa, who had long been called Pancho the Pistols. Murguía got the name because he preferred to hang prisoners rather than shoot them. He never lived up to his name as convincingly as in Chihuahua City one summer afternoon after beating us in a hell of a fight for the town. We penetrated deep into the city before his troops rallied and drove us back out, but 250 of our boys got trapped in town and taken prisoner. Pancho the Noose then announced to the townspeople that no Villista was worth a bullet, and he ordered all 250 men hanged. They were strung up in bunches from the trees along both sides of Columbus Avenue, one of the main thoroughfares. They say that when the executions were carried out, the Noose laughed and said, "Look at that—so many pretty trees so full of rotten fruit." After that, the street was known as the Avenue of Hanged Men.

Villa was enraged by the mass hangings. "So that's how this whoreson wants to fight, eh?" Two weeks later we got into a skirmish with a Carrancista patrol near Guerrero and took two dozen prisoners. Villa told them they were worth neither a bullet nor a rope. He had them buried in the sand so only their heads were exposed, then gathered the townspeople to watch our boys gallop their horses over the heads and crush them like melons. That's the kind of war it had become.

———

We attacked Ojinaga twice within a few months, both times with sufficient fury to send the Carrancistas running across the river to safety in Presidio. The first time, we looted the town, rounded up every horse in sight, loaded up every weapon we could find, and headed back to the mountains before Murguía showed up with reinforcements. The second time, we did the same—and got even luckier: we found two strongboxes full of silver bullion on an army train idling in the railyard. Some of it we used to buy more guns from a renegade gringo who brought the goods in through the Chisos Mountains. The rest we buried up in the sierras—me, Villa, Trillo, Rosalío, and Calixto. We had gold and silver cached all over Chihuahua. "For emergencies," Villa said, "and for our old age." The way the rest of us laughed at that put a scare on Trillo's face, which of course only made us laugh harder.

Around that time, Villa at last kept his vow to punish the men of the Herrera family in retaliation for Maclovio's desertion to the Carrancistas. We descended on Parral and routed the garrison force in quick order. Maclovio's father and two brothers were dragged out of hiding in their house and brought to Villa in the main plaza, where the town had been gathered to hear the usual speech about his undying devotion to the ideals of the Revolution and his promise to resist Carrancista tyranny to his last breath and blah blah blah.

"You invited me and my boys into your home and smiled at us like friends!" Villa ranted at the Herreras. "You raised your glasses to my health and good fortune. You swore my enemies were your enemies as well. And then you betrayed me!"

The elder Herrera pleaded for the lives of his two sons, begging Villa to be satisfied with killing only him. Villa shook his finger. "No—sons of a traitor grow up to be traitors. It is in the blood." Señor Herrera dropped to his knees, weeping and begging Villa for mercy—and immediately the two sons did the same. I felt the same disgust that showed on Villa's face. The crowd cheered when he drew his revolver and shot all three while they were still on their knees and begging.

As he reloaded, Pancho whispered to me, "Listen to them, our dear friends—so happy to see these traitors die. You have to wonder why *they* didn't do the job on them before I got here."

"They probably didn't want to deprive you of the pleasure," I said.

He nodded and smiled sadly at my sardonic tone. "Why don't they fight for themselves, Rudy?" he said. "I never understood that. Why they don't fight for themselves?"

I knew he wasn't talking only about the people of Parral— and it wasn't the first time he professed astonishment over something so obvious that I had to wonder if he was really serious or cleverly joking. He seemed serious, however, so I said, "Hell, Pancho, they're just *people*, that's why."

"Well shit, we're people too. But we don't let—"

"Us?" I said. "Man, they're not like us."

He gave me a look, then grinned, and then we both laughed.

"Hell no, they're not," he said.

The mayor was a Carrancista too, and many of the towns-people had deep grievances against him and wanted to hang him, so Villa gave permission and they promptly strung him up. As we watched them spitting on the dangling corpse and pelting it with stones, Villa said softly, "Well, maybe a *little* like us."

In the meantime Carranza kept right on reassuring the gringos that he had things well in hand and that there was no need to fret about the safety of U.S. citizens who wanted to do business in Mexico. He hated gringos as much as we did, but he liked the taxes and bribes they paid him for permission to operate ranches and mines on this side of the border. It irritated us to see gringos back in northern Mexico and making profits from our land. Pancho wanted to kill them all, but I suggested that kidnaping for ransom was a better idea. "That way, *we* get money from *them*," I said. "If they want to make a lot of money in Mexico, they'll have to pay a lot of money in Mexico—pay it to us."

"And if they choose not to give us a bite of their profits, it's their own fault they get shot," Pancho said happily. He was tickled by the whole idea. "Rudy," he said, "you should have been a god-damn businessman. Think how rich you could be by now if you had not settled for the honest life of a bandit."

Over the next few months we grabbed every rich gringo we could. It was such an easy way to get money—the bastards always paid. One of the first we kidnaped was a man named Knutsen, who owned a mining company near Laguna de Patos. We made him send a message to his brother, telling him to deliver $20,000 for his release. But we hadn't specified that the payment was to be in gold, and the brother showed up with a satchel full of Yankee paper money. Villa thumbed through the bills and then flung them angrily across the table. "I don't want this shitpaper!" he said. "It has pictures of gringos on it." We made him go back and get the ransom in gold coin. To make sure everybody got the point, we shot Knutsen in both feet before we released him. The word got around fast: if Villa grabbed you for ransom, you paid in gold or you paid in blood—and you paid quick or you paid in both.

———⟡———

Pancho still fell in love with a different woman every few weeks, but he hadn't gotten married in over a year. As far as he knew, only one of his legal wives was still alive and calling herself Señora Villa—Maria Luz Corral, the first wife he ever took, back before the Revolution. She was still living in El Paso, where he had long ago ensconced her to keep her safe from the perils of war. But though he had not recently married any of the girls he dallied with, he had not lost his sense of matrimonial honor. When the mother of a pretty sixteen-year-old girl came to him with the girl in tow and cursed him loudly as the devil who'd dishonored her daughter six months earlier and left her pregnant, Villa looked abashed. He neither denied nor confirmed the accusation, but he remembered the daughter very well and agreed that she was a good girl. To set the matter straight, he called for a priest—"the youngest one you can find," he ordered.

When the padre was fetched—a fellow barely into his twenties—Villa took him aside for a private chat. A few minutes later the faint-faced priest publicly confessed to his sin of deflowering the girl. He accepted the responsibility of his paternity, renounced his priestly vows, and begged to be permitted to marry her. "Well, *chica*," Villa asked the girl, "will you accept this honorable man, the admitted father of your child, as your lawful husband?"

When she hesitated, her mother gave her an elbow in the ribs and hissed, "Yes, yes, you little fool!" Five minutes later the mayor pronounced them man and wife and the whole thing was settled.

As the newlyweds were escorted away by a happy throng of well-wishers, Villa gave a contented sigh and said, "What else is so satisfying as doing the right thing? You should try to become a better person yourself, Rudy. We have much to atone for, you and me, and good deeds do much to redeem the soul." I didn't realize he was being serious until he responded to my laughter with a pitying look and shook his head in dismay.

His notion of goodness took a different turn a few weeks later in Jiménez when he spotted a beauty named Austroberta Rentería and was dazed at first sight. She clearly had eyes for him too, but he was set on doing the right thing, so he went to her father and asked for her hand. But the father, a tough horse rancher named Ignacio, despised Villa and berated him for a vile and evil man. "I'll never give my girl to you," he told Pancho. "The only way you can have her is by force—and that will only prove to everyone what a dishonorable brute you are."

I nearly laughed at the look on Villa's face. He was caught in the middle of three powerful urges—to do the right thing, to have the girl, and to kill this impudent old goat who dared to insult him so loudly. He resolved the situation to his satisfaction by ordering a few of the boys to take the old man into an alley, tie him down, and set fire to his feet. Within minutes, Ignacio Rentería was shrieking his wholehearted approval of the marriage.

That afternoon a husky pair of our boys carried him to the magistrate's office, his bandaged feet dangling, to witness the legal union, and that evening they bore him into the church for the religious ceremony, where he dutifully gave away the bride with full matrimonial propriety.

Pancho seemed truly in love this time. He bought a house
for Austroberta on a hill overlooking the town and held many
fine fiestas in its grand patio. She was not only lovely, she was as
lively and energetic as a pup; she had quick wit and an accommodating disposition. She delighted Villa with her skill at inventing
new lyrics to old tunes, with the funny faces she'd make when she
disagreed with something he said, and with her wonderful horse-
manship. They often went riding together, and he joked that she
must be part Comanche to ride as well as she did. I'd never seen
him so happy with a woman.

But of course he was not always with her, and marriage
neither neuters a man nor makes him blind to all other beauty
around him. A few months later, in Valle de Allende, he met a
young lovely named Soledad. Green-eyed and pale as cream, she
was unlike Austroberta in every way. She was moody and given to
outbreaks of temper—much as Villa himself still was, despite his
best efforts to rid himself of the troublesome trait. Their fights
resounded with curses, threats, breaking glass, and crashing furniture. They could be heard all the way out at the corral, a good
fifty yards from the house in which he'd established her at the
edge of town.

He invited me to live in one of the bedrooms of that house,
and the three of us often ate supper together in the main dining room. That's how I came to learn why he put up with her
wicked temper. He once had her remove her shoe, and he winked
at me when I saw the six toes on her left foot. He didn't see the
wink *she* gave me. Everybody in that part of the country knew
that a six-toed woman had secret sexual powers so pleasurable
they could turn men into half-wits, sometimes even rob them of
their souls. No man could refuse such a woman if she wanted
him. "It's the damned truth, amigo," Pancho told me one morning

after an evening with her. He was limping slightly and looked like he hadn't slept in a week rather than just one night. "That thing of hers—it's like some kind of crazy animal. Her tongue's a living sin. Her fingers know a thousand wicked tricks."

I believed every word of it. It was all in the spooky bitch's eyes. She'd give me looks behind his back, daring me, and I would have murdered any man besides Pancho to have her for myself. But those eyes were also full of crazy malice. I was sure she would let me have her just so she could rush to tell Villa for the pleasure of making him angry enough to kill me. And still I could not stop wanting her.

It was raining hard on the evening we heard about Zapata. We crowded into the sala of the main house of a hacienda where we were camped and got the story from a pair of Carrancista deserters who'd been at Chinameca and seen the whole thing.

Pablo González commanded the federal forces against the Zapatistas, and in many ways their war was even more brutal than the one we were fighting against Murguía. Every hacienda in Morelos was burned to the ground. Entire villages were put to the torch, and sugar fields were razed to black ash. Captive Zapatistas were beheaded. Federal prisoners were skinned alive. Women and children were bayoneted as casually as dogs. The Zapatistas were the nearest threat to the capital district, and the whitebeard was dead set on wiping them out once and for all. He gave González free rein to lay Morelos to waste—but the more savagely González campaigned, the more savagely the Zapatistas fought back.

When he heard that Zapata was making overtures to Obregón about forming an alliance against him, Carranza got desperate. Together with Pablo González and a halfbreed Yaqui colonel named Jesús María Guajardo, he came up with a plan. They cleverly leaked a rumor that Guajardo had fallen out with González and was ready to jump to the rebel side. Zapata was one of the most suspicious men I'd ever met, so even though he was in bad need of an ally with plenty of men and a steady arms supply, I never could understand why he fell for the trick and got in contact with Guajardo. But he did.

As proof of Guajardo's sincerity, Zapata wanted him to attack the army garrison at Jonacatepec. Guajardo did it, routing the federals and taking fifty-one prisoners. Then, as even greater proof of his allegiance to the Zapatistas, he shot every one of the captives. Zapata was both pleased and convinced. When they met face-to-face a few days later, Guajardo presented Zapata with a beautiful sorrel—and Zapata made Guajardo a general in the Army of the South. They then agreed to meet the next day at Guajardo's hacienda at Chinameca and celebrate their alliance with a banquet.

Guajardo greeted him at the front gate. There were soldiers all along the courtyard walls, and more soldiers inside, standing in ranks and at attention. When Zapata and an escort of ten men rode in, Guajardo's boys saluted them with their rifles held at "present arms." Zapata nodded and his boys smiled and waved. As the Zapatistas reined up in the middle of the courtyard, a bugle blared—and Guajardo's troops, over a hundred of them, suddenly took aim on them and opened fire. The Zapatistas were gunned down before they could even try to defend themselves. Their horses screamed and buckled. Even after Zapata was down and certainly dead, they kept shooting him, the bullets shredding his clothes and making his blood fly. The witnesses said that when the guns finally ceased, Zapata looked like he'd been savaged by wild beasts, that the ground under him was muddy with blood.

They threw his carcass over a horse and took it to Cuautla, where González was waiting. It was laid out on a table in the police station for everyone to see. Of course some of the peons whispered that it wasn't him, that the body was shot up so bad it could have been anybody. But the Carrancistas who told us the story swore it was him, all right. González ordered photographs taken of the body and wrote on them, "Emiliano Zapata— Dead!—10 April 1919." He had the pictures posted all over Morelos. In a picture he had taken for his own pleasure, he stood on the table and posed with one hand thrust in the front of his jacket and one foot on Zapata's chest. Two days later they buried him in the Cuautla graveyard. Carranza rewarded Colonel Guajardo with fifty thousand pesos and a promotion to general.

For a few long minutes after the Carrancistas finished their story, Villa didn't say anything. Then he called for a glass of brandy. He hadn't touched a drop since the time he took a drink with Zapata in Xochimilco. He raised the glass high and said, "To the Revolution and Emiliano Zapata who did not die on his knees!" He tossed off the drink, coughed hard, and smashed the glass in the cold fireplace.

SEVENTEEN

By June we were fifteen hundred strong and well-armed. Villa was dead set on making a major attack, and he decided we would hit Juárez. I had my doubts about moving so soon. I didn't think our boys were ready. They were tough, all right, plenty—but toughness alone isn't enough, not in the long run, and tough was all they were. Too many of them were Carrancista turncoats, and a man who turns his coat once can't be trusted not to do it again. Even worse were all the city trash we now had in our ranks. They were fierce as street dogs but just as wayward and without purpose. But like I said, they were tough, and that was good enough for Villa.

I was surprised that it was good enough for Felipe Angeles too. He'd finally rejoined us and was eager to get back to the fight against the whitebeard. During his stay in the U.S. he'd fallen in with a bunch of exiled Mexican intellectuals calling themselves the Alianza Liberal, and they'd persuaded him to act as their liaison with Villa. He talked about those guys like they deserved their own mosaic windows on a church wall. He'd changed—not very much, but enough so I noticed it, even if nobody else did. He was still the model soldier and the spotless dandy, but he'd been living the soft life in the U.S. and dealing with politicians for too long. That political group he was so fond of was full of fat men who had never been shot at in their lives, and it seemed to me they'd blunted his judgment of fighting men. In earlier days he would have been appalled by such lack of discipline as we had in our ranks now—and he would have been quick to caution Villa against sending his men into a major engagement until they had more training. I probably would have argued against him just for the fun of it, knowing Villa would wisely choose to follow his counsel. But now Angeles talked about the attack on Juárez as though it were only a board game, as though the quality of the men who would do the fighting were hardly important. "Once we control Juárez, my general," he told Villa, "we will be in excellent position to supply an organized advance into the interior" and blah, blah, blah.

And so we attacked Juárez, the town where the revolution against Díaz had won its first great victory and which in the years since had changed hands as many times as a durable old whore. We hit them in a night attack, Angeles' artillery aiming from east of town in order to avoid overshooting the river and hitting Yankee soil. El Paso was packed with gringo troops, and we didn't see any need to give them an excuse to cross over and join the fight against us. Just the same, Pancho had put out the word that if the Yankees helped out the federals with their damned searchlights again like they had in Agua Prieta, he'd turn Angeles' guns on El Paso without a second thought. Maybe the gringos believed he'd do it, I don't know, but there weren't any searchlights this time.

We took most of the town in a couple of hard hours, but at daybreak the federals counterattacked with everything they had and we had to pull back out of several sections of the city. We were in a stalemate till that afternoon, when Villa got fed up and sent our whole force at them all at once in a concentrated assault. It worked. The federals scattered in every direction like a flock of frightened birds. Some flew across the river and others went into the desert to regroup and think things over. In all the tumult, a few shells and rifle rounds carried over to the American side. We heard that a Yankee soldier had been killed by a stray bullet. "Only one?" Villa said. "They ought to thank us for missing so many." We were ready to get our boys out of there fast if the gringos sent their troops at us. But by evening they still hadn't come over the river, and we figured they didn't want to risk any more international incidents and we really had nothing to worry about.

Villa ordered camp set up at the Juárez racetrack. He greeted Angeles with a great *abrazo* in gratitude for his excellent artillery assault. Angeles was beaming with victory, bright-eyed, a man with a vision of more triumphs to come. He wanted to take some of the boys and advance immediately on the federal garrison in Villa Ahumada, the next town down the rail line leading to Chihuahua City. He would then attack Chihuahua City itself and get control of the state's entire supply line. He and Villa heated up each other's high spirits. Villa told him to take the men he wanted and be on his way. An hour later the hidalgo and his troops were a dust cloud on the southern horizon.

The boys of course wanted to celebrate the victory, and Villa didn't see any reason to keep them from whooping it up a little. He wasn't about to turn them loose on the town, however, not with all those gringo soldiers looking on from the other side of the river and just hoping for some fool to start trouble with them. Instead he let the local *cantineros* and whorehouses bring their wares to the racetrack. I thought he was making a mistake and said so. A bunch of drunks wouldn't be able to put up much resistance if the federals counterattacked in the middle of the night. Villa laughed at me. "When was the last time the federals attacked anybody at night? And they can't shell us—we've got all their artillery. Stop worrying, hombre. You're getting jumpy in your old age."

Pretty soon the cloying aroma of whore perfume was mingling with the usual camp smells of horseshit, unwashed flesh, hard drink and cook-fire smoke. Weaving through it all was the sickly sweet scent of marijuana smoke. Only the lowest of city trash smoked that shit. Like I said, these guys were a lot different from the boys we'd had in the old Northern Division. By nightfall they were all drunk in the thoroughly abandoned way only fools can be, drunk and smoked out of their minds. There were brawls everywhere. They were cutting each other up in fights over goat-faced whores.

By midnight the camp was an open-air madhouse. Towering bonfires cast long, wavering shadows and popped like pistol shots, arcing huge, showering sparks through the air. Here and there a tent burst into flame to the cheers of the drunken spectators. Even the musicians were cross-eyed drunk. Their miserable playing and singing could barely be heard above the caterwaul of howls and curses and threats, the shrieks of delight, the screams of fright and pain. Bodies sprawled everywhere—some passed out, some knocked out, some probably dead. Couples fucked in the open, mindless as dogs.

Villa stood in the doorway of the track clubhouse, absently doing rope tricks and staring out at his boys at play. He was not at all pleased.

"You were right," he said, not looking at me. "They're shit-heads. Win one little fight and they act like they won a war."

I was about to make some smart-ass remark, then thought better of it. It wasn't his fault they were such assholes. He always did the best he could with whoever he could get.

Despite his qualms, Pancho had given a few of the boys special permission to go into town. I said I wanted to go in and check on them, make sure they didn't set the place on fire or start shooting at the Yankee bastards on the other side for the hell of it. Villa said he'd go with me, and he ordered our horses brought around.

We'd ridden twenty yards from the clubhouse when an artillery shell came whistling in and hit the place deadcenter with a deafening explosion. Body parts flew by us. Our horses spooked and I nearly got thrown.

"Gringos!" Pancho shouted. "It's the goddamned gringos!"

Of course it was. In the next instant another round came in and hit the stands just behind the ruins of the clubhouse, blasting huge chunks of stone and jagged wood through the air. Something sliced my cheek like a razor swipe. My horse flinched and cried out at the shrapnel hits it took.

Artillery came pouring in. The gringo gunners had the racetrack zeroed in perfectly and were blowing us all to hell. The torn and dying were screaming all around us. To try to rally the boys and make a fight of it was out of the question. It was every man for himself.

We lashed our mounts through the camp with shells bursting around us and ripping people apart. We made it through the back gate and kept on going. Behind us, the artillery abruptly ceased and we heard the war cries of the Yankee cavalry as it charged into our drunk, dazed, and staggering boys—some of them still with their pants around their boot tops, armed with nothing but their dangling dicks.

Only a couple of hundred of us made it back to the sierras. A few of the others were scattered all over hell, but most had been killed or captured back at Juárez—or were hunted down by Carrancistas and killed or captured somewhere else.

Then came word that Angeles and his boys had run into a highly reinforced detachment of federals outside of Villa Ahumada (somebody had informed the Carrancistas of his coming) and taken awful beating. Angeles himself had been captured and transported to Chihuahua City to stand trial as a bandit and murderer.

"They won't shoot *him*," Villa said. "Even the whitebeard isn't that stupid."

He wasn't the only one who believed Angeles's reputation would save him from the firing squad. Angeles had many admirers in Europe and powerful friends in the U.S. We heard that the British consul pleaded on his behalf, that the French government sent telegrams urging Carranza to exercise clemency.

But the whitebeard was deaf and blind to all entreaties, and when the court convicted Angeles and sentenced him to death, he refused to intercede. "The Revolution was fought to establish the rule of law over the dictates of men," Carranza said, "and the law has had its say."

Witnesses reported that it was damn cold on the morning Angeles was taken out to the wall, bareheaded and in shirtsleeves. He smoked a last cigarette with the young squad captain and joked that he supposed he'd soon be plenty warm, considering his sinful life. (Villa sobbed on hearing that. "*Sinful?* Only Señor Madero was less sinful than Felipe!") He refused a blindfold but accepted the offer to give the execution commands himself. "Shoot straight, boys!" he called out to the riflemen, then gave the commands to aim and fire.

Apparently none of the shooters had wanted to share in his killing—because each one took it on himself not to shoot Angeles in the head or heart. By chance, they all shot him in the belly instead, which of course wasn't much of a favor. The volley tore him wide open but wasn't immediately fatal. They saw his guts spilled out like bloated blue snakes. He rolled and moaned in the dirt for several long seconds before the stunned squad captain finally regained his wits, rushed over to him, and shot him in the head with his pistol.

But the captain was so shaken that even at point-blank range he failed to deliver a proper coup de grâce, and Angeles began spasming horribly, his breath huffing whitely into the cold air. The spectators were crying with outrage and screaming at the captain to put Felipe out of his misery. The captain was now so thoroughly rattled he could hardly hold his pistol steady. He had to shoot Angeles three more times before he finally stopped twitching and died, and by then his head was as much a mess as his belly.

In a newspaper report, General Hugh Scott, Villa's old gringo friend in Texas, called Angeles the most cultivated Mexican gentleman he had ever met. He thought Angeles would have made a splendid president, perhaps Mexico's best ever, and he called his execution "a pity."

Villa was apoplectic over Angeles's killing. "To shoot a man like him is bad enough—but that was no execution, it was butchery! They *mutilated* him! They couldn't be satisfied with killing him—no, they had to piss on his dignity too, the bastard whoresons!"

He went crazy for a while. He muttered constantly about going to the capital in disguise and sneaking up on the whitebeard and cutting his throat. We heard a rumor that the people of Alta Loma, a small village north of Villa Ahumada, had been the ones to inform the federals of Angeles's whereabouts. It was only a rumor but Pancho didn't care. He ordered the boys to saddle up.

I wouldn't go. I told him I had a pretty little thing waiting for me in her bed and would rather spend my time with her than shooting a bunch of peons for no reason except that he was sorry he'd lost a friend. Villa roared that those peons were responsible for Angeles's death. "How can that be," I said, "when he could have chosen to stay in the U.S. and be a farmer?"

He was in no mood for philosophical argument. He raced to Alta Loma with a bunch of the boys and rode in shooting. Some unfortunate women and children were among the people shot or trampled as the boys went charging in. They hanged all the men and killed all the livestock and burned down all the huts and cornfields.

He offered ten thousand pesos to anyone, including the federals, who would deliver the captain of the firing squad to him alive, but a day or two later the captain was discovered in his quarters with his brains blown out and his pistol in his hand. "I wonder how many shots it took him to do *that?*" Villa said.

He learned the name of every man on the firing squad and offered one thousand pesos for each one's head and had them all within a week. One Carrancista sergeant tried to collect for a battered head he swore belonged to a member of the squad but which proved to be that of a petty thief known to several of our boys. "You should not tell me lies to try to make money from the death of my friend," Villa told the sergeant. He gave him the choice of a bullet in the head or cutting out his own tongue. The sergeant chose the razor and sliced up most of his mouth pretty good before he'd cut away enough tongue to satisfy Villa.

In Santa Rosalía de Camargo we overran the federal detachment but, as always, spared the soldiers' women. But one of their *soldaderas* hit Villa with a horseapple as he rode by, then cursed him for a bastard son of a diseased whore and said he didn't have the balls to fight her hand-to-hand. Pancho normally wouldn't even slap a woman, no matter how much she deserved it, but he was in no frame of mind to take this kind of shit from anybody, and he rode his horse over her. When the rest of the bitches raged at him for it, he had them shot, all forty of them.

He was like that for weeks—until the day we blew up a train carrying a shipment of silver to the federal garrison in Chihuahua City. We killed all the soldiers on board, of course, and Villa himself shot the freight guards, calling them no-good shits for working for the Carrancistas. The train was also pulling two coaches full of civilian passengers, and while I saw to the unloading of the silver, Villa told the boys to rob the passengers down to the last penny. By the time I had the strongboxes loaded on the wagons, he'd made the civilians get out of the coaches and line up along the train, and I knew what he had in mind.

There were no rich among them, no government agents. They were farmers and small ranchers, a few shopkeepers, most of them accompanied by their families. A little brown-haired girl of about four held a doll in her arms protectively, in the same way her mother was holding her.

Pancho rode up to me, his eyes as furiously bloodshot as they'd been since Angeles's death. "Whitebeard sympathizers," he said. "All of them. Do it."

"No," I said.

He had started to ride away, then pulled back hard and reined around to look me in the face. "*What?*" he said.

"I said no. You want to, you do it."

He looked ready to jump on me and bite my throat.

"Hey," I said, "I kill all kinds of sons of bitches. I'll kill any fucker who even looks at me cross-eyed. But these . . ." I gestured at the line of people and shook my head. "No."

"Damn you," Villa said. "This is still a war—a *war!*—and they belong to the other side."

"*This?* Bullshit. This isn't war. It's not even fighting."

"They killed Felipe! They shot his guts out!"

"Not *these* people! Jesus Christ, just *look* at them! Listen, you think Felipe would do this?"

I said it without thinking, but it stopped Villa cold. His face went slack, and for a long moment he simply stared at me, blinking slowly. Then he turned away toward the western sierras. When he looked at me again, his eyes had changed—and he was grinning. You never knew what to expect from him from one minute to the next, never.

"You're some killer," he said. "They say mothers use your name—your old name—to scare their children when they don't behave themselves. I can see why you changed it. Ramón Contreras, that's a good name for you now. It doesn't mean anything and it doesn't scare nobody."

I had to smile. "And I know damn well why you changed *your* old name. It didn't exactly freeze hearts with fear, did it? You'd say, 'Hands up, I'm Doroteo the bandit,' and they'd say, "*Doroteo?*" and start laughing like you told a joke."

"They fucking *died* laughing, you bastard. You got no respect for anybody. That's why you got no friends."

"I've always been lucky," I said.

He laughed again, then dismounted and went to the passengers and told them not to be afraid, he meant them no harm. He apologized for having frightened them, especially the women and children. Gently taking the little brown-haired girl from her mother, he cradled her in one arm and stroked her hair with his free hand. The murder of his dear friend Felipe Angeles, he told them, had made him insane with sorrow and driven him to intemperate acts of vengeance. The next thing you knew, he was telling them the story of his life, of killing the cruel landlord who violated his sister and thus being forced into a life of banditry, of the saintly Señor Madero who by his own example taught him the true spirit of the Revolution. He talked about his many dear friends who had been killed in the struggle to achieve the Revolution's grand goals of liberty and justice for all.

By then he was sobbing and slurring his words. The little girl in his arms had been watching his face with rapt attention. Now she reached up and wiped at his tears with her stubby fingers—and Villa's face brightened like the moon coming out from behind a dark cloud.

PART FOUR

. . . Or Until We Die, Whichever Comes First

"Death revenges us against life, strips it of all its vanities and pretensions and converts it into what it really is: a few neat bones and a dreadful grimace."

—Octavio Paz

EIGHTEEN

The stomping we took at Juárez ended all possibility that we'd ever get rid of Carranza before the end of his presidential term. The simple truth was that he beat us bad, him and the goddamn gringos. But the man's greed for power went deep into his bones, and three years of the presidency couldn't satisfy it. The constitution prohibited reelection, but it permitted a president to name the man he wished to run as his successor. Popular opinion expected Carranza to name Pablo González, who had served him so well and who wanted the nomination badly—and who was sure he could win. When the whitebeard instead selected a little nobody named Ignacio Bonillas, everybody realized he wanted a president he could control from behind the scenes. Bonillas was ambassador to Washington and had spent so much of his life in the U.S. that he was widely and disparagingly known as "Meester" Bonillas. He could speak impeccable English, and rumor said he had even applied for U.S. citizenship. Carranza defended his choice with the bullshit argument that Bonillas would do much to improve Mexico's relations with the U.S. "Shit," Villa said, "if *that's* the most important thing, why not elect Woodrow Wilson president of Mexico?"

González was furious at having been passed over and decided to run for the presidency on his own. That probably irked the whitebeard plenty, but González was a minor problem compared to Alvaro Obregón. A year before the elections were scheduled to take place, Obregón announced his candidacy and began campaigning hard. He railed long and often about the corruptions of the Carranza government. When reporters asked his opinion of Bonillas, he said the world was losing a superb bookkeeper and gaining one more worthless politician. It was a rough campaign full of dirty tricks on all sides—from tossing sneezing powder and setting off stink bombs at opponents' rallies to making death threats against opponents' supporters. But Obregón was clearly the most popular candidate. The whitebeard knew Bonillas didn't stand a chance unless Alvaro One-arm was in one way or another removed from the running.

The way we heard the story, Obregón was summoned to the capital to testify in the trial of an army colonel accused of subversion. Some of his friends warned him that it could be a trap of some sort, but One-Arm refused to believe that Carranza would try to harm him. From the minute he arrived in town, however, he was under surveillance by government agents, and on the first day of the trial it became clear that the prosecutors were going to try to implicate him in a conspiracy to overthrow the government. That night, with the help of a few close friends, he gave the slip to the men who were shadowing him and escaped from the city on a freight train. The next day Carranza telegraphed orders to all state governors to arrest Obregón on sight and send him back under guard to stand trial as a conspirator to subversion. If he resisted arrest, he was to be shot on the spot. When a friend showed him the telegram, Obregón reportedly said, "We'll see who kills who."

In addition to the allegiance of powerful fellow Sonorans like Plutarco Elías Calles—the bastard called the Turk, who beat us at Agua Prieta with the help of the gringo searchlights—Obregón still had many friends and supporters all over the country, and he called on them to join him against the whitebeard. Within days, like rats leaving a fast-sinking ship, most of Carranza's generals—including, of course, Pablo González—deserted him. Our old antagonist Francisco Murguía, Pancho the Noose, was one of the few who stuck with the whitebeard right to the end. I admired the bastard's loyalty.

When Obregón declared against Carranza and called for allies, Villa immediately wired him of our readiness to join the rebels. In return for our services, Pancho wanted recognition of our military ranks—and title to a hacienda where he could retire once the whitebeard was gotten rid of. The response came from Calles. He said they would make the deal if Villa would accept a hacienda in western Sonora rather than in his stomping grounds of Chihuahua. "Here you will have no enemies to cause you trouble," Calles said, "nor the sort of friends who might lead you into it." Hell, they just wanted him out of the way, someplace where he couldn't have much influence in politics and their boys could keep a close eye on him.

"They're damn right I have no friends in Sonora," Villa said bitterly, "but they're lying through their teeth about no enemies. *They're* in Sonora, aren't they?"

So we didn't join up with Obregón and Calles. We continued to give hell to any Carrancistas who ventured into our territory, of course, but otherwise we just sat back and waited to see how things turned out.

Pancho was fully fed up with our fugitive life. Miguel Trillo, that smart little jokester, was teaching him mathematics now, and introducing him to the Greek and Roman classics from his little collection of texts. Villa was awestruck by the *Iliad*. "Three *thousand* years ago," he said, "and men were killing each other for the same reasons as they are now: for glory, for honor, for revenge, or just to get their hands on a beautiful woman—or just because they were ordered to fight and had no choice. Sweet Mary, it's so *old* and still so true! It's so wonderful!"

He was more enthusiastic than ever about learning for the sake of learning. Ever since that little girl had wiped away his tears, he'd been talking about how foolish we were to continue living in the mountains as if we were still at war.

"You were right, Rudy," he said sadly, "this isn't the Revolution, not anymore. There's no honor in it anymore. Just a lot of greedy bastards fighting each other for whatever they can put in their pockets. All the good men are dead—and for what? Poor ignorant Mexico! All these years we've been fighting and killing so all Mexicans can have justice and their own land and the right to elect the leaders they want. So they can send their children to school. But how can they understand such things without education? I love them, Rudy, they're my people, but they're ignorant. And how the hell do we teach anybody anything about democracy by killing people?"

He paused and paced and gazed at the staggeringly beautiful panorama stretched out beyond the mountain rim we stood on—the lush narrow valleys and thickly wooded hills and snaking silver rivers; and, around it all, the high, dark sierras with their white peaks so bright in the sun.

When he spoke again, he voice was different, sounding suddenly farther away. "Do you ever think of how sweet it would be to live in peace, to live with a good woman, with a family of your own? If they gave us a hacienda, we could build a fine school on it, we could grow crops and raise good horses."

It was hard to believe he had ever been so naive as to think we were fighting for the poor. Of all the reasons men die in this world, to die for a cause is the most foolish, and the poor are the most foolish cause of all. Never did I fight for the poor. I fought *against* the rich—which of course isn't at all the same thing. In any case, the fighting was the point. You don't fight to *become* free—to fight is to *be* free. A man with a gun and the will to use it can't be mastered, he can only be killed. What other reason to fight does a man need?

Other than the pure pleasure of it, I mean.

Villa's problem was that he'd gotten too chummy way back when with eggheads like Abraham González and Madero and Felipe Angeles. They'd given him a headful of idealism and fooled him into believing he was fighting to make the world a better place. Jesus. Now he saw that stupidly pathetic notion for what it was and wanted no more of it.

On the other hand, I thought all his talk of retiring and having a family and farming and building schools and so forth was pretty damn foolish too—for men like us, anyway. But I have to admit that, sometimes, listening to him talk about it was almost like hearing a sweet and distant music that tugged me gently toward it in a kind of soft half-sleep. . . .

———>●<———

The whitebeard tried to make a run for it to Veracruz, but before he left the capital he looted the National Palace as it had never been looted before. He cleaned out the treasury to the last penny, of course, but also took the mint's dies, the currency printing

presses, the national archives, every piece of furniture, every paint-
ing, all the carpets, even the light fixtures. It took twenty trains to
carry it all—and another ten to carry the hordes of people who
went with him. In addition to his remaining troops, thousands
of friends and relatives joined the exodus, together with all their
personal possessions. Carranza's personal "Gold Train," as it came
to be called, led a rail convoy stretching more than twenty miles.
Sweet Mary. If he'd been satisfied with grabbing up the treasury
and taking only his family and his troops, he could have got out of
there fast and made the coast quickly. But, as always, his greed got
the better of him. It took days to load all those trains.

The back half of the convoy didn't make it but a few miles
past the outskirts of the capital before Pablo González's troops
overtook it. The forward trains that did escape found the going
slow and rough. They had to stop every few miles to repair the
tracks, and Murguia's boys were constantly fighting off attacks
by both rebels and bandits and taking heavy losses. Among those
leading the attackers was Jesús María Guajardo, whom Carranza
had rewarded so handsomely for his assassination of Zapata. We
heard that Obregón sent a wire to the whitebeard offering him
safe conduct to the coast if he would agree to exile himself from
Mexico forever, but Carranza refused.

The convoy got smaller and smaller as it made its laborious
way into the eastern sierras. Finally it could go no farther—the
tracks had been destroyed for miles ahead. By then Veracruz had
fallen to the rebels. Obregón's boys were closing fast from behind,
and more of González's soldiers were coming at Carranza from
the coast. The whitebeard and his remaining troops had to abandon the train and proceed on horseback, turning north, hoping
to make it all the way to San Luis Potosí, where they planned to
ask for help from the Yankee government. They took with them

only their weapons, their bedding, and a few basic supplies packed on mules—and a portable typewriter, which the whitebeard no doubt thought necessary for composing official presidential papers even as he fled for his life. They left four million pesos in gold on the train.

They pushed on up into the rugged mountains, slogging through a driving rain that never let up. The rivers were swollen and booming with white water, and several men drowned at each crossing. The whitebeard now had fewer than a hundred men with him, including Murguía and his remaining troops.

Somewhere in the interior of that harsh country they met with Rodolfo Herrero and his boys. Herrero was a local bandit turned warlord who had earlier been granted amnesty and given the rank of general in exchange for keeping this part of the country free of anti-Carrancista rebels. They say he greeted the first chief with a great show of affection and repeated avowals of loyalty to the death. He led the whitebeard and his party into a still wilder part of the sierra, where he assured him they would be safe from their pursuers. At a tiny deserted village called Tlaxcalantongo, they made camp for the night. Supposedly, when Herrero showed the whitebeard to the largest of the ramshackle huts, he said, "Tonight, Señor Presidente, this will be the National Palace."

A few hours later, in the middle of the night, the darkness was abruptly shattered by blazing gunfire. Through the alarmed outcries and screaming of the wounded, Murguía's boys were quick to fight back, though they weren't sure of where the attack was coming from, and in the darkness and the din of confusion some of them shot each other. When it was all over, Carranza was found dead on his pallet with a half dozen bullets in him. In the morning light it was discovered that the assassins had stripped him of his money, his spectacles, his watch. They even took the little typewriter. Murguía was said to have muttered that the bastards had stolen the last bit of the Carranza government's treasury.

Everybody knew Herrero had done the killing, although he denied it and insisted that the attackers had been unknown to him and his men. He swore he'd seen the whitebeard take a wound in the leg and then commit suicide to end his pain. But there was a story going around that Carrancistas had killed Herrera's two bandit brothers a year or so before, and Herrero had sworn revenge on the whitebeard. Obregón ordered Herrero taken to the capital for questioning, but all that came of it was that he was stripped of his military rank and allowed to go back home. About a year later Obregón would give him back his generalship.

Herrero's light punishment lent weight to the rumors that Obregón had given orders that the whitebeard not come out of those mountains alive. I'm sure he did. But who cared? Carranza was dead and that's all that mattered. Nobody gave a good goddamn about the minor details of how he got that way.

———⟶◆⟵———

On the same day Carranza was buried in Dolores Cemetery in Mexico City, the legislature elected Sonora governor Adolfo de la Huerta as interim president to serve out the last six months of the whitebeard's term. His close friends Obregón and Calles— the three of them were known as the Sonora Triangle—pressed hard for his candidacy and he won the election handily over Pablo González and two other candidates. The first thing he did was schedule a national presidential election for September, when, as everybody knew, Obregón would surely be the overwhelming winner.

Pablo González wasn't happy about the way things had turned out and Obregón and Calles knew it, so they retired him from the army and told him to go home and stay out of politics if he knew what was good for him. No sooner did he get back to his home state of Nuevo Leon, however, than he and his old partner Jesús María Guajardo started planning a rebellion against the new government. The Sonora Triangle got wind of it and moved fast to arrest both of them in Monterrey. They say that federal troops broke in on Guajardo while he was mounted on his mistress. They stood by and watched until he spent his load, then let him put his pants on before taking him away. That was at six in the evening. At six the next morning he was stood against a wall and shot. They say he died with a cigar between his teeth, and his last words were that he would yearn for his mistress's sweet ass in the grave.

Pablo González they found hiding in the basement of his house. He was taken to a Monterrey theater and there tried for treason. When he was convicted and sentenced to death, he wept and begged for mercy. The lucky bastard got it. De la Huerta thought it would be unseemly to impose the death penalty on so recent a candidate for the Mexican presidency, so he granted clemency and let him go into exile in the United States.

That's the kind of man de la Huerta was. Some say that the six months of his presidency were the most enlightened in Mexican history, and they're probably right. He granted amnesty to every Mexican living in exile and said they could come home whenever they wished, all was forgiven. He ordered the release of all political prisoners. One of them was Pancho the Noose, who'd been locked up since Carranza's death—first as a suspected accomplice in the killing, then for refusing to renounce his loyalty to the whitebeard. (Two years later he would publicly

accuse Obregón of murdering the whitebeard, call for an uprising against him, and for his efforts get put against the wall by
Obregón's boys.)

De la Huerta even made peace with the Zapatistas. The men of
Morelos had of course kept on fighting after Zapata's assassination,
but they'd lost much of their heart for it. The years of war had made
an ash pit of their *patria chica*; all their women were dressed in
black and their children were starving. When de la Huerta offered
them title to all the hacienda land they'd taken since the start of the
Revolution, the Zapatistas grabbed up the deal and laid down their
arms. When he heard of their pact with the government, Villa said,
"Good. They got what Emiliano always wanted, didn't they? I don't
blame them for putting down their guns."

We knew de la Huerta wanted to make peace with us too.
We were the only rebels left, and a compact with us would be his
crowning achievement: he would go down in history as the man
who pacified all of Mexico after ten bloody years. More important to us, we knew if we could forge a treaty with him, not even
Obregón would dare to violate it and be the cause of another
civil war.

In early July Villa wrote a letter to de la Huerta from our
secret camp in the sierras. We were ready to discuss terms of
peace, he told him, if he and Obregón and Calles were ready to
deal with us honorably. "If you are ashamed to be my friends,"
Villa wrote, "then reject me. However, if you would deal with me
as honorable men, send a letter saying so and we can begin to
discuss the future well-being of the republic. As of now, I am sus-
pending hostilities. I am a brother of your race who speaks from
his heart."

Obregón tried to dissuade de la Huerta from making a deal
with us, arguing that Villa couldn't be trusted to hold to its terms;

but the president wouldn't be swayed, and old One-arm finally gave up and pledged to honor the terms of any treaty made with us. Calles made the same pledge—and then immediately ordered his troops to fan out all over Chihuahua, find us, and get rid of us before any deal could be made. They didn't call him the Turk for nothing. Our emissary to de la Huerta was on the way back to us with a letter for Villa when he ran into a huge detachment of Calles's troops and learned they were hunting for us. He thought he gave them the slip, but less than an hour after he reached us with the warning, we spied the distant dust clouds of a cavalry unit closing in from the west. Our scouts had already reported federal patrols advancing from the north and south.

De la Huerta's letter was full of cheer and good wishes for us. He wanted Villa to contact him directly so the two of them could work things out without interference from underlings. But he also warned Pancho to be careful: "As always, my general, there are powerful people among us who would do all they could to prevent the realization of peace. Some of them even call themselves my good friends—but God spare us from such friends!"

De la Huerta's frankness and sincerity warmed Villa to him at once. "Our little brother," he called him.

We needed a safe place from which to deal with de la Huerta, but we sure as hell weren't going to find it in Chihuahua. Calles's boys were coming hard and fast. There was no way to go but east, into the neighboring state of Coahuila, but to get there we had to cross the Balsón de Mapimí, the meanest of all Mexican deserts.

We rode day and night, never resting, switching to fresher horses from our remuda as mounts foundered under us, until, 250 miles later and after losing fourteen horses and five men to the desert, we caught sight of Sabinas. To avoid being surprised by Calles's troops, we blew up the railroad tracks at points five miles from town in both directions. We posted lookouts all along a ten-mile perimeter, then rode in and took the place over without firing a shot. The only person hurt when we entered the town was a drunk who stumbled into the street and had his foot broken when Calixto's horse stepped on it.

The next day, Villa made himself comfortable in the telegraph office and sent a wire to de la Huerta, notifying him where we were, explaining why we had been forced to take the town, and assuring him that the townspeople had suffered no harm. "I am ready, Señor Presidente," Villa wired, "to continue the interrupted negotiations."

By evening the deal was done. They gave Pancho a pension of 500,000 pesos and a hacienda called Canutillo—250,000 acres of lush pastureland and rich farming soil in northern Durango State, not far from the Chihuahua border but well removed from both state capitals. We all received amnesty, of course, and a full year's pay. Villa was allowed to retain a personal escort of fifty men, but the rest of the boys were obligated to disarm and disband— though all of them were given the choice of joining the federal army under their present military rank. Villa's side of the deal was his promise to stay out of politics and never again take up arms against the government.

And then Pancho Villa's army—such as we were—made its last ride together. We slowly made our way back through western Coahuila and into Chihuahua, stopping at every little village we came to, basking in the cheers of "Viva Villa!" and accepting the people's warm hospitality.

We were eating lunch at outdoor tables in one little pueblo when a white-haired, one-armed former revolutionary shouted,

"Don't stop sleeping with one eye open, Pancho! The bastards will never stop trying to kill you!" Villa flung his tin cup high in the air, drew his pistol, and shot the cup three times—making it jump farther each time—before it hit the ground. He grinned at the crippled old rebel and said, "Let them try."

In Parral we were met by General Eugenio Martínez, de la Huerta's personal representative, who was to insure that all of the government's guarantees were met to Villa's satisfaction—and, of course, to insure that our boys either joined the army or turned over their weapons.

The town was crawling with reporters and photographers eager to cover the historic occasion. Villa had his picture taken shaking hands with Martínez, both men grinning and with an arm around each other, the very image of amiable fraternity. An impromptu fiesta got started. Bands blared and spirits flowed freely, firearms banged and people danced in the street.

That evening Pancho called his boys around him and said good-bye, wishing them long and happy lives. When they began chanting "Viva Villa! Viva Pancho Villa!" again and again, his eyes filled with tears and he hurried away.

And in the morning, we mounted up with our last fifty Dorados and headed south for our new home.

NINETEEN

And so we became *hacendados*.

Canutillo was a beautiful place suffering from years of neglect, but it didn't take us long to restore it to its old splendor and productivity. Villa let the boys have two-thirds of the land to farm for themselves and bought the best machinery on the gringo market for them—tractors, threshers, harrows, everything. They grew corn, wheat, squash, and potatoes, and the surplus brought the hacienda a nice profit. Villa bought angus cattle too, and blooded horses, and we did good business in beef and thoroughbreds.

He built a modern medic clinic on the place and staffed it with two doctors and a half dozen nurses, all of them American-trained. He put up a telegraph office and a general store, and permitted the small church alongside the residential housing area to hold daily mass. He was proudest, however, of the school he built for the children of the hacienda. On his orders, the schoolroom windows were set high in the walls so that the students could not be distracted from their studies. He liked to stop by every now and then and take part in the children's instruction. He might ask them to recite what they'd learned about Benito Juárez or

Francisco Madero or Abraham Lincoln, or to name the capital of
Argentina or England, or to compute how many meters there are
in a mile.

He was disturbed, however, that so many of the kids were
bastards. A lot of our boys had brought their sweethearts—
soldaderas, mainly—to live with them at Canutillo and had
fathered children by them, but few of the couples had married.
One evening Villa called all the boys to a meeting out by the main
stable and told them that any woman worthy of living under the
same roof with a man and bearing his children was a woman
worth marrying. "No child should be made to suffer the indignity
of having unmarried parents," he said. "Remember, boys, we're
respectable now and we should live as respectable men."

A bunch of the women had been listening nearby, and at the
end of Villa's little speech they all applauded loudly.

"Oh Christ, Chief," Calixto muttered, "now look what you've
done." Calixto's woman, Delia Ruíz—who had already borne him
two children and was as tough a *soldadera* as I'd ever known—
was at the forefront of the crowd of cheering women, jabbing
her finger emphatically at Rosalío and mouthing the words
"Pancho . . . means . . . *you*."

"Hell, boys," Villa said, "marriage isn't so bad, take it from me.
I've done it a dozen times and it hasn't hurt me yet."

A few days later he brought a judge out to the hacienda to
conduct a mass wedding ceremony. Villa had told the boys to
dress formally for the occasion and some of them were wearing
neckties for the first time in their lives. Most looked like they had
nooses around their necks. All the brides were pretty as doves in
their white dresses, but mine was resplendent.

Her name was Rosa Blanca Santiago. She'd been waiting
tables in a Parral restaurant when I met her a few months before.

Her reputation among the locals was of a stuck-up bitch who thought all the men in town were beneath her, and as soon as I met her I knew she was right. Her flowing black hair glistened like ink. She had fine, sleek haunches and quick, sure hands and the sharpest eyes I'd ever seen on a woman: they saw right to the truth of whatever they looked at. They couldn't be fooled. She wasn't brassy or loudly tough like so many of the *soldaderas*, but she took no shit either. It was common knowledge that she carried a razor and had once sliced a man's face to pieces when he persisted in putting his hands on her after she'd told him to stop. She hadn't had to use that razor since.

Within days of the first time we laid eyes on each other, she was living with me on Canutillo, in the little house behind the *casa grande*. One morning when Villa and I were having a cup of tea in my parlor, he said he'd appreciate it if Rosa Blanca and I got married along with everybody else. I said sure, why not. He'd been expecting an argument and looked damned surprised.

But Rosa Blanca said, "Not so fast, hombres—what about what *I* think?" She affected to study me hard and closely, propping one hand on her hip and thoughtfully stroking her chin with the other. She lightly kicked my wooden leg, then turned to Villa and said, "He's missing some pieces, but what the hell—there's still plenty of him left. I guess he'll do."

Villa roared with laughter and punched me on the arm. She looked at me with a wicked smile, brushed my cheek with her fingers, and left us with a happy laugh.

She had been a passionate lover from the start, but on our wedding night she was bolder and more ardent than ever. I mentioned it to Villa a few days later when we were overseeing the spring brandings, and he grinned brightly and said, "You *see*? You see what I've always said about marriage making a woman happier in bed? You and Tomás used to make fun of me, eh?—but *now* you see what a wise man Papa Pancho is, eh?"

Our first child was a boy, and Rosa Blanca insisted he must be baptized, so of course I asked Pancho to be the godfather. When the priest asked the child's name, just before dipping the holy water on the baby's head, I said, "Doroteo. Doroteo Ramón Contreras Santiago." Villa gaped at me. I grinned and put my hand on his shoulder. "If he strikes fear in any hearts," I said, "he'll have to do it on his own, with no help from his name."

His eyes brimming, Villa embraced me hard and whispered in my ear, "The kid's going to hate your guts, you cruel fucker."

⟶◦◦◦◦⟵

Villa of course lived in the *casa grande*, which he renovated, from its red roof tiles to its massive mahogany doors to its colorful floor parquetry. With him lived Austroberta Rentería, his young bride from Jiménez. He called her Nana, because she was, he said, the *nana*—the caretaker—of his heart. She called him Panchito until they had their first child, then called him Poppy. They had two children in two years and adopted three others. She got him interested in gardening, and he planted and tended a lush rose garden behind the main house. He took up birdwatching too, and read books about ornithology. He built an aviary in the side patio and stocked it with parrots, canaries, and doves. But his favorite birds were a pair of cardinals—a blood-red male and a rust-colored female—that he'd raised from babies after a storm blew their nest out of a tree. Their home was a large white cage whose door was always open, and Austroberta laughed as delighted as a child every time Villa whistled for them and they flew out to feed from his hand.

He raised fighting cocks too, which he kept roosted behind the main stable, where Austroberta wouldn't have to see them

whenever she took a stroll in the rear patio. But there was no way
to keep her from hearing their crowing. She thought cockfighting
was cruel, and had asked Pancho to please get rid of the bantams,
but he had only patted her hand and kissed her forehead and said
no. There's only so much a man can do to please a woman, after
all, no matter how much he loves her.

Books filled his study, and his teak desk was as big as a bil-
liard table. Every evening he studied for several hours under
Trillo's tutelage—history, economics, science, the stars; he was
interested in everything. A portrait of Madero hung on one wall,
and on the mantel across the room stood a bust of Felipe Angeles.
Another wall was covered with framed photographs, including
the one taken of Villa in the president's chair on the December
day in 1914 when we entered Mexico City with Emiliano Zapata
at our side. There was a picture of him and me and General Hugh
Scott at the races in Juárez. Most of our old friends in the pictures
were dead.

He corresponded on imported stationery, his name embossed
in the upper left corner, just above a small picture of Lady Justice
with her sword and scales. "How do you like this?" he'd asked me
when the stationery first arrived from London.

I carefully examined the sheet he handed me and said, "I like
the way her gown clings to her tits." He snatched the paper from
my hand and called me a hopeless brute—which of course made
me laugh. It was fun to kick his *hacendado* pretensions in the ass
every once in awhile.

Because we so often had to go to Parral on business, a round-
trip of a hundred miles, Pancho bought the Hotel Hidalgo for
the boys to live in during our stays in town. He also bought a
new Dodge motorcar to take us there, an open touring model,
and he had the old road from the hacienda to Parral smoothed

and graded. Rosalío loved the car so much—he took it on himself
to wash it every day and clean off the seats and floorboards—that
Pancho gave him driving lessons and then made him the official
chauffeur.

Business wasn't the only thing Villa tended to on our trips
to Parral. He'd bought a nice house on Zaragoza Street for Soledad, his wife from Villa Allende, whom Austroberta knew nothing about. If she'd known Villa was accommodating another wife,
Austroberta was the sort who would have been deeply hurt, and
Pancho would have done anything to keep from hurting her.
Anything but give up Soledad. Every time we were in town, he
spent his nights with her. Who could blame him for his arrangement? I'd lie in bed in the room directly beneath theirs and listen to the bedposts thumping against the wall with their furious lovemaking—always culminating with Soledad's piercing
yowl and Villa's explosive gasp and heavy, bed-rattling collapse.
I'd watch the shadows dancing on the walls while images of her
nakedness slithered through my mind. I'd smell her perfume, her
hair, her skin, even her sex, as keenly as if she were there in the
room with me. At the breakfast table in the mornings, she'd glance
at me with such wicked pleasure I'd feel like both grinning at her
and crushing her insolent lips between my teeth.

According to Villa, Soledad knew all about Austroberta but
didn't give a damn. I didn't say so, but I didn't think she gave a
damn about anything except making fools of men for the fun
of it. If she'd demanded to live out at the hacienda with Villa, I
don't believe he would have been able to refuse her, despite his
desire not to offend Austroberta. But Soledad didn't want anything to do with the hacienda. "Your country hen can have that
big house in the sticks with all those animals and stupid peons,"
she told Villa. She said she'd had enough of that kind of life to

last her forever. She liked the streetcars and the music halls and the restaurants, the fashions, the radio programs, the big markets, everything about the city. "This is the place for me, Francisco," she told him. She always called him Francisco—except during their fights, when she'd call him horse-ass or shithead, among other things. Villa called her his *chulita brujita*, his "sweet little witch"—except during their fights, when he'd just call her "you crazy bitch."

He was always being asked for interviews. Requests arrived in the post every day—from newspapers all over the country, from European publishers, from South America, and of course from the United States, which couldn't seem to get its fill of stories about the "Centaur of the North." They're a confused people, the gringos: one day they're sending thousands of soldiers to try to kill a man they hate, and the next they're treating that same man like some kind of storybook hero. They never know what they really think about anything, not for long.

In the first year of his retirement, he granted an interview to a group of gringo reporters who drove out to Canutillo from Parral after receiving permission to come see him. A large table with chairs and refreshments was set up in the main courtyard, and Trillo served as translator for the gringos who couldn't speak Spanish. Pancho had expected them to ask him about life on Canutillo and wanted to show the place off, but all their questions were about his views on Mexican politics. They wanted to know what he thought of the new president, Alvaro Obregón, who'd been his friend in the wars against Díaz and Huerta, then his enemy in the war against Carranza, and was now, presumably, his friend once again.

Villa refused to discuss politics and Obregón. He reminded them that he was completely retired from politics and was now dedicated "in body and soul" to work and study. "Ask me about my farm," Pancho said, "ask me about my fine racehorses."

But gringos being gringos, they persisted in their line of questioning: one of them wanted to know if there was any possibility he would ever take up arms again. Villa gave him an exasperated look. "Listen, shitface," he said, "the only reason I'd ever go to war again is if your troops invaded Mexico again. I'll fight to the death against you gringo bastards."

Trillo edited the profanity out of his answer, but there was no hiding the anger in Villa's face. I could see him trying to get his temper under control. More calmly, he said that the only other reason he'd ever fight again would be to help "my little brother Fito," meaning Adolfo de la Huerta. "Unlike some politicians who I won't name," he said, "Fito is a man I trust completely. He is much like Madero: his only faults come from his goodness, his trust in men who don't deserve it. I think he would make a wonderful president, and if he should ever need my help in any way, he knows he can count on it."

Trillo didn't want to translate that, and I knew why. He was worried it would get back to the capital and stir alarm among the many enemies Pancho still had in the government, including Alvaro One-Arm himself. But a couple of the reporters understood Spanish well enough to tell the others what Villa had said, and they all scribbled hastily in their little notebooks. Trillo shook his head at Villa in reproval, and Pancho's face got dark and tight with the realization that the reporters had got the best of him, after all. Then one of them who knew some Spanish said he'd always heard that Villa was a great shot with a pistol and asked if he'd put on a shooting exhibition for them.

That did it. "Fuck you!" Villa shouted. "I'm not some god-damn circus performer! Did you come here for me to *amuse* you? Get the hell out of here, all of you—*now!*—or I'll show you some fucking shooting!" He stomped off into the house, and Trillo hustled the gringos back to their car and sent them on their way.

After that, all mail requests for interviews were answered with a dignified form letter written by Trillo for Villa's signature: it very politely explained that he was retired from all political activity, and expressed regret that his duties and responsibilites at Canutillo kept him much too occupied to grant interviews to anyone.

———— ><>< ————

Not long after the interview with the gringos, Villa received a present from Alvaro One-Arm—a pair of American machine guns. They arrived with a note saying, "Some men feel safe with only God's protection; others of us require a little more than that." He signed it, "Your old and sincere friend, Alvaro." Trillo thought the gift was Obregón's way of showing Pancho he'd taken no offense at what he'd told the Yankee reporters, but I figured it was a warning to Villa to keep his mouth shut if he didn't want the kind of trouble not even machine guns could deal with.

We took the guns out behind the stables and had a good time firing them for about thirty seconds—they just *poured* bullets with a squeeze of the trigger—and then they jammed, both of them. It took a good five minutes to clear them, and then, after firing another few fast rounds, they both jammed again.

"I get it," Villa said with a laugh. "My old and sincere friend gives me guns that don't work worth a shit to defend myself against my enemies. I get it."

Some of those enemies were damn close by—like the friends of Maclovio Herrera's family who hadn't forgotten that Villa had personally shot all the Herrera men in revenge for Maclovio's desertion of us. There was a small army garrison on the edge of town under the command of Colonel Felix Lara, but as far as the army was concerned, Villa's protection was his own business.

That was the way we preferred it. I was chief of the bodyguards—a cadre of seven sharp-eyed Dorados who would not have hesitated to shoot their own mother if they thought she was trying to harm Villa. On the hacienda, they carried carbines and pistols. They kept him in view at all times when he was outdoors and posted themselves around the house when he was inside. In town, I had them flank him close on all sides and made sure there were always at least two shotguns in the party. But when he went to the house on Zaragoza Street, I took only our two best *pistoleros*—Claro Hurtado and Daniel Tamayo—and left the rest of the boys with Trillo at the Hotel Hidalgo.

On our first visits to Parral, people nearly ran to get the hell away from us wherever we went. It bothered Pancho that the sight of him caused such fearful stirs among the citizens, and so he made it a point to stop in at a variety of shops whenever we were in town; he'd buy things he didn't really need, just for the chance to chat pleasantly with the proprietors and the other customers. Most of the townspeople gradually got used to us and came to see Villa as the benign fellow citizen he insisted he was.

The children all loved him, of course. As soon as our motorcar rolled into town, they'd flock to it like magpies, shoving and elbowing each other for the privilege of riding on the running board. Rosalío hated having all those kids hanging onto "his" automobile, but Villa was delighted by their excitement and would chide Rosalío for trying to smack them away. He made sure we never left Canutillo without a sack of wrapped candies in the front seat of the car, and he'd fling handfuls of it into the mob of kids every time we arrived at the Hotel Hidalgo. In no time at all he knew every boy in town by name.

———⊶⊷———

Trillo was not only the most educated among us—and one of the funniest storytellers—he was for damn sure the biggest worrier. One of the things he used to worry about was that three men weren't enough to guard Villa on the nights he spent with Soledad. We'd been living the *hacendado* life for about six months when he finally got all the proof he needed that Pancho was sufficiently protected at the Zaragoza house.

Late one afternoon, after concluding some business with a Durango cattleman and putting him up for the night at the Hotel Hidalgo, Villa got behind the wheel of the Dodge and headed for Soledad's house across town. I sat beside him, and Claro and Daniel sat in back. The sun had gone down behind the distant mountains but the dusty evening light was still rosy. The air was full of the smells of good cooking. Swallows were flocking to their roosts in the trees. A few fireflies were already flashing in the shadows. Daniel was telling a story he'd heard from Trillo about a blind whore and deaf and dumb customer.

Villa parked in the alley alongside the house and gave a couple of urchins a silver peso apiece to wipe the dust off the car. Daniel was just getting to the punch line of the story as we walked to the front corner of the building. He and Claro were two steps ahead of me and Pancho. As they started to turn the corner, Daniel suddenly shoved Villa back toward me and Claro yelled, "Assassins!" I grabbed Pancho by the shoulders and wrestled him back into the alley in the same instant that Daniel and Claro opened fire with their shotguns and pistol shots rang out from the front of the house. They scuttled sideways into the street, moving fast, pumping and firing from the hip, the shotguns thundering and muzzles flashing—and then they dropped the empty shotguns and pulled their .45s and ran forward, shooting as fast as they could pull the trigger, no longer drawing fire. Villa wrestled free of my grip, cursing me hotly, and we both dashed around the corner with our pistols raised and ready.

But it was all over. Claro was sliding a fresh magazine into his pistol and jacking a round in the chamber while Daniel kept his other pistol—a revolver—trained on the four bloody bodies sprawled in the street, all of them in postures only dead men can assume. Claro stepped up and shot each one in the head once more, just to be sure.

It looked like they'd been lying in wait for us in the alley on the far side of the house, not sure which side of the building we'd park on, since sometimes Pancho used one side and sometimes the other. He still kept to his old practice of never following a routine. When they saw us turn into the other alley, they'd decided to come around in front of the house rather than wait for us to step out into the open, like they should have done. Stupid clumsy amateurs. They never stood a chance against the likes of us.

After giving the last coup shot, Claro looked at Daniel with a grin and said, "So what *did* the blind whore say, anyway?"

"Oh yeah," Daniel said, holstering his pistols. "She says, 'Well, for Christ's sake, amigo, why didn't you just *tell* me that's how you like it?'"

They laughed like happy schoolboys who'd just won a ballgame. Claro had a bloody sleeve, but the round had torn through the flesh without hitting bone, so it wasn't anything serious. Daniel would later find two bullet holes in his jacket, though he hadn't gotten a scratch.

A crowd had begun to gather, and the two kids who'd been wiping down the car were running around the bodies, aiming their index fingers at them and yelling, "Bang-bang-bang!" while a frisky pup chased after them, barking and barking.

Daniel gave me a cigarette and struck a match to light it for me. As I took a deep drag, I saw Soledad standing in the front doorway as Villa mounted the steps toward her, her hands to her mouth, her eyes huge and bright with thrill.

The gunmen turned out to be two cousins of Maclovio Herrera and two of his close friends. Their bodies were put on display in front of the undertaker's parlor the next day so everybody could have a good look at what happened to fools who thought they could kill Pancho Villa.

Nobody tried it again. Not for more than two years.

TWENTY

The Parral cockpit was in a converted warehouse alongside the railyard. There were matches every night of the week, but the Sunday afternoon fights always drew the best cockfighters in the region and attracted the biggest crowds of bettors. The pit itself was enclosed by wooden walls three feet high and surrounded by tiers of dimly lit bleachers. On those packed afternoons the air was hot and thick with smoke and sweat, and the place reverberated with the roars of the spectators. We showed up every Sunday with a few of Villa's best birds—and our shotguns—and usually came out well ahead at the end of the day.

Until Villa began pitting his birds in Parral, the champion cockfighter had been Melitón Lozoya. He was a vain man with a tough reputation who owned a large and profitable cattle ranch a few miles from town. Like Villa, he had his share of enemies—and like Villa, he never left home without an escort of bodyguards. Occasionally, one of Villa's birds would lose a fight to one of Lozoya's, but during the three years we'd now been living in the region, it was mostly the other way around—which gave Pancho great pleasure because he'd disliked Lozoya from the moment he met him. "He's a phony bastard," Pancho said. "A cheat, a back-shooter. It's in his eyes."

Lozoya usually accepted his losses with an exaggerated shrug of indifference. He was one of those guys who preferred to swallow his anger rather than give anybody who'd got the best of him the satisfaction of seeing it. But one Sunday his cool facade failed him badly. He bragged that his new cock could beat any bird Villa pitted against it, but Pancho was so confident in the superiority of his roosters that he put his second-best bird—a muscular red named Chico—against Lozoya's new champion. In less than five minutes Chico crippled Lozoya's bird to win the fight—and a stake of a thousand pesos in addition to the side bets.

Lozoya hadn't shown much emotion during the fight, but when his maimed rooster couldn't face off anymore, he began cursing loudly, then stalked into the pit and kicked the bird to death.

Villa laughed out loud and said to me and Trillo, "Now, there's a guy who could do with a little self-control"—which, coming from him, made me laugh even louder than I had at Lozoya.

On the following Sunday Lozoya brought another new cock to the pits, a big black named Brujo which we heard he'd bought for five thousand pesos from Durango's best breeder. He challenged Villa to put up his best bird in a match for a thousand-peso stake. Villa said, "Hell, son, I'll put up Chico. And why not make it two thousand?" Lozoya said, "Why not?" And the cocks were pitted.

The black cock flew at Chico like something set loose out of hell. They smacked together in a scattering of feathers and slashing steel spurs, and it was over in less than a minute when the black put a spur through Chico's eye. As Brujo stood over Chico's corpse and crowed in triumph, Lozoya swaggered over to our side of the pit to collect the stake. It was the first time in a long while that Pancho had lost—and the first time in an even longer while that anybody had smirked at him like Lozoya was doing as he stood in front of him with his hand out.

"Two thousand pesos, my general," Lozoya said. "And better luck next time."

Trillo started to extract the money from his coat pocket but Villa stopped him with a raised hand, his eyes hard on Lozoya. "Another match," Pancho said. "I'll bet three thousand against your two."

Lozoya dropped his hand and quit smiling, as though he'd suddenly remembered who he was dealing with. But his eyes met Villa's steadily and he said, "Very well, General, as you wish."

Pancho's best rooster was a golden brute named Dorita, and his match with Brujo was a cockfight to remember. It lasted almost an hour and they fought in a frenzy the whole time except for the brief respites when their handlers were permitted to pick them up and wipe them with cool wet cloths and blow cigarette smoke in their faces to keep them in a fury. Near the end, both of them were badly torn and bloody, and each had lost an eye—and still they lunged at each other, pecking and slashing. The crowd's yelling had gone hoarse.

Suddenly Brujo made a desperate rush that staggered Dorito. The black struck him again and knocked him down. Brujo leaped on Dorito, slashing and stabbing with his spurs, and in a few seconds more it was over. There was cheering and groaning and cursing, and lots of money changing hands.

Brujo stood swaying over the dead cock and crowed weakly. Then his head blew apart in the blast of a gunshot.

The whole place went silent as Villa stood up and reholstered his pistol. He turned to Trillo and said, "Pay the fucker for the damn bird too."

Claro and Daniel had smoothly and quietly edged up beside
Pancho, smiling and bright-eyed, holding their shotguns down
along their legs. They and I and Rosalío were the only guards he
kept around him anymore. I'd already drawn my .45 and thumbed
off the safety. Beside me, Rosalío had his hand in his jacket and on
his gun. Lozoya's boys looked fearful that their boss might say the
wrong thing, but he was wise enough to keep his mouth shut. The
only sound in the place was of Trillo's boots as he walked across
the pit, stepping carefully around the two dead cocks, and handed
Lozoya ten thousand pesos. And then we left.

For the first few miles of the ride back to Canutillo, Villa stared
out at the passing landscape and didn't say much. The road was
in rough shape—it hadn't been smoothed in weeks and a long
dry spell had baked it to powder. The Dodge trailed a high plume
of pale dust as it clattered along. A pair of hawks spiraled slowly
over a patch of yellow pasture. Pancho sat against the passenger-
side front door, with Trillo squeezed between him and the driver,
Rosalío. Claro and Daniel were in the backseat with me, joking
and talking about some girls they'd met at the riverside park the
day before.

Finally Pancho said, "That was a damn fine rooster, that black,
a real bravo. I shouldn't have shot him. It's just that son of a bitch
Lozoya. I can't *stand* to lose to him."

"He's a cheeky spitface," Trillo said. "Don't waste your time
thinking about him."

"Fucker thinks he's big just because he's got some cattle,
plenty of money in the bank," Rosalío said, wrestling the steer-
ing wheel over the bumpy road. "But he was nothing but a damn
bootlick when he lived on our place."

"What are you talking about?" Pancho asked.

"Lozoya. He used to be a foreman for the family that owned Canutillo before the Revolution—the Jurados. You didn't know? Marianuela told me—my woman in Parral. She used to work for the Jurados too. She says Lozoya was a bully, all the workers hated him. But he was always kissing the Jurados' asses, and damn if it didn't make him a rich man."

According to Rosalío's woman, when the Revolution broke out and started moving toward the south of Chihuahua, the Jurados grabbed up all their money and fled for Mexico City. A few weeks later they sent a telegram to Lozoya authorizing him to sell every last head of stock, all the farm implements on the place, and every piece of carved Spanish furniture in the *casa grande*. For this service, the Jurados permitted him to keep half of all the money he got for the sales; the rest he sent to them in Veracruz.

The hacienda property had fetched a great deal of money, of course, and it was widely believed that Lozoya had kept more than his rightful share of it. The Jurados, after all, had been in no position to do much about it, even if they'd suspected they were being cheated. "Marianuela says it's a fact he kept the best of the Jurado cattle for himself," Rosalío said. "Those were the animals he used to start his own ranch."

The story infuriated Villa. The way he saw it, even though the stock and property had been sold years before Canutillo was deeded to him, it all would have come to him with the estate if Lozoya hadn't sold it. His logic could work like that when he was angry, and when it did, it wasn't any use to argue with him. "That son of a rotten whore stole from *me!*" he thundered. "Drive to his place," he told Rosalío. "Now!"

Trillo started to protest, but the look Villa gave him changed his mind. He shrugged and pulled his hat down tight.

The road to Lozoya's ranch was hardly more than a rutted
wagon trail, and the Dodge bounced and banged the whole way,
raising even more dust than before. They must have seen us coming from a long way off. When we finally rolled into the courtyard
and came to a stop in front of his big house, Lozoya was standing
in his shirtsleeves at the top of the steps to his verandah, wearing
a pistol on his hip. His boys were positioned everywhere, about a
dozen of them that I spotted at a glance, all of them armed with
rifles. Claro and Daniel were smiling tightly. Each held a shotgun
across his lap and out of sight, and they had their feet set, ready
to jump out of the car. I was holding my cocked pistol between
my knees and silently cursing Villa. There were at least thirteen
of them, probably more, against us six—and they were spread out
while we were bunched in the car. Horseshit odds. An image of
Rosa Blanca's finely smooth ass, naked on a moonlit bed, flashed
through my mind—and of Soledad's wicked smile.

"You!" Villa called out, and beckoned Lozoya to the car. Lozoya
hesitated, then slowly came down the steps. He didn't look afraid,
just wary, like he was expecting Villa to start shooting at any
moment. He stopped a few feet from Pancho's door. Now he could
see the guns in our hands and for a second he looked sad.

"You've got thirty days," Villa told him, "to return every head
of Canutillo stock you sold, every piece of equipment, every
fucking stick of furniture, you understand? Anything you can't
return—a cow, a shovel, a rocking chair, I don't care what—you're
going to pay me for it. In gold."

Lozoya gaped at him. Of all the possible troubles he might
have imagined having with Villa, this one had obviously never
crossed his mind. "Return the stock?" he said. "Pay you . . . ? But
I was authorized, you see—Don Jurado, he . . . Oh hell, if I'd
known *you* were going to be the next—"

"Thirty days!" Villa said. "Or I'll fertilize my rose garden with you." He tapped Rosalío on the arm and gestured for him to drive off.

As the car wheeled around, I was sure Lozoya would order his boys to open fire, but he didn't. He just stood there and watched us go, his face hard and full of hate.

As soon as we were out the courtyard gate and jouncing back toward the main road, Claro and Daniel broke out laughing. "Did you *see* that fucker's face!" Daniel said. "He couldn't *believe* we went right in there and told him pay up or die!"

Villa was staring at the road ahead, smiling, looking well satisfied. Rosalío was pouring sweat and grinning like an idiot as he drove.

Trillo mopped his face with a handkerchief and gave me an arched-browed look over the front seat. Within the next few days he would persuade Villa that he hadn't been wronged; that if Lozoya hadn't sold the property as he had been ordered to do by his *patrón*, the federal army would soon enough have taken it all for itself; that in any case, nothing that could be rustled or stolen would have remained on the place for long. Villa would come to agree with him, but he would tell Trillo not to let Lozoya know he was off the hook. "Let the bastard sweat out the thirty days."

As we got back to the main road Daniel uncorked a bottle of tequila and we passed it around. Even Pancho took a drink—and got a chorus of cheers for it. We were singing "Valentina," a great song of the Revolution, as we headed down the road and into the blaze of the setting sun.

<hr>

While Lozoya was sweating out the ultimatum Villa had no intention of enforcing, Trillo made a trip to the capital to close a deal for a new thresher and to buy a boxful of new books. He also brought back some interesting news about the upcoming presidential election. At the lunch table under the patio oaks, he told us that Plutarco Calles, who had been serving as minister of government for Obregón, would certainly be Obregón's choice to succeed him. But there were some in the capital who were strongly opposed to Calles and had been encouraging Adolfo de la Huerta, who had done such a wonderful job when he was interim president, to run against him.

"Excellent!" Villa said. "Fito was a great president for six months; he'll be an even greater one for four years."

"Except he doesn't want the job," Trillo said. In fact, de la Huerta had discouraged his supporters from pressing his candidacy, and he had assured his old friends Calles and Obregón that he had no ambition to be the president.

Villa shook his head and said it would be a damn shame if Fito didn't run. "I'd do anything to help him get elected."

Trillo stared at him glumly and said, "Yes, I know you would. *Everybody* knows you would. That's the trouble. Obregón knows it. Calles knows it."

Pancho made a face of mock fright, and then shrugged, but Trillo didn't smile.

"Hey, *compadre*, what are you worried about?" Pancho said. "Fito told them he wasn't going to run, and if he doesn't run, Old One-Arm and the Turk don't have any reason to worry about us."

"No, they don't." Trillo said. "But then they're not the sort of men to take anybody's word for anything, not even de la Huerta's."

"Oh hell, Miguelito, you worry too much," Villa said. "And I'll tell you one damn thing: if they ever do come after me, they'll need better guns than what they gave me for a present." Daniel and Claro chuckled at that. Villa looked at me and said, "Right, *mano?*"

I smiled.

He gestured at me and said, "This one can't be killed by bullets, did you guys know that? It's true. He's made of magic. As long as I keep him next to me, I'll always be all right." He turned back to me and said, "You and me, little brother, we're going to live forever, aren't we?"

"Certainly," I said. "Or until we die, whichever comes first."

The boys all got a good laugh out of that.

———— ⟫•⟪ ————

In July, about three months after our visit to Lozoya's, we received an invitation to the christening of the infant son of one of our old *compañeros,* Jose Sabas, whom we'd always called El Flaco because he was skinny as a sugar stalk. He wanted Pancho to be the boy's godfather, and he invited him to bring all the boys to the celebration. He lived on a small farm near the village of Río Florida, about ten miles outside of Parral. Pancho accepted, of course—he never turned down a *compadre's* request to sponsor a child's baptism, and by now he had nearly a hundred godchildren. He was in the mood for a fiesta and wanted to make the trip on horseback. Such fine summer weather was just right for a ride in the saddle, and he thought we ought to make a grand show of ourselves, as in the old days. Trillo dissuaded him from that idea, reminding him that Flaco was a poor man who would be unable to provide for so many guests and horses. He had invited all of us only out of politeness, Trillo said—if we went there by the dozens we would only embarrass him. Pancho realized Miguel was right. He decided Rosalío would drive us there in the Dodge—him, me, and Miguel. And, of course, Claro and Daniel.

⸻⸻⸻➤●◀⸻⸻⸻

Flaco was something of a famous man in Río Florida for having served in Villa's elite corps of Dorados, and when the villagers learned that Villa himself would be in attendance for the christening and the celebration to follow, they all contributed what they could to help Flaco provide a proper banquet for so illustrious a guest. There was kid roasted on spits, platters of grilled chicken, bowls of pork-in-chile stew, pots of rice and beans, stacks of tortillas. There were jugs of beer and mescal, and to make sure the supply of spirits would not run out, we'd brought several cases of tequila. Garlands hung from the trees and rooftops. A string band played at one end of the street, a brass band blared at the other, and a team of boys were kept busy sprinkling the street with water cans to keep down the dust raised by all the dancing feet.

Villa danced and danced, as always. The only dancing I'd done since losing my leg was with Rosa Blanca—at her relentless insistence—but only in the privacy of our house. It was fun to whirl her slowly about the parlor, and she always praised my grace. I knew she'd never admit it, but what she really meant was "Not bad for a guy with a wooden leg." I had steadfastly refused to dance in public. I remembered too well when I had danced with grace.

When he took a break to eat a bowl of beans and a few tortillas, Villa prodded me to dance with the girl he'd been spinning around. She was standing under a nearby tree, watching us with a smile and still panting from the last wild dance with Pancho. She was a light cinnamon beauty with tight, hard Indian tits.

"She has eyes for you," Pancho said. "She asked me who you are and I told her Napoléon Juárez, grandson of Benito and the greatest wooden-legged dancer in all Mexico."

"I'm a philosopher," I said, sipping at my tequila. "Philosophers sit and think and drink—they don't dance."

"*Bullshit!*" he said—and the way his face brightened I knew it was one of those times he loved best: when he had some bit of knowledge at hand that would win him an argument for certain. "Socrates learned to dance when he was eighty years old, I bet you didn't know *that*. An eighty-year-old philosopher learning to dance must look pretty ridiculous, no? But he didn't give a shit how funny he looked, and he didn't give a damn how bad he did it, he just wanted to *dance*. And you know why? Because a life without dancing is a life not fully lived, that's why. *Socrates* said so. You think you know better than Socrates? Like hell you do!"

Trillo joined us at the table as Pancho was making his argument. He was gasping for breath and sweating like he'd been rained on from the effort of his dancing, but he was beaming with happiness. The pretty thing he'd been dancing with sat on his portly lap and patted his face dry with the hem of her skirt.

"You're responsible for this," I said to him, gesturing at Pancho, who was smiling smugly.

"It's always gratifying to see one's student apply his learning so effectively," Trillo said. The more he had to drink, the more he talked like a professor. The girl yipped at his light pinch of her breast and playfully slapped at his hand.

"You can't look any more clumsy dancing on that piece of wood," Villa said, "than Miguelito here looks doing it on two good feet. But I'd like to see you enjoy yourself half as much." He leaned across the table and said just loud enough for me to hear: "How good do you think *I'd* be dancing if you hadn't kept Garcia from cutting off *my* leg, eh? I'll tell you one damn thing: if I had *no* legs, I'd still go on dancing—I'd dance on my hands—I'd dance on my ass."

"General Juárez?"

The girl was standing beside me, her blouse pasted wetly to those wonderful tits, her eyes hot and bright. "General," she said, "will you dance with me?"

Villa grinned. "Listen," he said, "if she laughs at the way you dance, you can always shoot her. That'll prove to everybody you're still the man you used to be."

Bastard.

So I danced, if dancing you could call it. More accurate to say I lurched around. The girl tried to go easy, but her natural spirit was a lot stronger than her good intentions, and she couldn't help dancing with more vigor than Rosa Blanca and I ever did in our parlor. I hadn't been out there two minutes when I made a hard misstep and went sprawling on my ass.

I heard laughter all around us. A red haze closed over me, a rage so strong I felt myself trembling with it. But when I saw the girl gaping down at me, wide-eyed with fear, my anger gave way to a sudden rush of shame. How unmanly to make a lively young girl afraid with a show of bad temper. How shameful to be so cruel as that, even unwittingly.

Villa was looking at me, not laughing, waiting to see.

I clapped my hand over my bicep and raised my fist at him: fuck you.

He laughed and returned the gesture. I smiled at the girl and reached my hand out to her. She grinned happily and helped me up with both hands and we laughed along with everyone else as I adjusted my leg and brushed the dust off the seat of my pants.

And then we continued our dance. And whether anyone else could call it dancing didn't mean shit to me. I lurched and stumbled about and staggered badly every once in a while. I swayed unsteadily and bumped against her and the dancers around us, and several times almost fell again. But I wouldn't have cared if I had. I would have gone right on dancing—dancing on my ass.

⟫●⟪

The next day we drove directly to Parral and took care of some business, then enjoyed a sumptuous supper together in the dining room of the Hotel Hidalgo. Trillo had been nursing a monstrous hangover all day, and suffering further from Villa's incessant teasing. "You were so drunk," Villa said, "I bet that poor girl who took you away to her bed last night finally had to mount the bedpost to get some satisfaction."

Trillo said he was certain he had done his manly duty, even if he couldn't recall the details too well.

Claro and Daniel recalled very well their wild night with two pairs of sisters who were determined to outdo each other in acts of wickedness. They'd been reminding each other of it all day, not that they needed much reminding—they both had slight limps and tended to grimace whenever they sat down and their pants tightened in the crotch. It must've been some night. When Trillo began to drone at the supper table about the latest market prices for beef, Villa nudged Daniel and said in a stage whisper, "A man can only do so much with one dick. While you were busy with one girl, didn't the other one get bored?" He'd never been one for such exotica as three in a bed, but he was always curious about everybody else's sexual escapades.

Daniel said both sets of sisters were too imaginative to let
things ever get boring. They knew exactly what to do to keep
everybody happy all at once.

Claro said the girls were all so experienced he'd felt like an
ignorant child getting very advanced lessons in female geography.
"Ay, but what teachers!" he crowed.

Villa shook his head in disapproval. "In *my* youth, country
girls were sweet and innocent," he said. "Only in the cities could
you find girls who did such sinful things. Isn't that right, little
brother?"

I nodded and said sure, but gave the others a wink and they
all laughed. Most of the country girls we'd had our fun with in the
old days had been about as innocent as Jezebel.

"You laugh," Villa said, "but it's a hell of a thing when young
country girls carry on like all those sisters did with you guys."

"It sure is a hell of a thing," Claro said. "A hell of a *fine* thing!"

We laughed all through supper, each of us getting mocked in
turn by the others. The plates were cleared away and all of us had
brandy except Villa, who stuck with his usual herb tea. I accepted
one of Trillo's cigars—and though he didn't light his, Pancho
took one too, to play with and roll in the corner of his mouth as
we joked and told stories of the old days and made plans for the
future of Canutillo. It was one of those evenings nobody wanted
to see come to an end.

Around midnight we headed for the house on Zaragoza,
Villa and me, Claro and Daniel. Rosalío drove us there and then
took the car to his woman's house, where he spent his nights
when we were in Parral. Villa told him not to be late getting there
in the morning. He wanted to get an early start back to Canutillo.

TWENTY-ONE

A loud bang woke me in the dead of night. I bolted up in bed with my pistol in hand, whirled toward the next two bangs at the window, and very nearly shot the shutter slapping hard in the gusting wind. I let out a long breath and went to the window, leaned out and latched the shutter back in place against the outside wall.

The trees were swaying in the wind, and silent lightning lit the distant mountains. The moon flashed in and out of a rushing tangle of thick violet clouds. The air smelled of impending rain.

I'd been dreaming of the time we rode triumphantly into Mexico City, our horses prancing through a tide of flowers, the air shaking with the capital's cheers. But in the dream, everyone around me—Villa, Zapata, Urbina, the people lining the streets, *every*body—was already dead. They were nothing but skeletons wearing clothes. "Pancho!" I shouted to Villa, riding beside me, "You're dead! Everybody's dead!" He turned his grinning death's head toward me and his laughter sounded like the clatter of dry bones. He raised a bony hand and pointed to the large glass window of a building we were passing. In it I saw our reflections— saw that my head too was only a grinning white skull. Villa's laughter grew and grew, and then I was awakened by the banging shutter.

I craved a drink, so I pulled on my pants, slipped a pistol into the waistband, and went shirtless to the kitchen, passing through the front parlor, where Daniel was sleeping on the sofa. I heard his breathing change and knew he'd come awake the instant I stepped into the room. He was a cat, that guy—him and Claro both. Claro was the outside guard and slept in the open shed behind the house. Whenever we were at the Zaragoza house, they slept with their shotguns at their sides.

There was a light already burning in the kitchen. Soledad was sitting at the small table against the far wall, her chair turned outward, her legs crossed. Her hair was tied back with a black ribbon and her silk silver robe was parted at the top of her long, smooth thigh. She was sipping a glass of wine. When she saw me standing in the doorway, she made no move to cover the exposed leg. It was the one that ended in six toes, and she was swinging the foot from side to side like a cat switching its tail.

She watched me pour a drink of tequila, then raised her glass to me in a silent toast. I returned it and we drank.

"Tell me," she said in a low voice, smiling wickedly and gesturing at my pistol, "do you sleep with that thing in your pants?"

"That depends."

"Yes, of course. I suppose it would."

She was staring at the scars across my chest and belly. "How is it," she said without a trace of mockery, "you're still alive?"

I pulled out a chair and sat facing her, my knee almost touching her bare leg. I seized her swinging foot gently and held it still. When she didn't pull away, I stroked her six toes. "How is it *you* are?" I said.

"I don't live as dangerously as you do," she said.

I ran my eyes over her leg and said, "The hell you don't."

She smiled her wicked smile. "Well, maybe sometimes."

"Let's just see," I said, and poured a dollop of tequila on her leg. It rolled along her thigh and under her robe. I slid my finger down the thin, bright tequila trail on her skin, all the way to the part in the robe, then paused a moment, pushed my finger on down into the nest of hair, and touched her sex. She was moist with more than the tequila. I moved my finger over her in a small slow circle. She shut her eyes and sucked a breath between her teeth.

"He'll kill you," she whispered, tightening her legs around my hand.

"I damn sure will," Villa said.

Her chair scraped backward and bumped hard against the wall as she snatched her robe closed over her legs.

I thought, Oh fuck, and slowly turned around in my chair.

He was shirtless too. And pointing a revolver at my head. "Some friend you are," he said. He sighted carefully, and drew back the hammer with a loud double click.

"Bang!" he said, and lowered the gun and laughed. "Oh brother, you ought to see your face."

He looked at Soledad and quit smiling. "I promise you, my love, with all my heart: next time I *will* shoot. I'll shoot *you*."

She stood up and warily eased by him, then scurried out the door, nearly running into Daniel, who was standing just beyond the doorway with his shotgun. Daniel watched her go, then turned and looked from one to the other of us, shook his head, and went back to the front parlor.

Villa poured himself a glass of water and sat down in the chair Soledad had vacated. He eased the hammer back down and set the pistol on the table. "Now *you've* looked the Mother of

Bones right in the eyes," he said, "just like I did in front of Huerta's firing squad. How did *you* feel?"

"Like a fool with nothing to shoot back with but a sticky finger." I wiped it off on my pants. "Listen," I said, "I, uh . . ." I shrugged.

He waved away my apology. "A man can't be blamed for wanting to try with her. You might as well blame a hawk for hunting rabbits, or a compass for pointing north. Anyway, you couldn't have touched her if she didn't want you to. It's always up to the woman— except when it's rape, and even then it's sometimes her idea."

He took a deep drink of water and studied my face closely "Hell, *I'm* the one with the problem. I'm crazy for the bitch. I don't mean in love with her, I mean *crazy* for her. You know what I mean?"

I nodded. "The gypsy love curse."

He nodded glumly. The gypsy love curse was what a man had when he desired a woman so badly he'd put up with any sort of shit from her—any misbehavior, any amount of infidelity, any humiliation—just to still have her himself. Just to be able to fuck her once more—and then still once more. A man can't get any more pathetic than that. We'd laughed at a lot of fools who'd been struck with the curse, but Villa wasn't laughing now.

"You're the first to touch her as far as I know," Villa said, "but not the first she's made eyes at. I've warned her a half dozen times. I gave her a beating the other night that left me crying harder than her. But she doesn't scare, this one, not for long. I know she can't help what she is, but that doesn't make it any easier to take."

He stared off at nothing for a moment, then he fixed his gaze on me and asked what the hell I was doing up at this hour anyway. I told him I'd awakened and couldn't get back to sleep, so I came down for a drink.

"You better watch you don't turn into a rummy in your old age," he said. "Me, I can't sleep too good tonight, either. I keep having these wild dreams. I keep dreaming about Tomás—and Zapata, and Maclovio—a lot of guys—a lot of dead guys. It's funny, they're nothing but skeletons in the dream, all of them, but I know who each of them is, even though all skeletons look alike. I start walking toward them, but they wave me away, like they don't want me with them. Then I wake up feeling damn strange but I don't know why. Then I go back to sleep and have the same fucking dream again."

All I could do was stare at him.

He looked at me and grinned. "Then I come down here for a drink of water and find my good friend with his hand between my wife's legs. Jesus, what a night."

We laughed so loud, Daniel shouted out from the parlor: "For Christ's sake, let a man get some sleep!"

———❧———

Soledad's maid Chata arrived at her usual early hour and made us a breakfast of fried chiles, scrambled eggs, tortillas, and coffee. She was complaining about the dogs in her neighborhood over by the river bridge and the Juárez Plaza. They'd awakened her before dawn with their incessant barking.

"Those stupid animals usually sleep till the middle of the day before they start with their infernal barking at everybody who passes by," she said. "But something got them stirred up before daylight this morning and they wouldn't shut up for love or money. When they finally stopped, it was time for me to get up."

"Quit your complaining, Chatita," Villa said, "you're not the only one who didn't get much sleep last night." He grinned at me across the table. For a man who only a couple of hours earlier had confessed to me that he was suffering from the gypsy love curse, he was in pretty high spirits.

"I know *I* didn't get any sleep worth a damn!" Daniel said, and Pancho and I laughed at his disgruntlement.

Claro said he didn't know what everybody was complaining about, he'd slept just fine except for the brief rain which had leaked in on him through the shed roof.

We heard the rattling arrival of the Dodge in front of the house, and Rosalío honked the claxon. He usually ate breakfast with Trillo at the Hotel Hidalgo when he stopped there to pick him up. As we passed through the parlor on our way to the front door, Soledad appeared on the stairway. Villa paused at the door to return her glower. She was sporting a fresh black eye, and she made a vicious "evil horns" sign with her fingers. I didn't know if it was intended for me or Villa—probably, it was meant for us both.

"Keep that silly witchcraft to yourself, woman," Pancho said. He slapped at the pistol on his hip. "And remember what I said about next time."

As he went out the door, I smiled at Soledad and blew her a kiss. If looks could kill, hers would have hacked me to pieces on the spot.

———>•<———

Villa felt like driving, so Rosalío got out and stood beside him on the running board and held on to the windshield brace. He still got a boy's thrill out of riding that way, even for the entire fifty-mile trip. Trillo was seated in front with a large satchel at his feet containing twenty thousand pesos for the payroll at Canutillo. I sat behind him, Daniel next to me, and Claro behind Villa, against the other back door. Daniel and Claro put their shotguns on the floor.

Villa let out the clutch too quickly and the car jerked sharply and stalled. Rosalío squatted slightly to peer in at him with a severe expression. "Easy does it, Chief. You have to *eeease* the clutch out."

"I'll be goddamned," Villa said to me over his shoulder. "*I* taught this puppy to drive, and now he thinks he can tell me how to operate this machine." The truth is, he rarely drove anymore, and Rosalío had become the better driver.

Pancho eased the car into motion, accelerated slowly, shifted smoothly into second gear, and sarcastically asked Rosalío if he was driving well enough to suit him. Rosalío grinned into the car and said he was doing fine, that the trick was not to be nervous. "A motorcar is much like a horse, my chief—or a woman. It must always sense that you are in command or it will refuse to show you proper respect."

"Just like some impudent bastards I could name," Villa muttered, turning onto Juárez Avenue. Three short blocks away, at the Juárez Plaza, the avenue ran up against Gabino Barrera Street. There, a little dogleg turn to the right would take us over the Parral River bridge and out of town.

It was a pretty Friday morning, the sunlight angling softly yellow through the trees. Except for a few women in black rebozos, scurrying in the direction of a church bell tolling on the next block, the streets were nearly empty. Farther down the street, a sidewalk vendor stood by his little cart of goods in front of an alley bordering the plaza. "Where *is* everybody?" Trillo said. "It's seven-thirty, for Christ's sake."

"The army went out on maneuvers yesterday," Claro said. "The garrison workers don't have to go there today."

"Well hell, *everybody* doesn't work at the garrison."

"It's just laziness," Daniel said, lighting a cigar. "People are getting lazier all the time. Used to be they'd go to work before the sun came up. Now they stay in bed till the sun comes through the holes in their roof and hits them in the face."

"Listen to you," Claro said. "We thought we'd have to use a lasso to get you out of bed this morning."

As we came abreast of the vendor, he took off his hat and waved it enthusiastically. "Viva Villa!" he shouted. "Viva Villa!"

Pancho raised his hand to him. A flock of mourning doves fluttered up from the street ahead of us.

Daniel said, "Hey, *I* wasn't lucky enough to spend the night out in the shed where you don't have everybody in the house waking you up in the middle of the goddamn night."

"Oh Christ, do we have to listen to this again?" Villa said—and then stomped on the brakes sharply to keep from hitting a mangy dog that dashed out of the plaza and into the street. The sudden halt threw us all forward—Trillo's head thunked against the windshield, and Rosalío nearly fell off the running board—and the car stalled.

Rosalío bent down and gave Pancho a reprimanding look, but Villa put a finger in his face and said, "Don't—don't say a word." He brought the finger around to Trillo and said, "You either."

Trillo rubbed his forehead, looking at him accusingly. Then he silently mouthed the word "Ouch." Claro snickered—and then we all laughed like hell, even Villa.

As Pancho restarted the motor, I looked through the rear window and saw that the vendor was gone. The car got moving again. Directly ahead, on the other side of the dogleg turn, stood a high stone house with doors at either end and a pair of wide shuttered windows facing the street. Villa drove slowly into the turn and the car's left side was barely fifteen feet from the house as I opened my mouth to yell that it was an ambush—but in that instant all the shutters and doors banged open and rifles thrust out of the darkness and opened fire.

Blood sprayed off Rosalío's chest and he tumbled from the car. Clara's lower jaw vanished in a splatter of red bone and he spasmed as he got hit again and fell over on the shotguns. The windshield blew apart. Trillo shrieked. I saw Daniel's thumb vanish from his left hand. I took one in the shoulder and felt a chunk of my cheekbone get shot away. Blood flew off Villa's head. The car veered sharply and crashed into a tree alongside the house and Daniel fell hard against me, cursing through the cigar still clenched in his teeth.

The gunmen came running out of the house, now shooting with pistols. Villa raised his revolver and shot one through the eye. I shoved my door open and rolled out with Daniel right behind me. Two of them came running around to our side of the car, and from flat on the ground I shot one through the throat as Daniel stood up and shot the other in the heart. Then Daniel's hair jumped and he fell dead with blood pouring from the side of his face. Trillo was hanging backward over the car door as if his spine were made of rubber, his arms and necktie dangling below his head.

I got up and saw three men standing by the driver's door and shooting Villa again and again even though he was already as dead as a man can get. Two others stood beside them, firing into the back of the car. One of the men shooting Villa was Melitón Lozoya. I tried to shoot him but my .45 was jammed. One of the men beside him saw me and fired through the car, hitting me in the belly and knocking me down. I got up again and staggered across the street, expecting bullets in the back any second. I fell at the foot of the bridge and tumbled down the incline and into the scrub brush along the muddy river bottom.

I lay there staring up at the clouds sailing slowly across the sky. The shooting stopped. I expected the bastards to appear at the top of the embankment and finish me off. I heard a horse blowing and I pushed the brush aside and saw a rider leading a group of saddled mounts out from under the bridge and up the incline.

I figured I might as well die on the move as not, so I got up and made my way along the lower bank, away from the bridge, until I came to a set of old wooden steps leading up to an alleyway. There was a doctor named Montero whose office was just off Juárez Avenue. He'd tended lots of Villa's people. I'd met him once when Calixto carelessly gashed his own foot with an ax and I'd brought him to the office to get stitched up. That's where I headed.

I made my way through the back alleys, the insides of my boots filling with the blood running down my legs. When I reached the rear door of the doctor's office, I beat on it with my fist until he jerked it open and said angrily, "I told you tramps not to come begging for food from me anymore, damn you!"

Then he saw my bloody face and the sopping belly wound under my hands and his eyes went wide. And then he recognized me. "Captain Contreras! My God, man! Here, let me help you."

I fell forward in a whirling faint.

⟶═◦═⟵

Witnesses said the killers mounted up and rode away as casually as you please. That was about the only point the witnesses agreed on. Some said there were as many as twelve of them; some said there were only eight or seven or six. (I recall nine, including the one holding the horses under the bridge.) Some said the ambush took place right in front of the plaza and the car kept going into the curve and hit the tree. Others said the assassins had been waiting at the bridge, that the car had backed up in an attempt to turn around and get away, then crashed into the tree. And so on.

Nobody mentioned a survivor who staggered away from the scene and went rolling down the bridge embankment, and none of the newspapers said anything about the twenty-thousand pesos Trillo had been carrying in his satchel. Maybe the killers took it, or maybe some brave and quick-witted citizen of Parral simply picked it up and walked away with it.

Photographers had swarmed to the scene like buzzards and taken dozens of pictures before the dead were taken to the Hotel Hidalgo and stripped and washed fairly clean of blood, then laid out for public display. And the photographers took more pictures. Within hours of the shooting, they were hawking the photos on the street. The most popular was the one captioned "The Forty-Seven Wounds of Pancho Villa." Montero bought one of them and brought it to me in the back room of his house, where he and his brother had taken me after he'd extracted the bullets from my stomach and shoulder and sewn me up.

The picture showed Villa lying on a bed, a portion of sheet covering his privates, his flesh rent with gaping wounds still oozing thin streaks of blood. One of the holes in his side was bigger than my fist, and the viscera bulged from it. A dumdum wound. The pillow under his head was so thickly clotted and dark with gore I knew the back of his head had been blown off. The body on the bed to his right was so shot up it took me a moment to recognize it as Claro's. The photo was the first vision of death that ever struck me as obscene, and I ripped it to pieces. The doctor made no objection. I'm sure he'd bought several more.

Nobody knew who'd done it. Obregón sent a special investigative commission to Parral to question witnesses and study the evidence. He told the newspapers he would not rest until the assassins of his old friend and comrade General Francisco Villa were brought to justice. The investigators stayed in Parral a week, then went back to the capital and announced their findings: the bullets used in the murders were the same sort used by the federal army, and the killing was "probably motivated by political reasons."

A Mexico City newspaper published a cartoon in which one man asks another, "Who killed Pancho Villa?" and the other, with a finger to his lips, answers, "*Calle . . . se, amigo*" a response that starts out sounding like the name Calles, then quickly becomes the warning to "Shut up, my friend." The joke became famous all over Mexico. A lot of people knew damn well that Calles— with Obregón's blessing, naturally—had arranged for Villa's killing. It was common knowledge that they'd had a falling out with their old friend Adolfo de la Huerta, who any day now was expected to announce his candidacy for president. Faced with that likelihood—and with Villa's avowed devotion to his "little brother Fito"—they decided to make sure Pancho wouldn't interfere with Calles's presidential ambitions.

That's the way a lot of people saw it. Me too. I sure as hell couldn't prove it but I knew that's how it was. It was something they'd been wanting to do for a long time anyway. They had always been afraid of him. All they had to do was find a guy who would be sure not to splash any blood of suspicion on them.

———※———

The guy was Jesús Salas Barraza, a Durango state congressman. On the ninth of August, nearly three weeks after the killing, the capital newspapers announced that he was the man behind the assassination. By then I was recuperating in the house of Rosa Blanca's sister in Santa Barbara, a pueblo a few miles south of

Parral. Calixto and a couple of the boys had taken me there in a truck after I got word to them of where I was.

Salas Barraza had surrendered to the federal police and confessed everything in a letter to president Obregón. Reporters were permitted to interview him in the penitentiary, where he was awaiting trial, and the man talked and talked. He said he had surrendered voluntarily in order to "protect the good name of the government" and prevent any further suspicions from falling on "certain guiltless public officials."

He claimed that his fiancée had been raped by Villa back in the early days of the Madero Revolution, and when he went to Villa's headquarters to protest, Pancho had pistol-whipped him nearly to death. He called Pancho a "dog," a "hyena," a rabid animal who had deserved killing for a long time. He said that, over the years, he had become acquainted with many other men of property and social station whose wives or daughters or sweethearts had also been violated by Villa the Brute—or whose property had been stolen by him. When Pancho retired to Canutillo, Salas called some of these men together and offered to get rid of Villa if they would put up the money to pay for gunmen to help him and to buy military weapons and dumdum bullets. They agreed, and Salas hired a man in Parral who had his own good reasons for hating Villa. (Melitón Lozoya, of course!) That man in turn enlisted seven trusted friends into the plot.

Salas said he and his hired killers spent several weeks in Parral, studying Villa's habits and schedules, planning their ambush. They rented the house on Gabino Barrera Street and posted a lookout disguised as a vendor in front of the plaza. On the morning of 20 July 1923, when Villa and the unlucky friends with him drove down the Avenida Juárez, the lookout waved his hat and yelled "Viva Villa!"—a signal that Villa himself was in the car. When the Dodge entered the slow turn right in front of the building, the men inside were perfect targets.

All told, the ambushers fired more than two hundred rounds. Salas said he himself gave Villa several coup shots in the head.

That was true—I recognized his picture in the paper. He was one of the men I'd seen shooting Villa from point-blank range. He was the one who'd shot me.

"I'm not a murderer," Salas told the reporters. "I rid humanity of a monster."

They locked him up in the Chihuahua State Penitentiary, and then, less than nine months later, gave him a pardon and a commission in the federal army. Not too long after that he was elected to Congress. The son of a bitch lived to a ripe old age. Just before he died in bed in 1951, he still insisted he alone was the "intellectual author" of the assassination. Lying bastard. I could have gone to him and killed him, of course, but what for? *Revenge?* That's stupid. Revenge for what? For shooting Villa? For wounding me? Villa's enemies had been trying to kill him all his life—it's what enemies are supposed to do. Pancho knew that better than anybody, but he got careless. I was fair game because I was with him. Hell, Salas didn't know me from Adam; he shot me because I damn sure would have killed him if that worthless .45 hadn't jammed. They got the jump on us and they won. When they killed Villa, it was over. Revenge—bah! Only women and fools seek revenge for a lost fight.

I do like to think that when Salas got to the gates of hell he found Villa waiting for him, with the devil's permission to kill him again and again for all the rest of eternity. For damned sure, I'll find out.

EPILOGUE

I dug up one of our gold caches in the sierras and bought a small ranch a few miles outside of Juárez. I would have preferred to live farther south, but Rosa Blanca had relatives in Juárez and in El Paso, and it pleased her to live near them. I hired wranglers and raised horses. I listened to Rosa Blanca's happy gossip. I taught Doroteo to ride and shoot as soon as he was big enough to hold a gun in both hands. In the evenings I'd read from one or another of the books I'd taken from Villa's library. My favorite is still *Moby Dick*.

Rosa Blanca and I shared the same bed for the first few years, but she finally had enough of being awakened by my thrashing every night when the dreams came to me, and she moved to another bedroom. I'd dream of blood and fire and laughing skeletons—and sometimes, later on, of Villa's decapitated body wandering through the windy desert night, searching vainly for its head. Three years after his death, somebody broke through his concrete tomb in the Parral graveyard, pried the lid off the coffin, and cut the head off the corpse. An American adventurer named Emil Holmdahl was arrested as the chief suspect. Rumor had it he'd been hired for the job by a powerful Mexican general who hated Villa and wanted to use his skull as a bowl in which to feed his dog. Or by a group of U.S. scientists who wanted to study Villa's head to learn the source of his primitive genius. Or by a secret society of American rich men who collected the skulls of notorious killers. Or by . . . oh, hell, who knows? In any case, the evidence against Holmdahl was strong but circumstantial, and he had influential friends who interceded on his behalf, and so he was released. But the way the story goes, not long after leaving Parral he turned up at the Sheldon Hotel in El Paso and showed the head to a couple of friends before vanishing into the night with it. Maybe the story's true, maybe not, but what happened to the head is still a mystery—except, of course, to those who know.

———>●<———

Obregón, that sly bastard, decided to run for president again when Calles's term ran out. His buddies in Congress amended the constitution to allow for presidential reelection after at least one term out of office. While they were at it, they extended the presidential term from four to six years. It all looked like a cozy arrangement to have Old One-Arm and the Turk alternate the presidency between them for the rest of their lives.

But they still had some serious enemies, among them the Catholics, whom Obregón had repressed mildly during his first term of office, and whom Calles, in his term, antagonized into a ferocious uprising. By the time Obregón was reelected, the Cristero Rebellion had been largely put down, but the Catholics' hatred of him and Calles still burned hot as hellfire. Less than two weeks after his election, Obregón was being honored at a luncheon in a Mexico City restaurant when a Cristero fanatic pretending to be a sketch artist stepped up to his table and emptied a pistol in his face.

Calles continued to be a political power behind the scenes until 1936, when President Lázaro Cárdenas, who'd once been his protégé, got fed up with his old mentor's interference in the government and gave him a choice: live in safe exile in the U.S or die immediately in Mexico. It was a far more generous choice than he would have been offered by anyone else—especially yours truly. The only choice he'd have got from me was whether to be shot in the head or the heart. But of course not everybody gets what he deserves, so Calles escaped killing.

———⊰⊱———

About the time the Turk was thrown out of the country, Doroteo drowned in one of the ranch *resacas*. I'd always meant to have somebody teach him to swim, but Rosa Blanca always argued against it because she was afraid he would drown while learning. Her only fears in life concerned our son, and although those fears were often absurd, I doted on her too much to countermand them. And so the boy drowned when he was thrown from his horse in three feet of water and could not get his footing. And she, who was so strong in so many ways, lost all spirit. She wore black for the rest of her life—another ten months. She rarely slept. Her face aged years every week. She ate nothing and shrank to a bundle of sticks. Nothing I said to her made any difference. Her heart was beating against her will. My own heart withered with the realization that I was not enough reason for her to go on living. When the winter got into her bones, she caught pneumonia. She died on a dark day in February while a blue norther howled at the windows.

———⊰⊱———

Now I'm *old*. Every morning I wake up in utter astonishment at my continued existence—and at how nothing changes but the flesh: the Olympic Games are to be held in Mexico City next week, but yesterday soldiers opened fire on a student demonstration in the Plaza of Three Cultures and killed hundreds.

My gut hasn't worked properly since taking that bullet at Parral. My ears never stop ringing. My joints ache constantly. It's a bitch to piss. Life goes on until it no longer does, but I hope I die before I'm completely blind. The sunsets are the only thing I can still see without difficulty, although maybe the sunsets I see are mostly a mix of memory and imagination, I don't know. There's one other thing I still see clearly—the photograph taken of us in the National Palace on the glorious day we took possession of Mexico City. Sometimes I bend over it with a large magnifying glass, and sometimes I just shut my eyes and look at it in my head. Either way, I look hard and close at our faces, Pancho's and mine, and I see everything in them but tragedy.